THE RUTHLESS

THE RUTHLESS

A BRUNO JOHNSON NOVEL

DAVID PUTNAM

OCEANVIEW PUBLISHING

SARASOTA, FLORIDA

ISBN 978-1-60809-406-6

Published in the United States of America by Oceanview Publishing

Sarasota, Florida

www.oceanviewpub.com

10 9 8 7 6 5 4 3 2 1

PRINTED IN THE UNITED STATES OF AMERICA

This book is dedicated to Pat and Bob Gussin.

My rocky journey to publication started decades ago, involving four literary agents and 156 rejections (before I quit counting). I was writing my thirty-eighth manuscript when Pat and Bob picked up *The Disposables*, fulfilling a lifelong dream. Thank you, Pat and Bob, for helping me—and so many others—see dreams come true.

THE RUTHLESS

CHAPTER ONE

IN THE ERRATIC world of a criminal, the bond of friendship is always tenuous; loyalty often tested by fire and blood. In the case of my friend Nigel Braddock that unfortnate trial came much too soon.

I sat behind the wheel of the stolen Monte Carlo, my head on a swivel, watching, waiting. Nigel sat in the passenger seat, unable to stop moving. He fidgeted constantly, shifting in the seat, scratching his cheek, his neck, the top of his head. His long, sandy-blond hair was stringy and greasy and hadn't been washed in at least a week, a classic paranoid tweaker on meth who perceived danger at every turn.

"Come on, let's get moving," he urged. "We're sitting ducks back here. The cops are always comin' by this place. They're always cruising this parking lot. And I mean all the damn time."

Odd, the term he chose. The cops called a stolen car without a suspect in it a "duck." He was right that if a cop cruised the back parking lot of the Crazy Eight, there would be trouble. A black guy dressed as a trucker, sitting with a white meth freak in a new Monte? That scenario would pique any cop's interest. No way could I afford to be caught in a stolen ride. I still had too much left to do.

A strong chemical odor emitted from Nigel, from his clothes, from the pores of his skin, and from his breath when he spoke.

Everyone on the street knew him as Nidge. He'd been chasing the dragon: smoking meth by heating it up on a piece of foil and inhaling the vapors.

For the thousandth time, he spun in his seat to look out the back window. He spun back and checked the mirrors. I reached over and put a hand on his shoulder. "Stop. Just stop, sit back, and take a breath." I knew it was impossible for him, no matter how hard he tried. He was in the grip of a five-day bender, probably on the verge of seeing phantoms and ghosts. In another day, if he made it that long without crashing, imaginary bugs would crawl out of his skin. Before his heart exploded, I needed to score him some downers and insist he take them. He'd sleep for a week—and that was something else I didn't need. Nigel was too important to what I had going on.

"I told ya," he said. "I could cop you a gun just about anywhere. Even at the Big O Donuts on Alondra. We don't *neeeed* to be doing this right here, right now. Not in the back of the Crazy Eight, not in a hot short, for cripes sake. This is crazy, man. And I mean crazy with a capital K."

He was an old hippie, a throwback from the seventies who came to meth late in life.

"Shut up and sit tight," I said, looking up in the rearview. "Here he is now. It'll only be a minute more and we'll be gone." I opened the door and got out. I closed the door, bent at the waist, and leaned back in. "You all right?"

"Yes, yes, I'm good. Just get 'er done so we can make like babies and head out."

I slapped the open windowsill. "Good. Two minutes, then we're outta here."

The front of the Crazy Eight sat on Central Avenue at the corner of Eighty-First Street. No one parked out front: Central was too busy and the curb was painted red. The back of the bar comprised the bottom lip of an "L" configuration to a dilapidated strip center filled with parlors—one tattoo, two massage, and one beauty. The rest was made up of a donut shop with grease-smeared windows, a check-cashing place, and a pawnshop. The two high windows at the back of the Crazy Eight sported heavy wrought iron, the same as the door. Weeds grew in the cracks in the asphalt in the underused part of the parking lot, and artistic gang graffiti tagged the walls with brightly colored names that visitors from another country might misconstrue as intentional.

The BMW that had parked in front of Jerry's Pawn Shop fit right in with the other patrons of the strip center. It had scarred and sun-faded red paint and old crash damage to the right rear. I'd been hoping for a newer car, something to indicate a higher level of professionalism. The closer I got to it, the harder I ground my teeth. I'd been misled. This guy was a down-on-his-luck PI out there taking the dregs, the cast-off cases. I knocked on the passenger window, bent, and peered in. A woman—not what I expected from the street-side referral. She was a brunette who looked sixteen but was probably twenty-six or even thirty. She pushed the button on her door. The window came down so we could talk. "I'm Karl Higgins." I lied about the name. "I'm the one who called you."

I couldn't see her left hand, which she kept down between her seat and the driver's door. "Pick up your shirttails," she said, "and let me see your waistband. Then turn around slowly."

"Not gonna happen. I know you got a gun in your hand, so you don't need to worry about me. I'm going to reach into my back pocket, so just take it easy." I pulled out a bundle of hundreds, folded in the middle and kept together with a red rubber band. I tossed it on the seat. "Here's my good faith. Now can we talk?"

Her eyes never left mine as her hand snaked over to snatch the bundle off the passenger seat. She thumbed it with one hand seeing that it wasn't a grifter's con, that the bills in the center weren't ones and fives. "Okay, step back. We'll talk outside." She rolled up the window.

She wasn't a fool. To let me into the car would've been a dangerous rookie move. She met me around the front of her battered heap and kept her distance. She wore a loose-fitting shirt that hid her curves and any weapons she carried. She had intense brown eyes and little dimples at the corners of her mouth. "You said you wanted someone found, a child, is that correct?"

"That's right," I said. "But I have to tell you that for this kind of money I was hoping for"—I glanced back at her banged-up Beemer— "Ah . . . someone a little more professional."

She smiled even though I had disparaged her character. It changed her entire personality. "So, let me get this straight. You are paying me in cash, meeting behind a bar that in the last year has had a murder in this parking lot and one inside, not to mention the nine other felonious assaults and two solicitations for prostitution, and I don't meet *your* expectations?"

So she *was* professional and smart and had done her homework. I liked that.

I looked around and didn't see any cars in the area that she might have brought along to back her play.

"I'm here by myself. Who do you want found?"

"Like you said, a child."

"For what purpose?"

"Doesn't that kind of money preclude me from having to answer that question?"

"Male adult, sure. Kids and women, not a chance."

I liked her more and more, but I couldn't tell her the entire truth. Not with what I had in mind. "The child is in foster care right now, placed there by CPS, which is fine. For now, anyway."

"But soon," she spoke the rest for me, "this child is going to be released into . . . a hostile environment?"

"That's correct. There is a very real possibility the child is going to be released to a dangerous predator and then Alonzo will be in severe danger."

"I see."

"No, you don't." I raised my voice. Just that quick I'd let loose some of that pent-up rage Doc Abrams talked about. I held up my hands. "I'm sorry. Really. It's just this is a hot-button issue with me."

"Is this child your son?"

"No." That wasn't a lie. From the way she handled herself, and based on the questions she asked, I wouldn't be able to hide my identity from her for very long, not once she found Alonzo.

"What's going to happen when I find this location and give you the address?"

I stared her in the eyes. "I have nothing but goodwill toward this child. I promise you nothing bad is going to happen to him. I only want to ensure his safety and have only the best intentions. There's no subtext here, no hidden agenda."

She stared at me. The moment hung fat between us. I didn't look away and returned her gaze.

She took out a notepad and pen. "Okay, what's his full name?"

"Alonzo Sams."

"Black male? How old?"

"Yes, and he's just under two years old."

She closed her notebook and put it in her back pocket.

"Wait. What's wrong? Don't you want the rest of the information?"

"I'll have the address where CPS has placed Alonzo no later than tomorrow." She moved around the car and opened the door and stood looking over the roof of the Beemer.

"Hey," I said, "you don't know how to contact me."

She reached into her pants pocket and took out the wad of cash I'd given her. She tossed it to me. I caught it, stunned. "No, please, I need your help." I couldn't get anywhere close to Alonzo without someone recognizing me or I'd have already found him myself.

"The beard threw me off for a minute," she said. "Bruno, you're money's no good with me. I used to work LAPD. Ned Kiefer was a great guy. I was there that night Ned died. That same night you beat JB's ass in your front yard. I'll get you your address. And if you need anything else, anything at all, you just ask." She turned around to face Eighty-First Street and a used car lot on the south side. She stuck her index finger in the air and twirled it. A sleek, late-model black BMW with smoked windows, hidden among other cars, pulled out and drove away. She got in the banged-up red Beemer, started up, and followed.

Huh.

I got back into the stolen Monte and was met with the sweet scent of marijuana smoke. Nigel sat mellowed out and reclined in his seat smoking a fatty of high-grade sensimilla Kona Gold that we'd scored shortly after he picked me up in the Monte Carlo. I started the car. Nigel's head slowly came around. "Where to now, Bwana?"

"You said you were going to take me to get some guns."

"Yeah . . . yeah . . . that's right. No. Wait? Did I say that? You sure I said that? That's some heavy shit you're asking for this time." His eyes were mere slits.

"Yeah, you did say that, and yeah, you're going to do it. Now tell me where we're going."

He stayed slumped down below the window ledge. "Take it easy, big man. Cool your jets, okay? Jumbo, man, he can get you whatever you want. Long as you got the green. You got the green, big man?"

"Just tell me how to get there, Nigel, and let me worry about the rest."

"Jumbo's got everything you need. He took off a train car of military-grade shit. You want M-4 rifles, nine-mil pistols, he's got a ton of 'em." He laughed. "Literally a ton. Get it?"

"Just give me the directions."

Nigel tried to slap my arm and missed. "You got it, big man, head east. Jumbo's got an auto parts place over in Norwalk. He's sellin' 'em out the back door."

I pulled out onto Central and turned south. I'd only gone a block when the quick chirp from a cop car's siren caused me to check my rearview. An LAPD patrol car right behind us turned on its overhead red and blues, no siren. He wanted me to pull over.

"Ah, shit."

Nigel, still scrunched down in the seat and unaware of the threat, said, "Hey, you know, I could eat. You wanna stop and get some tacos?"

I pulled to the curb and stopped. "How does a sack lunch with a bologna sandwich on dried-out white bread sound?"

"Nah, man, I ate enough of those in jail. Let's get us some tacos."

CHAPTER TWO

BODY ODOR AND the sour essence of vomit never leaves the jail, no matter how hard the trustees scrub and scour. The scent particles permeate the natural pores in the concrete and tile grout. It stays there until the building grows antiquated and when demolished dies a silent death. Within months of opening a new jail, it too takes on that same essence, one that represents hopelessness and despair and all too often becomes a symbol of lost lives.

I sat on the concrete bench in a holding cell next to my partner in crime, Nigel Braddock, and fifteen other unfortunates. Some of them sat on the floor or stood against the wall. A fat black man with his shorts down to his ankles shamelessly stood over the stainless-steel toilet, urinating. The humid reek rose up and mingled among the other men, who had nowhere to go to get away from it.

The right side of my face throbbed from the kick the LAPD officer delivered while I lay facedown on the pavement, my hands out from my sides in a classic felony prone position. I had been taken out of a "rolling stolen" at gunpoint, and the cop gave me a little extra just because he could. Or maybe he had a thing against blacks or black truck drivers. I understood the concept, the theory of "them against us." Had it been twenty years earlier, the odds were better than even that I'd have ended up in a hospital jail ward with sutures and broken bones. Back then, this little bit of curbside justice was the reason why some GTA—Grand Theft Auto—artists preferred to take their chances running rather than take a well-deserved beating. Now they just ran so they could be on live news and enter the jail a newly minted television star.

The LAPD jailer, an older man with glasses and hair going gray, came to the bars with a big brass Forge key in his hand. "Karl Higgins? You got a visit. Get your ass up here." Most LAPD stations had their own holding cells where inmates were kept for court or before catching the chain to County. This jailer had worked too long in one of the world's many dungeons, and I could tell by the way he treated people that he no longer believed in the good of man; that, for him, only the dregs of humanity existed.

I got up. My old bones popped and creaked as I moved slowly toward the bars. "A visit?" I prayed to God it wasn't Dad. If he saw me like this—the guilt and shame of it—I'd melt into the concrete floor leaving behind tooth and bone and a pile of worn-out clothes and shoe leather. Then I realized the jailer called me by my aka instead of my real name. I let out a long breath, one I didn't know I'd been holding. The jailer opened the heavy barred gate. I didn't step out and held my ground.

"Who is it?"

"Not my problem, pal. You want the visit or not?"

I leaned my head out and looked down the hall. "Ah, shit."

Robby Wicks, my old boss from when I'd worked the violent crime team, stood with his thumbs hooked in his belt. He shot me a hateful glare. He shook his head in disgust. He waved for me to come out.

I stepped back into the cell. "I don't want the visit."

The jailer looked down the hall to Wicks and nodded. Then he looked back at me. "You don't have a choice. You come out on your own, or I'll get a couple of meat eaters and drag your ass out."

The day wasn't working out like I planned. I trudged from the cell, not looking forward to the berating I had coming. Wicks turned and moved into an alcove where all the incoming fish were photographed and printed. My fingertips still carried smudges of black ink. I'd never been arrested before, and it made me sick thinking about that damn booking photo being part of public record. How it now stood a good chance of getting leaked. I just didn't want Dad to see it.

Wicks wore his trademark brown polyester Western-cut coat and pants and ostrich cowboy boots. He must've just come from court. Today he also had on a bolo tie with a gold nugget clasp he'd always said was real. He'd lost some weight, and the suit hung off him.

He stood a head shorter than me and emitted a burnt tar and nicotine odor. His skin had aged faster than the rest of him, the ill effects of SoCal sun, cigarettes, and bourbon. He was one of that rare breed who thrived on the hunt, running down violent men, who, when cornered, would turn and fight. That's what he lived for: that violent confrontation. For him, nothing else mattered. It wouldn't be long before he was too old. He had already slowed too much and now survived merely on instinct and guts.

We'd been a great team. I had grown up in the street and knew how the animals we hunted thought and moved. I acted as his bird dog and led him to the wanted murderers where he, or sometimes the both of us, took them down. Too many times we had stood in the parking lot of a liquor store or grocery after a violent takedown, drinking beers in a celebratory ritual. Through the long hours of tracking and surveillance—the microseconds filled with gun smoke, filled with air so laden with fear you could smell it—we'd developed a special bond that could never be broken. One that many wouldn't understand.

Looking back on that life, coupled with what had happened in the last few months with my daughter, Olivia, and grandson, Albert,

I marveled at how it overshadowed everything else and made what Robby Wicks and I had been through seem juvenile and senseless, a couple of grown children playing at cops and robbers only with real guns and real blood and bone. What had it really accomplished?

He stared at me, not talking, waiting for me to admit the errors of my ways, the equivalent to kneeling and kissing his ring. He'd be waiting a long time. I liked him and respected him, but in the last couple of years—and more so in the last few months—he had not acted like a friend. When I left his violent crimes team to work in the courts so I could give my daughter, Olivia, the parental time she needed, time that she deserved, Wicks took it personally.

In the end, it didn't matter. I came up a day late and a dollar short with Olivia. That was my burden to carry and no one else's. Now I could only do my best to make it right. Find her some small iota of justice. Going to jail for a G-ride threw a big monkey wrench into things. And now I had to deal with Wicks. No way would I let him deride or belittle me.

"Well," he finally said, "what do you have to say for yourself?"

I stared at him and said nothing.

"Bruno, what the hell were you doing in that stolen car?"

I didn't have an excuse, not for him. I shrugged.

"You were driving it, for Christ's sake. You know how hard that's going to be to fix?"

I held his bitter glare. "How did you find out?"

But I knew. I'd made a small mistake by using the undercover name Karl Higgins when I was booked. Wicks had eyes and ears everywhere; that's how he'd survived the politics for so long. He had not, however, tumbled to my big secret, or he wouldn't be standing there talking to me. He'd be angry beyond belief that I had once again left him out of a major decision in my life.

He waved his hand in the air and didn't answer.

I said, "You never returned my calls."

He took a step closer, his lips tight. He pointed a finger toward the floor. "That has nothing to do with this right here right now. So, buddy boy, don't try and change the subject."

"Robby, what did you find out about Albert and Olivia?"

I couldn't get anywhere close to that investigation because of the huge conflict of interest, and the fact that I'd be arrested for obstruction if I tried. I could only sit in the courtroom and watch Derek work the system that favored the ruthless and the profane. So I'd asked my friend Wicks to look into it for me, do what he did best: figure out what had really happened. Who better to ask than your closest friend, a bulldog of a cop who wouldn't let go once he caught the scent of a crook? But something had happened, and I hadn't heard from him. For some unknown reason, he'd cut me adrift. Good thing I had already decided to go the long way around, through back channels in order to find out what really happened. I'd taken a big step in that direction just before the arrest in the Monte Carlo ruined all I'd gained.

"I looked into it." He turned uncomfortable and looked away. I knew him well enough to know the next words from his mouth would be a well-rehearsed lie. "And you just need to let it go. There's nothing there. It's just as the reports said—those two incidents, your daughter's overdose and your missing grandson, are unrelated."

"Did you get a chance to interview Sams and put the heat to him?"

"Stop it. Bruno, let it go. I told you that it would be this way and that you were barking at the moon. I told you to let it go and let the court handle Derek Sams.

"Now look at you. What the hell were you doing driving that stolen car? You give up your star after all those years of service, and what? You turn into one of them? You revert back to type."

Back to type? I wanted to slug him.

With him, it had always been us against them, and now, in his mind, I'd become one of *them*. Blind anger fueled his hateful words, so I didn't take them to heart as maybe I should have.

"I don't think you looked into it at all."

He brought his finger up and stuck it in my face. "I warned you this would happen. Didn't I? I told you that if you left the department, you'd go back to the street where you came from. Now I can't help you. Not with all of this." He waved his hand around as if the jail was the evil I had chosen over him.

"I asked you to help me with Albert and Olivia. I never asked you to look out for me. Please, just go. Walk away. You don't have to worry about it anymore. I'll take care of the final disposition of what happened with Albert and Olivia."

He pulled his head back. His mouth sagged open. "Don't you dare talk to me like I'm some kind of ignorant mope, not after all I've done for you."

"I don't work for you anymore, Robby. I can talk to you any way I choose."

He clenched his teeth, grabbed me by the throat, and shoved me up against the wall. He moved in close, his breath laden with burnt tobacco and expensive bourbon. "I have a good mind to leave you right here and let you rot."

I tried not to choke and sputter. "That's fine by me. Do it. Get the hell outta here."

The jailer came into the alcove. "You okay, Lieutenant?"

"Yeah, I got this." The jailer left.

Wicks let go, stood back, straightened his suit coat, and adjusted his tie. "For old times I should fix this for you, but I'm not going to, Bruno. Not this time. Before anyone can help you, you have to hit rock bottom, and I don't think you're there yet. Not with the way you're talking to me. You understand? I'm sorry, my friend, you got yourself into this, so you're just going to have to pay the price."

I rubbed my throat and said nothing.

He said, "And now, what I'm going to say next, I am not talking to you as a friend, I'm talking to you as a cop. Don't go near Derek Sams or his court case. If you do, I will personally get your bail revoked for this stolen car caper and see that you get the aggravated term in Chino."

He turned and walked away.

"Hey?" I said.

He turned back. "Keep your head down, huh?" A term of endearment we used to say to each other.

He started to come back, anger and violence in his expression.

I waved. "Don't. Just let it go."

Wicks hesitated, watching me. He turned and left.

The jailer came back into the alcove to put me back in the cage. "Can I get my phone call now?"

"Sure, why not?" He pointed to the pay phone on the wall. "You know the routine, dial 'O; it's got to be collect, pal, or not at all."

The guy wasn't doing me any favors; the law mandated two calls. I waited for him to leave or to at least step back out of range. Once he did, I dialed a number I had memorized. Since all phone calls in the jail are recorded, I whispered coded words into the receiver to Black Bart.

CHAPTER THREE

I STEPPED OUTSIDE the back gate of the jail, never happier to breathe the fresh air of freedom. I propped Nigel up with one hand under his arm. Two and a half days without meth and he looked like a tornado had scooped him up and set him down twenty miles away, raggedy, torn, and ready to fall to pieces.

We were arrested on Friday, and the system didn't kick us both out until Monday afternoon. I could've gotten out earlier, but I needed to stay close to Nigel so he wouldn't get eaten alive inside the human zoo. I took partial responsibility for his involvement. He'd stolen the car all on his own, but I'd been the one to arrange the meeting with the PI behind the Crazy Eight or we wouldn't have been there.

We were both given public defenders and arraigned in court. They released us on our own recognizance with a promise to appear at a later date. I should've felt worse about having a criminal record; instead more guilt piled on over missing the Monday morning court session to Derek Sams' trial for the murder of a dope dealer, William Percy, aka Bumpy Spanks.

Nigel made a phone call and got us a ride. After forty minutes, a young woman pulled up in an old Toyota Corolla. She looked thirty-five or so, dressed in denim jeans with holes in the knees. She wore her mouse-brown hair in a ponytail so severe it tugged back the skin from her face. She didn't smile and only grunted for us to get in. Nigel got in the front seat. "Thanks, kiddo, I owe you." He leaned over to give her a quick peck on the cheek.

With one hand, she shoved his face away. "Don't. Who's he? You didn't say anything about someone else. I won't have any of your doper friends in my car, especially . . . especially him." She looked over her shoulder at me and sneered. "Get out, mister, no free rides."

"I'm sorry to inconvenience you, but I really need this ride, and I'm willing to pay for it." I reached into the plastic bag that contained all my property and pulled out a separate envelope with *$3000.00* noted in black ink on the outside by the booking officer. Good thing that PI refused to take my money. I pulled out three bills and showed them to her. "I can pay my own way. It's worth fifty to me."

She looked at the money as if it were a cheeseburger and she hadn't eaten in a month. Then she looked at me. "You're not one of Dad's regular friends. You're not a doper?"

"I am your dad's friend, but you're right, I'm not a doper." I moved my hand with the money closer. "Here. Take it, please."

She snatched it away. "Thanks, mister." She turned in her seat, pulling the Corolla away from the curb and putting distance between the jail and us. Fine by me.

Nigel said, "Karl's a good Joe, Penny. He works at TransWorld Freightliners. He's giving me some work. It's piecework, sure, but it's still work. A place to start anyway. I'm finally getting my life back together. I am, you'll see." The lie flowed from his mouth smooth as liquid silk.

"Shut up, Dad. Just shut up and sit there. I had to take a half-day off work to pick you up. I said I'd never do it again and here I am doing it again." She looked in the rearview and caught my eyes. "I'm sorry, I shouldn't have talked to you like that. It's just that Dad has priors, if you know what I mean?"

"That's okay, I understand."

"Where to?"

"Sorry, but it's a little bit of a drive to my place. Shoot over to Alameda and take it south. This time of day, that'll be the fastest. The freeways will be jammed already."

We drove, and for a little while, no one spoke. Nigel had withdrawal symptoms; his hands shook and his facial muscles twitched. He put his head against the window and eased down a little in his seat. He closed his eyes, his lids fluttered, the picture of someone in the throes of night terrors.

Penny maneuvered through the afternoon traffic and spoke over her shoulder. "It wasn't always like this. Dad used to work for Boeing. He had a great job as an aerospace engineer. We had a nice . . . a nice life. Until he lost it all." She snapped her fingers. "Just like that, his house, his family, everything, gone. Dope ate it all. That stuff is insidious."

"Hey, kiddo, I'm sitting right here." He didn't open his eyes when he spoke. He'd heard it too often. Her disparaging words no longer carried the same sharp-edged bite.

But for me, what she said did pile on another layer of guilt. I wasn't Nigel's friend, not really. I was only using him as a conduit into a criminal life where I didn't have access.

I'd heard his story, or ones just like it, again and again throughout my years in law enforcement: coke, heroin, meth, and ruined lives. Not just the users but entire families were impacted for decades to come. South of the border, hundreds of thousands of people died and continue to die over the United States' gluttony for drugs. Sometimes I thought it might be better to just legalize all drugs. That way only the person who made the poor choice would take the hit. Legalize it, tax it, and put all the money toward rehabilitation. Society would be better served.

But my worldview was tainted now. Drugs had stolen my little girl from me, along with my grandson.

From Friday to Monday afternoon, I could only catnap. I had to stay vigilant to the dangers in the jail. Now fatigue hung off my bones like a blanket soaked in warm water. I fought the urge to curl up and sleep. Anywhere would be fine. Only there wasn't time. I had to get home, shower and change, and get down to Compton court to see the tail end of today's session of the Derek Sams trial. If I hustled, I could catch the last witness for the day.

My biggest problem right now was Dad. I'd have to explain where I'd been. He had to be worried sick. He'd be angry and justifiably so. I considered making something up, a whopper of a lie. But lies diminished Dad's integrity, his honor. I couldn't take much more guilt before I spun deeper into the depths of despair, unable to dig out. I *would* have to tell him the truth, at least a small portion of it. Later on, he'd find out the rest.

Nigel started snoring.

I leaned forward in an attempt to stay awake. I caught Penny's eyes in the rearview as she watched me. "Sit back, please."

I stayed.

She nodded as if she understood my decision and accepted it.

I asked, "So where do you work?"

She looked to the road then back. "Why?"

"Just making conversation."

"I work two jobs. I'm a legal secretary during the day; and on weekends, I'm a hostess at Stars, a night club in Hollywood. I'm going to law school at night."

"Geez, when do you sleep?"

"Yeah, and I need this right now like a hole in the head."

"I'm sorry."

"What happened? Which one of you stole the car?"

"I'm going to let your dad tell you that one."

"I get it. That means he did. You seem like a nice enough person. I'm sorry he dragged you down with him. Take some advice, get as far away from him as you can."

A sad admonishment coming from his own daughter.

"I like your dad."

"He's a drug addict." She checked the mirror. "Do you use?"

"No."

"Addicts are good at lying."

"I don't know you so there's no reason to lie."

"Unless you want something you haven't asked for."

"I don't want anything but a ride home."

We'd made it to Alameda and headed south. "When we come to Imperial, take a right; then to Wilmington, take a left; then a left on 120th. You can let me off there, a few blocks in."

"Is that where you live?"

"Close enough." I didn't want Nigel to know my address.

"That's not a very nice part of town where you live."

"I grew up there."

"What does the company you work for do? What did Dad call it, TransWorld Freightliners?"

"It's an import-export business that's mostly logistical. We move things around, store it for a while, then sell when the market for that item heats up."

"Huh? Never heard of anything like that before."

"Yeah, whoever thought it up is making a fortune. I'm just a small cog in the big machine."

"Is Dad really working with you?"

"He's making some money here and there."

"That's good, I guess, but he's still using. I can smell it on him."

"It's hard to kick when you've been at it as long and hard as he has. It's really good of you to help him out like this, giving him a ride. Being there for him when it counts. It tells him that you still care. He needs that."

"You think he'll ever come out of it? You think he'll ever quit?"

"There's always hope." I didn't know why I said it. Hope no longer fit anywhere in my vocabulary.

She checked her mirror and locked onto my eyes. "Why did you get arrested? Why were you in the car? You don't seem the type."

"I'm sure you've heard it before, but this time it's the truth: wrong place, wrong time."

She smiled and looked as if she believed me. She had great eyes, and seeing into them gave me a glimpse of a world that used to exist and no longer did, not for me. Not until I finished what needed to be done, and maybe not even then.

CHAPTER FOUR

TEN MINUTES LATER, she pulled over on 120th Street. I got out and stood by her open car window. "Thanks again for the ride. You saved me a lot of trouble."

Through the driver's window, she handed me a business card for a law office down the block from CCB, the Criminal Courts Building in downtown Los Angeles. "This is where I work. My home number is on the back. If you could look out for him and let me know how he's doing, I'd really appreciate it." She smiled big for the first time. She stayed a half beat longer and drove off. I watched the car until it made the first turn.

I looked at the card and played back in my mind what she'd said. A part of me wanted to think there had been a subtext to her request, that we'd somehow, in that short car ride, connected. I looked down the street where the car had made the turn, then back at the card. I crumpled it up and let it drop in the gutter.

Twenty minutes later, I opened the door to our house on Nord. Junior Mint, Olivia's big dog, jumped me and wanted to play. He was a real handful, a hundred pounds of pure muscle. I got down on the floor and wrestled with him until I ran out of steam and called it quits. He'd play all day if I let him. I opened the back door to let him out in the yard to do his business. He wouldn't go until I stepped out on the porch. He had an unwarranted fear I'd close the door and lock him out of my life. He'd only started acting that way after Olivia passed.

He moved around sniffing the shrubs and trees out back. Olivia loved Junior, and to see him and to touch him reminded me so much of her it continued to bring burning tears to my eyes. He had the red bandana tied to his collar that she put there. I'd never take it off. I'd given him to her when he was just a pup. Back then, almost three years ago, he was small and fluffy and mostly black with a tinge of brown. He had huge paws. The first time she saw him, her face glowed with genuine joy. She held him up to look at him. "He looks just like one of those Junior Mint candies. I'm going to call him Junior Mint." She brought the puppy in close and let him lick her face. She giggled. I could still hear that wonderful sound and hoped like hell time wouldn't diminish the memory.

I called him and he came running. I filled his food and water bowls, then went in to take a much-needed shower. He followed my every step. Lately, I'd been too busy to give him the attention he deserved. He needed a home with children to run him ragged. He'd been great with Albert and Alonso, my twin grandsons.

The shower never felt better, and I ran the water heater out of hot water. I got dressed in a clean pair of denim pants and a khaki shirt with patches that said *TransWorld Freightliners* and *Karl*. I stomped on my heavy black work boots and laced them up. I headed for the front door when fatigue again took hold and tried to drag me back to the bed.

The phone rang.

I didn't know where Dad had gone. It had to be one of his friends on the phone. No one ever called me anymore. I answered it.

Harry Dolan, a newspaper reporter, said, "Hey, Bruno, I missed you in court today."

"How's it going, Harry? Yeah, I ran into one of life's little complications."

"I know how that is, but with you to miss this show, it had to be a helluva complication."

During my two years as bailiff in Judge Phillip Connors' courtroom, I'd met and befriended Harry who worked the crime beat. Compton court had more than enough crime to keep him busy. He gave Derek Sams' case a little extra attention for my benefit.

"Maybe I'll tell you about it someday."

"I'm always looking for a good story. Do you know why they recessed the Sams case today? I asked the DA, and he gave me the high-hat routine."

"No, I don't."

This new information meant I no longer had to hurry to court. My body relaxed all on its own and allowed fatigue to take first priority and start to cloud my thoughts.

"You know as well as I do, those kind of things happen all the time. I'll call a friend of mine in the court and find out. If its anything out of the norm, I'll ring you back. Thanks for the call."

"You got it, Bruno. Will I see you in court tomorrow?"

"I'll be there."

I hung up and dialed Esther, who worked for Judge Connors in a different court than the Sams trial. The phone rang and rang. That was odd; she ate her lunch at her desk and always answered during business hours. Even with court in session, I'd seen Esther lower her head, cup her hand over the phone, and whisper. Connors' court must be dark for the day. I started to dial Connors' home and changed my mind.

I looked around for Junior and found him sleeping on Olivia's bed. We had not touched her room; it remained the same as she left it the day she died six months ago. Junior missed her too.

Seeing Junior on O's bed made me realize I wouldn't be able to sleep. I left Dad a note on the kitchen table. Junior, sensing I was leaving, ran and stood by the door. He liked going along. "All right, but this time you better mind your manners. No biting the bad guys, you understand?" He turned his head sideways as if trying to understand. We went out, got in my truck, and headed for TransWorld Freightliners in Lakewood. Another reason I wouldn't be able to sleep. I needed to explain to my boss about the three thousand dollars in my pocket.

CHAPTER FIVE

OUT OF INSTINCT and habit I drove in and around TransWorld Freightliners checking for people or cars I'd recognize, checking for a threat. Looking for furtive people, the dregs of society who skulked about looking for a target of opportunity. The possibility of an attack from an angry customer remained foremost on the minds of everyone who worked at TW. According to James Barlow, "Trans-World is a septic tank that draws in every turd from miles around." Based on this analogy, Barlow, a man who never missed a Sunday prayer meeting, referred to the people we dealt with as "Brown Trout, who had the inalienable right to be flushed."

Junior Mint sat up on the front seat of my Ford Ranger, his eyes on full alert as if he, too, knew the dangers that lurked around every corner. I continued to make my usual circuit of all the buildings in the complex.

Barlow's Harley Davidson Softail Deluxe sat around back of TW in the same place he always parked.

TW, a storefront operation, was buried deep in a light industrial area of Lakewood and didn't sport any signage other than a stenciled name painted in red above the smoked double glass doors in front. The back door was kept heavily barred, and no one was allowed to use it.

TW sat at the far end of a cul-de-sac and had CCT cameras that covered the approach of all cars and pedestrians. Even so, I always played it safe. It was better to handle a problem when it was small rather than wait until it spun out of control, something Dad pounded into my head from a young age.

Without a word of advertising, TW depended exclusively on word of mouth for business. If the good people of Lakewood knew about us, they would raise "holy hell and we'd all be looking for a new job," this also according to Barlow, our boss, who went by the street name Black Bart. That's why we kept our presence on the down low.

I didn't mind walking in from two or three or even four blocks out. I parked the Ford Ranger under a magnolia tree at the side of B and R Plastics, a factory that made ballpoint pen bodies, key chain fobs, and their bread-and-butter item, a variety of bobblehead dolls that mounted on car dashboards or in back windows. I parked in a different spot each time, always someplace in the same industrial park. I didn't want my truck to be associated with TW's criminal enterprise. After Friday's arrest and incarceration, my choice to join TW was turning out to be a bigger mistake than I had anticipated.

I walked a block on the sidewalk and cut in, moving down the asphalt access through the long concrete tilt-up buildings. Junior stayed at my side without a leash. He wanted to run off and sniff the shrubs and walls and fire hydrants. Every time his curiosity got the better of him and he'd veer off, I'd say, "Junior." He'd come right back to my side.

The big roll-up door to Sparkle Plenty, a place that customized chrome for antique car bumpers, car trim, and anything else people wanted chromed, stood open to let out the heat from the liquid metal vats inside. Leonard Martinez Jr., the owner's son, waved. "Hey, Karl, wait up a second." He came out and hurried to catch up.

Junior let go with a low growl. He possessed an inborn crook alert that had not been wrong yet.

"What's going on?" I asked. But I knew, and I didn't want to have this conversation. Leo wore all black tattoos on his arms and neck, the kind obtained almost exclusively in the joint. If I wanted to play the odds, I'd bet money he was still on parole. His dad, Leo Senior, a helluva nice guy, made him show up for work every day whether he picked up a tool or not. He just wanted to keep an eye on his son, to keep him out of trouble.

"Hey, can you stop for a second? I need to talk to you."

"Sorry, man, I'm late for work."

Leo followed along in quickstep. He looked back twice to the open bay door to his dad's business. He licked his lips, his tongue was dry and caked, and his body hummed with anxiety. All subtle symptoms of a casual meth user, one who stood on the razor edge ready to take the final plunge into full-on tweaker.

"Hey, ah . . . word on the street is that you guys over at TransWorld buy guns and the like and—"

I stopped and rounded on him. "Go back to work, Leo. You don't want any part of what I'm buying over the counter at TW."

"So it's true?"

I tried to think of a way around the problem while Black Bart's voice boomed in my head: "We buy from any and all Brown Trout that swim our way, no exceptions. You hear me? None, zero. You turn someone down, the word goes out, and it'll ruin our reputation. And in this business, reputation is everything."

"What do you got?" I reached down and took hold of Junior Mint's collar so he wouldn't lose his cool and bite Leo. Two weeks earlier, he'd bit a skinny black guy named Trunk, who Nigel had brought into TW to sell a gun. Trunk didn't ask permission before he pulled the Desert Eagle .44 from under his Raiders football jersey. Bad manners on his part that could've gotten him killed. Before anyone could stop him, Junior Mint leapt and took hold of Trunk's arm. Twenty-seven sutures later, Black Bart said Junior Mint was no longer allowed out in front of the counter. For morale purposes, he stopped short of complete banishment; everyone in TW loved Junior Mint.

Leo once again looked down the row of businesses to the open bay of Sparkle Plenty to see if his dad had noticed him missing, and then back at me. "I might have a few guns."

"What are they and how did you get them?" Parolees and ex-cons weren't allowed to possess any type of firearm.

"Let's just say . . . that . . . well, you know, I found them abandoned in an alley." He winked at me. He'd taken them in a residential burglary to supplement his income and support his drug habit.

"What exactly did you find in this alley?"

"I can bring 'em over tonight after work. You going to be open late?"

"We can be. Handguns, rifles, what?"

"Yeah, some of each."

"How many?"

"Twenty pistols and eleven rifles. How much do you think I can get for them?"

"We'd have to see them first, but I'm going to tell you up front; if they're hot, you're not going to get anywhere close to wholesale value."

"Yeah, yeah, I get it. Gimme a guess? Ballpark?" His eyes glowed with greed.

"Fifty each for the rifles and seventy-five for the handguns. Was anyone hurt when you found these guns in the alley?"

His mind spun trying to do the math in his head.

"Around two grand," I said, to save him from having part of his brain blow out his ear from the effort.

"Two grand, huh?" He licked his lips again. "You know the going rate on the street is two hundred each. I can get more on the street."

"Then why are you talking to me?" I took a step to leave. He took hold of my arm. Junior let loose with a soft rumble. I'd low-balled Leonard on purpose. I really didn't want his father going through the kind of pain his son's poor judgment would cause.

"Can you do a little better?"

"Not up to me, it's up to my boss. Was anyone hurt?"

"What? Nah, nothing like that, it's all cool."

"Come around about eight tonight, and we'll fix you up."

He took my hand to shake. Junior growled and lunged at him. I pulled him back and told him no. I said to Leonard, "I have to get to work. See you tonight."

"Yeah. Hey, Karl, don't say anything to my dad, okay?"

I just stared at him. I couldn't imagine what it would do to my dad if I'd committed a burglary, stolen a bunch of guns, and sold them for dope. Dad wouldn't say a thing, but the look in his eyes would have the same effect as a Mack truck falling on me.

"I'll catch ya later, Leo." I tugged Junior around and we headed for TW. I could feel Leo's eyes on my back until I made the turn in between the buildings.

CHAPTER SIX

I CAME OUT in front of TW, opened the door, and entered. Rodney Davis stood behind the counter. He went by the nickname RD while working TW. "Hey, Karl. You're late. Bart wants to see you ASAP. Hey, Junior, come here, boy."

I let go of Junior, who took off running. He rounded the corner of the counter and tackled RD. I stepped over them and went into the back, past the break room that opened to a huge warehouse area with rows and rows of cheap gray shelving, eight feet high, that contained every kind of used and new household item: power tools, TVs, stereos, silverware, you name it. Even a couple of banged-up yard gnomes. Their eyes seemed to follow me as I walked by. Against one wall of the warehouse stood a row of seven gun safes, all purchased at the same time, all with the same combination. Three stolen cars sat in the bay close to the roll-up back door: a Honda Civic, a Dodge minivan, and a shiny new yellow Corvette with Arizona plates.

Black Bart spied me from his open office door. "Karl, get your shabby black butt in here."

"Yes, sir." I entered and closed the door. The burly James Barlow never shaved or cut his shaggy black hair and looked more like Chewbacca's long-lost brother than a D-3 from LAPD. He could burn right through a person with his wet brown eyes. A scar peeked out the top of his beard on the right cheek, the end result of a broken beer bottle in a Pacoima bar fight when he wore a uniform. He had knuckles the size of quarters and was one person I never wanted to go up against—not without something long and heavy in my hand. Even then, maybe not.

"You got yourself arrested in a G-ride?"

"Sorry, boss."

"What did I tell you? That arrest could've gone a lot different. You know that, don't you? You could be in the hospital right now, but I'm not telling you anything you don't already know. Where would I be without my best field man?"

I sat in the chair in front of his desk and held up the flat of my hand. "I know. I said I was sorry. It won't happen again. Nigel was too loaded for me to let him drive. He'd have piled up the Monte for sure. I didn't know he'd bring a hot ride to our meet, and I couldn't leave it there." Bart didn't know about my meeting with the PI. That was strictly personal business conducted on company time.

Black Bart eased back in his chair; the butt-chewing portion of the meeting was over. "Get me the report on your version of what happened ASAP, and I'll have the DA do a no-file. But I can't get the record in CII expunged until—"

"I know all of that. I knew the risks when I signed up for this detail. It's just the cost of doing business."

Nobody could know about TransWorld. The storefront acted as a criminal magnet drawing in the bad guys like moths to a flame. The city of Lakewood would be furious if they knew. If word ever did get out that TransWorld Freightliners was a front for a sting, all of our time and the federal grant money would be wasted.

Cops, probation, and parole officers were the worst gossips, so they, too, were left out of the loop. The edict for all personnel involved in

the sting—no exceptions—was that nobody was to know, not even
wives or family or best friends. If one person slipped and word got
out, it would spread around the street in a nanosecond.

"Enough said on that point. Now onto the only stuff I really care
about, the money. RD says you checked out three grand. You have
chits to cover that amount? I told you, I need to know about it before you take it out."

I reached into my pocket, pulled out the envelope, and tossed it
on his desk. "It's short fifty. I had to get a ride back from the jail. I
needed the money for flash on a gun deal."

He eyed me, opened his desk drawer, raked the envelope in, and
closed it. He wanted in the worst way to do a count. I could see it in
his demeanor, but out of good leadership, he'd wait until I wasn't
present.

"Fifty's pretty heavy for a ride home from the jail."

I shrugged.

"Chit it and I'll approve it."

"Thanks, boss."

If the PI behind the Crazy Eight had taken the money, we'd have
been having an entirely different conversation. Didn't matter. I was
willing to risk it to find out where Social Services had placed my
grandson Alonzo. He didn't need to be in someone else's home
being raised by people he didn't know. An absolutely horrible situation I needed to rectify one way or another.

Black Bart leaned back and put his heavy black motorcycle boot
up on the desk, and for the hundredth time, I wondered what the
people of his church thought of him looking the way he did. I
wanted to hear the wild explanation he gave them as to what he did
for a living looking like an escaped black bear from a zoo.

He said, "Nigel give up his big gun connection he keeps bumpin'
his gums about?"

"He was taking me there when two of your brothers in blue pulled us over and ruined our weekend."

"Excellent. Get Nigel back online and let's set up a deal with his connect."

"Nigel says this Jumbo took off a train car loaded with government M4 rifles and 9mm pistols. Said there was literally a ton of the stuff."

Black Bart brought his leg down and came forward, his eyes going larger than normal. I had never seen him get excited about anything. "You've got to be kiddin' me? That kind of deal will put us on the map." He waved his hand. "It'll make all this other stuff we've done look like child's play."

"Not to mention taking a butt-load of guns off the street."

"Yeah, that too." He pulled a notepad over and started writing. "Did he say where and when this heist went down? Never mind, there can't be too many. If this isn't pure braggadocio then it's probably the only one of its kind. This is big, Karl, my friend. This is huge."

"If it's true, we're not going to have enough money to flash for the buy bust, not for a deal this large."

Black Bart waved his hand as he continued to write. "If I can confirm this, it won't matter. We can get ATF to come in and front us the bread we need. I just have to make a few phone calls. You go find Nigel and make nice with him."

"If I treat him nice, he's going to know something's up."

"I don't care then, slap him around, just do what you do best and get him to intro you to this Jumbo dude. Also, get RD to work on identifying Jumbo."

I got up and opened the door. "I don't like the idea of the feds coming in on this. It'll be harder to keep Nigel out of it. I won't put Nigel up front."

"I'll do the best I can on Nigel, you know that."

"I know you will." I turned to go.

"Bruno?"

I turned. Black Bart was death on maintaining our cover names, so him calling me by my real name caused my back to stiffen. "Yeah, boss?"

"I heard about Wicks coming to see you in the can. That wasn't right, what he said to you."

I said nothing and stared at him. The boys in blue had a serious pipeline for underground information.

"I know how hard that was not to tell him about this operation. I just want you to know I appreciate it."

Black Bart didn't ask if I had told Wicks. In the six months we'd worked together on the sting, he'd come to know the way I worked. I nodded and left his office to go find Nigel.

CHAPTER SEVEN

I walked back the way I'd come through the warehouse area to collect my dog. Rodney Davis, an LAPD D-2, still sat on the floor behind the TW counter playing with Junior Mint, play-slapping his face. Junior whined and nipped at him with pure glee in his eyes.

The other side of the counter, the public area, contained three rows of standard gray shelving that held cheap auto parts and supplies: car batteries, jumper cables, cases of motor oil and the like. All of it from China, used only as window dressing to disguise the operation, things nobody in their right mind would purchase.

Rodney Davis wouldn't answer to his other nickname, Stool Sample, a tag his good friend Black Bart had bestowed upon him. I never asked the story behind it and didn't want to know. RD was the sting operation's house mouse; he never left the environs behind the counter. He liked the thrill of the job but didn't have the instinct, or if it ever came down to it, the emotional ability to pull the trigger. If out on a food run and some thug approached him and said, "Gimme your lunch money," RD would comply without a peep. The way Wicks had always broken down the divisions of society, there were only two classifications of people: the victims and the predators. These two groups existed in the cop job, with

civilians, and with the bad guys. RD just happened to be a victim
who carried a badge.

RD loved dogs, so he couldn't be all bad. He handled the lion's
share of paperwork the operation generated, and there was a ton of
it. He kept track of all the evidence, the money, the scheduled larger
deals that happened over TW's counter, and he collated and filed
all the reports in thick three-ring binders. There were ten of them so
far filled with six hundred and fifty-seven buys. We'd seized just
under two thousand guns, and, counting Nigel's Monte Carlo,
fifty-six stolen cars. Everyone who did business with TW walked
away with cash money in their pockets. RD was also tasked with
identifying all the crooks, a monumental job in itself. No one would
be arrested until the final takedown unless that person was deemed
a threat to public safety. Then an anonymous call would be made to
the appropriate law enforcement agency.

Two other Los Angeles Police detectives worked as I did in the
field as ropers directing unsuspecting crooks to TW. Two more Los
Angeles County Sheriff detectives borrowed from Metro worked
the office doing the deals and acting as cover and control and site
security. They hung out in TW's office with the one-way mirror,
smoked, ate street tacos, and played gin. And through it all, RD did
his best to keep up with us and keep us organized.

When the sting started, Black Bart only let us bring in one
sucker at a time to keep things from getting out of hand and to let
us get used to working together. The other rule he had was that no
matter how small the deal, at least two undercover cops had to be
on the premises when a deal went down. Usually three or four
stood close by.

One of us always stood behind the one-way glass with a shotgun
shouldered and pointed at the crook out in the lobby doing the deal.
What Black Bart feared most was a rip. When you dealt with

nothing but life's bottom feeders, a holdup became a very real possibility. The crooks would view it as a freebie. Since we were hip-deep in nefarious criminal activity, or at least the appearance of such, they would easily figure that if they robbed us, we'd never call the police. This made our cash operation four or five times as dangerous as a regular undercover assignment in narcotics. The threat remained high, always there hanging over our heads.

On a shelf right under the counter, resting on a piece of soft green felt, sat a pistol-grip 12-gauge shotgun with an extended magazine. Black Bart had also installed a button to electronically bolt the front door for anyone who did try to do a hit-and-run.

After the first week of roping and bringing in crooks to sell their stolen property, word spread countywide. Soon we had walk-ins who brought everything you could imagine, items stolen from all over the greater Los Angeles metropolitan area. Every day at eleven o'clock in the morning, a throng of criminals stood outside the door of TW waiting for it to open. They smoked and twitched and scratched, most all of them jonesing for their next fix.

"RD," I said, "let go of my dog. I gotta go."

He put his arm around Junior. "I don't think so, big man. Junior wants to stay here with me; he told me so. Right, Junior?"

I whistled. Junior jumped up and tried to break free. RD held on, his arms around his neck.

"I wouldn't do that if I were you; he's going to nip your nose."

"He won't. We're pals, aren't we, Junior?"

I slapped my leg. "Come."

Junior again tried to pull away. RD held him for a second too long. He jumped back just as Junior whined and nipped at his face.

RD released him. "Cripes, Karl, you didn't have to sic him on me."

"If I'd have sicced him on you, you'd know it. Listen, at eight tonight, Leo Martinez from Sparkle Plenty is coming in with twenty handguns and eleven rifles. I forgot to tell Black Bart; would you mind telling him? I plan on being here, but if I don't make it back in time, maybe he could have a couple of the other guys here to make the deal?"

"Hey, I know Leo. I can do that deal myself."

I stared at him. He nodded. "Okay, I'll tell Bart."

"Thanks, I'm beat. Bart left me in jail over the weekend, and I didn't get any sleep. I'm going home to get some sack time but I'll be back."

I moved around the counter and headed for the front door.

"Hey, Karl?"

I turned. Junior stopped and sat next to my leg, his head turned upward to see what I'd do next.

"I heard what happened over at Southeast Division, what your old commander said to you."

The jailer had been eavesdropping and had told Bart about an ex-deputy who'd been arrested and then Bart had told Stool Sample. I didn't know how to respond.

RD lost his smile and said, "You don't have to worry. I'll take care of it."

I walked back to the counter with him still on the other side. "I don't want you to do anything. It's over. Done." RD didn't understand the relationship I had with Wicks; I wasn't sure anyone would.

RD shrugged, pasted on a fake smile. "I gotcha."

"Really, I'm not kidding."

RD's work at TW kept him constantly on the move, but somehow he still found time for practical jokes, the kinds of pranks cops were known for. In fact, he'd pulled one too many and had gotten bounced from an already career-killing assignment working downtown forgery. Black Bart and RD had been friends for years, went to the same church, and ran in the same social circles. TW was RD's last shot before his department dumped him in the Motor Pool checking cars out to the real cops.

Last Christmas, while working forgery, RD bought a slew of ten-dollar coffeehouse gift cards and put each one in a Christmas card. He addressed and signed them as if they came from the captain of the division. He put them in the individual detective bureau mail slots, all except for two detectives who constantly made fun of him. The day he did it he made sure he stood next to the mail slots when those two detectives arrived for work. He pulled out the Christmas card he'd given himself and said, "Oh, look, a card from the captain. Hey, a ten-dollar gift card, that's really cool." The two detectives checked the other mailboxes and found everyone had received the coffeehouse gift card except them. They fumed for a couple of hours until they'd had enough. They stormed into the captain's office and slammed the door. Yelling ensued inside the glassed office while RD told everyone in the bullpen what he had done. When the two detectives came out, all the others laughed. The two immediately figured out they'd been had by RD and chased him from the office. The next day, Black Bart got RD assigned to TW. That had been six months ago.

"You sure?" RD said.

"Yes, I'm sure. Leave Wicks alone. He doesn't have a sense of humor. Now I gotta go. Don't forget to tell Bart about the deal tonight at eight."

He nodded. "You know, you spent the weekend in the can, and today, just walking into this place you hooked up a deal with thirty-one guns. The three days you were on ice, Jack and Frank combined didn't do that well."

"I didn't do anything for that deal, Leo ran *me* down."

"That's exactly what I'm talking about."

I turned and walked away. I raised my hand in the air as a good-bye. I didn't want to leave. I really didn't want to go home either.

But my body demanded it. Sleep had become the worst part of my life. I had no control over my dreams. Guilt reigned king over those night terrors. Each and every time I nodded off, Albert and Olivia, with their ghostlike pallor, visited me. Both in eternal slumber with their eyes open. Their silent entreaties let me know I had failed them. I could only apologize again and again and wish like hell I had a chance to do it over. Only life didn't allow do-overs.

Instinct had told me what to do and I didn't listen. Three years earlier, I had stalked and then grabbed Derek Sams out in front of a pager store on Central Avenue. I took him for a ride, intent on resolving the problem by dropping a sealed drum stuffed with his lifeless body into San Pedro harbor. He'd been going out with Olivia, dragging her down into the gutter. The day before I'd grabbed him, he had jeopardized her safety by taking her into a rock house where she'd been held against her will.

But after talking to him, seeing the youthful exuberance in his eyes, I couldn't do it. I let him go with the sternest of warnings and a very serious threat to his life. The moral compass Dad had instilled in me would not allow me to go through with the plan. The biggest single mistake of my life. I would much rather have had to live with *his* death on my conscience than the deaths of my daughter and grandson.

I walked back to the Ford Ranger in a daze, no longer on alert for any kind of threat, no longer caring. I really did need some sleep.

CHAPTER EIGHT

I PULLED UP in front of our house on Nord, the place where I'd grown up with my brother, Noble. I couldn't live in my apartment in South Gate, not after what had happened there. Too many bad memories.

Junior barked and scratched at the truck window. He'd seen Dad standing in the front yard. Dad had some kind of sixth sense that at times freaked me out. After I'd been gone for almost three days, how did he know I'd be pulling up at that moment?

I leaned across Junior and opened the passenger door. He barreled out and ran toward Dad. Dad went down on one knee to pet and wrestle with him, all the while not taking his eyes from mine. He was upset about my three-day absence and had every right to be. An easy solution would be to tell him about TransWorld, tell him that I hadn't really resigned as a deputy. If I told Dad and asked him not to tell a soul, I knew without reservation he would keep his word. And that was why I had to keep mine to Black Bart.

I got out and tried not to trudge over to Dad and failed miserably. Junior sensed the shift in mood and stopped playing. His tongue lolled out as he sat next to Dad's leg. He'd look at Dad then back at me.

"Where you been, Son?"

His question hit like a lash.

When we were little, Dad had explained to us about truth, and how an omission or an economic truth could be deemed the same as a lie.

"I don't think you want to know." My voice came out low and then tapered off.

He glared at me. I wanted to melt into the ground.

He finally said, "You weren't in court today?"

"That's right. For some reason the judge put it over. I'll be there tomorrow."

He nodded. That wasn't what he meant with his question. He knew I'd never miss a court appearance, not when it concerned Derek Sams.

"You look like hell. Maybe you should go in and get some sleep. We can talk about this when you get up."

"Thanks, Dad." A lump rose in my throat. He could've put the screws to me, and in my state of fatigue, I would've crumbled like a piece of blue cheese. I would've violated my code of honor and told him everything. I walked by, stopped, and put my hand on his shoulder.

He gripped my arm. "Get some sleep, Son."

"Thanks, Dad."

I continued on and stepped up on the little wooden stoop at the front door.

"Bruno?"

I turned.

"Judge Connors called."

Connors, unlike Wicks, had been a good friend, and every few days since Olivia passed, he'd call to see how I was doing. He also knew what I was capable of and was worried I'd go off the reservation chasing parties unknown who'd committed the most heinous act upon my family.

"When?"

"Friday morning, early. I haven't seen you to tell you."

"Okay, thanks. Could you wake me at seven, please?" I could hardly keep my eyes open. I half-stumbled up the steps, through the living room, and down the hall to my room and fell on the bed. What I had failed to tell Dad guaranteed a nap filled with nightmares of evil deeds.

*   *   *

Derek Sams didn't go far to lose himself, about a hundred miles from Los Angeles to a city at the top of Cajon Pass called Victorville. With an elevation of four thousand feet, the night was bitter cold, and I could see my breath. With the ocean influence so close, that rarely happened in South Central LA. I'd tracked him through people on the street in Willowbrook where he sold rock and heroin and where he still kept in contact with those who sold for him. Nineteen years old, he had never learned right from wrong; he just knew how to lie and cheat to get what he wanted, what he needed to feel good in that fleeting moment and to hell with what came after.

He'd come out of a fleabag motel called The Green Spot a block in off Seventh Street and cruised around until he spotted a Hispanic hooker on D Street who wore a dirty coat with fur trim and not much else underneath. He picked her up and brought her back to his room. Number seventeen painted by hand in white on a green door.

I stood behind a telephone pole in the shadow of a streetlight, wearing a navy-blue nightwatchman's cap and an army surplus green fatigue jacket, waiting until he had enough time to get his pants off. I'd been warned multiple times to stay away from the investigation. And as far as anyone knew, I was. I hadn't come for the purposes of investigating.

I stood in the cold doing a slow burn. A hooker, someone who could have hepatitis C or AIDS, diseases easily transmitted to Olivia. I clenched my fists. Derek was my seventeen-year-old daughter's boyfriend, the father to my twin grandsons, Albert and Alonzo. Two weeks earlier, Albert had disappeared from our apartment in South Gate. South Gate PD had exhausted all avenues in the missing persons investigation, going so far as to polygraph both Olivia and Derek. They passed. But I knew Derek better than most. He was a sociopath and more than capable of telling a perfect lie while drinking a glass of whole milk. I'd waited until there was nothing more South Gate could do before I intervened.

Then Derek had gone missing. He'd known I would step in.

He should've been at home consoling Olivia and taking care of Alonzo when he just took off. And that's when I found him in the high desert with a hooker.

I left my gun in the car, afraid of what I'd be tempted to do. I checked my watch again: ten long minutes had lapsed, plenty enough time to conclude his business. I stayed in the shadows, going behind the cars in the parking lot, and moved up to the flimsy wood door that had been kicked in before. More than once. The frame had been repaired and not replaced. I took out a Buck knife and quietly stuck the blade in between the jamb and the plate and worked back the bolt. I eased the door open.

On a swayback bed the naked Hispanic hooker straddled my daughter's boyfriend, her hips moving back and forth. Derek laughed and reached around and slapped her naked butt cheek. "Come on, girl, move your ass. What do you think I'm paying—" He stopped. Through the open door the cold December air penetrated the thick and smothering heat put out by the wall heater. He looked around the fleshy side of his night's entertainment and saw me as I eased the door closed. His expression shifted from glee to pure terror. The hooker looked over her shoulder and said, "Take a number, mister." She looked down at Derek. "Hey, what happened? Where'd you go?"

I said, "Grab your clothes and take a walk."

Derek made his move. His hand shot out to the nightstand for the black automatic he'd put there just in case. I moved faster and put the knife to his throat, my other hand on the gun. His finger was already through the trigger guard.

The hooker yelped. "Aye yai yai. Just wait, mister. Just wait. Don't do nothing until I get out of here." She swung off Derek, took up her clothes, and hopped trying to get her shoes on. She fled the room into the bitter cold, semi-nude in a flurry of brown skin and loose clothes. With the knife at his throat, Derek struggled into his pants while still lying on his back. I saw enough to know he'd not been using a rubber.

I took the gun from the nightstand and held it on him as I backed up and closed the door. Derek sat on the edge of the bed trying to button the top of his pants. "You can't do anything to me. I'll tell O. O will never forgive you if you do anything to me. You know that." He pointed his finger at me. "You know that."

I hit the release for the gun magazine. It dropped to the floor. I released the slide and tossed all the other parts. They clattered against the wall. I took a giant step and grabbed a hold of Derek by the ear. "Now you're going to tell me what you did with my grandson."

"Ouch. Hey. Hey. Let go of me. What are you talking about? I didn't do anything with him. He just went missing. We'll find him. He'll come home. I passed the damn polygraph, didn't I? You were there, you saw it. I passed."

"A monkey can pass that test." I dragged him over to the bathroom door. "I'm going to administer a different kind of polygraph, one that

isn't used near enough and should be on people like you. Do you know what the odds are in a child abduction that one of the parents did the deed?"

"Oh, no. No. No. No. Don't do this. I didn't do it, I swear."

I got behind him, put my arm around his neck, and squeezed just a little to let him feel his helplessness and his vulnerability. I gave him a little taste of what Albert had to have experienced. I grabbed his hand, and before he could retract his index finger, I stuck it in between the jam and the hinged edge of the door. I applied pressure with the door, moving it a millimeter toward closing it. He yelped. I let go of his hand and let the door do the work holding him. His legs did a jig. "No. No, no no. Don't do this. Pleeease don't do this."

"Now, you can save yourself ten broken fingers by telling me the truth. The truth is the only thing that will set you free."

He looked up at me, his eyes pleading just like he did three years before when I had him in a similar situation and I chickened out. I hated myself for that one mistake. I wouldn't make it again.

"One chance on this finger. Tell me. Where's Albert?"

"I swear to—"

I moved the door another millimeter.

"Aiy! Aiy! Aiy!"

"You going to tell me?"

"I swear—"

I shoved the door closed. His finger crunched. He screamed. I opened the door. He slid to the floor cradling his crushed finger. Before he could react, I quickly reloaded the next finger in the slot and held the door.

"Nine more. What's it going to be?"

He'd turned ashen, his face wet with tears.

CHAPTER NINE

WHAT SEEMED LIKE two minutes later, Dad had a hold of my leg and shook. "Bruno, you wanted me to wake you."

I struggled up and opened my gummy eyes. Darkness more than light filled my room. I'd slept four hours and could've gone another twelve or so.

I got up, swung my legs over, and sat on the edge of the bed, rubbing my face with both hands.

Dad moved back to the bedroom doorway. "Where is it you have to go?"

A question I dreaded because I didn't want to lie to him.

I stood and stretched. "Let's go into the living room and talk."

We sat on the couch. We left the lights off and let the living room continue to dim as the orangish dregs of dusk faded in the windows.

I put my hand on Dad's leg. "Okay, here it is." He looked far older than his age. He looked like an old man who'd had the life stomped out of him. I had not told him everything and for good reason. Mostly shame over what I had done, but I also wanted to shield him as best I could from truth's unkind reality.

He waited for me to continue while I tried to muster my strength and lost my resolve.

Too late. I couldn't do it.

"You see," I said, "I don't think Olivia died of an overdose."

He sat back a little. "Not this again. Son, we've been over this and over this. The South Gate Police said it was an accidental overdose. The coroner said the same. What do you know that they don't?"

He knew that wasn't true; the coroner ruled it "undetermined."

"Olivia didn't use drugs, Dad."

His head shook almost imperceptively. "She was upset, despondent about her son being taken, about Albert being gone. He was never coming back. She knew it. I don't blame her for what she did, using drugs to escape from this mess, and you shouldn't either. You need to accept it or it's going to eat away at you until you have nothing left inside. It's going to ruin your life. Think about little Alonzo. We need to think about Alonzo now. We're all he's got."

And he *was* all we had left.

In the fading light, Dad looked worse. He hardly looked like the same man. Flesh had melted away and skin hung from bone where muscle once thrived. All of this had taken a huge toll on him, and I wasn't helping matters by not letting a sleeping dog lie.

"You're not a cop anymore," he said. "If you look into this, it's only going to cause this family more heartache. Please, please, Bruno, let the court take care of Derek. If the system doesn't get him this time, he'll screw up again. That's how it works. That's his life, not ours. We have to be better than that."

"I just have to find that witness I talked with. That's all. Then I'm through, I promise. Then I can get Derek charged the way he should be charged." Someone on the street would eventually tell me who Derek had used to overdose Olivia.

"And here I thought you had something else to tell me. Something new."

I was tired of fighting it. I opened my mouth to finally tell him the whole ugly truth, the story I'd squeezed out of Derek. The one I'd never told Olivia.

After crushing Derek's fingers, I couldn't very well accompany him inside South Gate PD, so I had shoved him in through the front door, telling him, "For once in your life, do the right thing." He cradled his damaged left hand and promised to go in and cop to what he'd done, said he'd tell them everything he'd told me he'd done to Albert. I believed him.

But instead, Derek had gone into South Gate and copped to a murder all right—only not the one with my grandson Albert as the victim. A different one to keep Derek in custody, to keep him safe from me as I waited outside the PD just in case he lost his nerve.

The court was now trying Derek for the death of a fellow dope dealer, Percy Williams, who they called Bumpy Spanks out on the street. Bumpy fronted Sams some dope, and Sams never paid him back. This had been a common ploy for Sams, and it finally caught up to him. Bumpy came after him and Sams shot Bumpy dead. After all, Bumpy's murder was self-defense, and worst-case scenario, the most Derek would get was seven to twelve. He'd do three and a half years and get out. A much better deal than if I again caught up to him on the street. I wouldn't hesitate this time.

Olivia had visited Derek in jail where he awaited trial. I never knew what he told her, but shortly thereafter, Dad found her unresponsive with a syringe in her arm. I knew my darling daughter—she would never do something so extreme. Since he was in jail, I knew Derek didn't have a *direct* hand in it, but he had plenty enough motive to *have it* done. Maybe Olivia knew something about what really happened to her son, Albert—what only Derek and I knew as the truth. That Derek had killed their son, put him in a satchel, and tossed him off the San Pedro bridge into the ocean. Maybe she got Derek to tell her the ugly truth of what he'd done, or maybe Derek just wanted to get even with me for three crushed fingers. What I did know for sure was that he had something to do with my daughter's death. I didn't believe she would use drugs. He'd made a phone call or had a visitor in jail. He'd had one of his cronies do the deed.

Now I couldn't get at him again until his court case was adjudicated. For once I hated myself for hoping the jury would cut him loose for killing Percy Williams. Derek Sams needed my help to be shuffled off this mortal coil. I was more than happy to assist. I would not miss a third chance.

When I wasn't working at TW, I was hunting and taking down people associated with Derek. I'd ferret out the truth. I'd find the one who did it.

Now Dad was waiting to hear whether *I had something else to tell him. Something new.*

No, I couldn't tell Dad what happened to little Albert. South Gate PD still considered the case a simple missing person.

I hadn't had the fortitude to tell Olivia, either, and now she was dead. I had wanted to protect her. If I had told her, would my daughter still be alive?

And now, sitting on the couch next to Dad, I again lost my resolve to tell him the words he needed to hear. I couldn't pass on that kind of heartache, the kind of emotional pain that wouldn't let me sleep at night, the kind of pain that left permanent emotional scars. For Dad, the way he understood what had happened was far better than the truth. As far as Dad knew, Albert had never been found. Dad still held out that faint glimmer of hope that somehow his grandson was still alive. What Dad knew allowed him to believe a blind justice system would take care of the likes of Derek Sams. If I told Dad the truth, all those misperceptions would dissolve and he would float down to join me at the bottom of an emotional quagmire. I couldn't allow that to happen. I had to continue on with my monumental charade choosing to leave him in the dark. Even if it meant telling him a good-intentioned lie.

I shook my head and looked away from him.

"Then are you going to tell me where you're going tonight? You're not going back to that dive bar over on Central, are you, Son?"

He tried real hard to keep tabs on me when that wasn't possible, not with what I had going on. "I think I'm going to just drive around a bit to clear my head."

"Stay away from there, Bruno, please?"

A couple of weeks ago he'd gotten lucky and just happened to be driving by as I walked into the Crazy Eight to get a beer and talk with some people. He'd parked around back and came in to confront me. He thought I'd turned into a closet drinker keeping from him a burgeoning need to smother my sorrow at the bottom of a brown bottle. That day it hurt to see his expression of disappointment. He'd caught me there two more times since, sitting in that dark bar among others of the street drinking cheap beer and whiskey, frittering away our lives in our own prison without bars.

I'd seen his reflection in the mirror behind the bar when he came in, the way he froze when he saw me with a drink in my hand. And all I could think about had been the misdirection I needed to feed him to get him to walk away and leave me be.

At what point does an illusion cross the line into a lie and that lie becomes a reality?

Now I looked back at him and said nothing. I couldn't tell him I wouldn't go there, not when I had to run down Nigel. I was forced to play two games. In order to keep my badge and my connection to law enforcement resources, I had to keep Black Bart happy. All the while, I continued to work on Olivia's death. Even harder now since I no longer had help from my old boss Robby Wicks.

Tears welled in Dad's eyes. "I miss Alonzo. Have you talked to Social Services about our supervised visits? You said you were going to try and talk to them again."

I'd screwed that up, too. That was another part of what I couldn't tell him. South Gate PD took into consideration Olivia's death and the disappearance of Albert, and the lack of evidence to support Derek's claims that I had crushed his fingers, and decided not to prosecute me for torturing him. South Gate settled for my badge, which had only been an elaborate ruse to pacify them.

I was lying low, working undercover at TW for a while until the heat died down. Black Bart had struck a fortuitous deal with a favorable deputy chief that knew my background on the violent crimes team, all of our many successes.

South Gate informed Social Services of my violent nature, and Social Services would not, under any circumstances, allow visits with Alonzo. The violent nature that helped keep the neighborhoods safe from class-one predators now worked against me. I had spent all of Olivia's college fund and my savings on attorney fees trying to secure our custody of Alonzo. The way it looked, Alonzo might ultimately end up with Derek's relatives. And that wasn't going to happen, not while I still stood upright.

If I told Dad any part of it, I'd have to tell him all of it. The shame of what I had done would come out.

The telephone rang.

Salvation.

I didn't jump right up; I let it ring a couple more times. I got up and walked to the kitchen. I picked up the phone. "Johnson residence, this is Bruno."

Breathing came over the phone line.

"Who is this?"

The voice came across hoarse and almost unrecognizable, strained and angry. "You are . . . you are one vindictive, arrogant asshole, and I will make you sorry you ever heard my name."

"Wicks? What are you talking about?"

"Don't you dare play coy with me. You know exactly what you did."

I swallowed hard. He'd found out about my undercover assignment with TransWorld. Now he knew the real reason why I took the arrest for the stolen Monte Carlo. And even though he had not acted like a friend when he had pulled back from Olivia's investigation, friends did not keep those sorts of secrets from other friends like I had done with him.

"I . . . I . . ."

"What? Don't you want to gloat? You don't want to laugh and throw it in my face? It's not funny, Bruno. Not one damn bit. You really jammed me up here. I get it that you're mad at me for not helping out with that G-ride beef, but this . . . you pulled Barbara into it, and now she's jammed up right alongside of me. Did you even think about Barbara?"

"*Barbara?* What are you talking about? How did I jam you up?" Barbara was his wife. She worked for Montclair, a police department located just across the county line in San Bernardino County.

"Don't play dumb. I got the cops out in front of my house right now ready to run us both in. What the hell's the matter with you? You've really lost it, pal."

"Robby, I really don't know what you're talking about."

He went silent except for more mouth breathing. "You didn't park a stolen car in my driveway, a bright yellow Corvette with Arizona plates?"

Stool Sample. Rodney Davis.

I put my hand over the receiver and tried not to laugh too loud.

CHAPTER TEN

I left Junior Mint with Dad and walked away from the house without looking back. I headed over to Wilmington and the parking lot of Martin Luther King hospital where I kept a cold car TW supplied for roping, a real beater with 200k miles on it, a faded orange Opel Kadett.

I circled the Crazy Eight checking for anything out of the ordinary, a police stakeout, or scandalous folks who could mean trouble. There wasn't any way to know if Nigel was in there; he never drove the same stolen car twice. I parked down the street on Central Avenue in front of a defunct secondhand clothing store with a For Lease sign in the soaped-over windows, and walked back.

I still wore my TransWorld khaki shirt and denim pants. In my waistband, I carried my second Smith and Wesson .357. My first one I had stuck under the front seat of the Monte just as LAPD pulled us over, three days ago. I wouldn't get that one back until the sting concluded. I felt half naked without two of them.

The most dangerous time of day happens when dusk hands off to night. Your eyes play tricks on you with fleeting images that aren't always there. The ones that are there are the ones to worry about.

I entered the back door of the Crazy Eight and stepped into a short hall with male and female bathroom doors on either side and waited until my eyes adjusted to the dark.

Ralph Ledezma, the owner-operator, kept the place dark. His clientele didn't want to see life pass them by while they hid in a bottle of watered-down liquor. Ledezma stood behind the bar wiping down elbow prints and bits of peanut shells with a dirty rag. He kept his red curly hair cut close to the scalp. One of his blue eyes worked, the other never followed along and must've been glass. So many freckles covered his hands, they looked suntanned. He always wore a blue bowling shirt with "The Crazy Eight" embroidered over the pocket and scrolled large across the back in faded yellows and oranges. He nodded when he saw me.

Nigel wasn't among the fifteen or twenty patrons. I bellied up to the bar, nudging the stool aside. Sitting takes away a huge advantage if someone comes at you. Not having your feet on the floor leaves you without balance and support.

Ledezma put a draft beer down in front of me with white foam overflowing the rim. I took up the mug and drank down half of it. It tasted wonderful and went down too easy. Before the TW sting had started, I wasn't a big drinker and usually only imbibed at the conclusion of a takedown with Wicks. My cover now required that I blend in with the criminal element. I didn't fight the alcohol as much as I should have, not with all that had happened, a weak-kneed excuse to avoid dealing with the curveballs life tosses you.

I set the mug back on the bar and wiped the foam from my mouth with the back of my hand. "You seen Nigel?"

"Not since you two left out of here the other day. Heard you got jacked right down the street. Heard that car you were in was stolen?"

I took another drink without taking my eyes off of him. The other patrons stopped drinking and talking to listen in. I finished the beer and set the mug on the bar. "Wasn't the first time and it's not gonna be the last."

Ledezma set another beer on the bar in front of me and nodded down the bar to his left. "Johnny Sin has been looking for you."

"Who's Johnny Sin and what does he want?"

"That's between you and him. I'm staying out of it. I told you before, as far as you're concerned, I'm Switzerland. I stay neutral on all matters that don't concern this here bar."

"Tell him I'll buy him a drink."

Ledezma looked down the bar. "Hey, Johnny, this here is Karl, the guy you were looking for."

I turned perpendicular to the bar and let my right hand casually drift under my shirt to the stock of my .357 in my waistband. From down the bar came a white guy who didn't fit in with the mostly black drinkers. He had a hop in his step and a light swing in his shoulders mimicking cool black men from a bygone age. He wore clothes from the seventies in a retro look, a long-sleeve red dress shirt with four buttons undone, exposing his chest and a thick gold chain around his neck. He was lean and raw-boned with dirty brown moussed hair spiked in every direction. His pants were flared at the bottom and his shoes had three-inch heels, making him five foot ten. I couldn't see anywhere he could hide a gun except in an ankle carry. He came toward me with a fake movie star smile. A tooth on the front left side was black and dead. The guy really stood out. Not a good profile for a high-end criminal. Or maybe it was smart. If he ever had to run, he could easily change clothes, cut his hair, change his walk, and most people wouldn't recognize him. Except for that tooth. He'd have to knock out that tooth, and with a smug grin like that, he wouldn't have a difficult time finding someone to oblige him.

"You lookin' for me?" I asked.

"That's right." He held out his hand to shake.

I turned, faced the bar, and took up my beer. I watched him in the mirror on the wall behind the bar. "How can I help you? I'm kinda busy."

Johnny Sin lost his smile. "Not here."

I turned back to face him leaning against the bar, mug in hand, and looked him up and down. "I'm not going anywhere with you. I know better."

"What do you mean?"

"You could have a couple of your thug buddies waiting for me outside."

"Don't be ridiculous," he said. "I don't even know you."

"Hell, you could be a cop, for all I know."

"I'm not a damn cop," he said. "I look like a cop to you?"

I shrugged. "Who looks like a cop nowadays? Hell, I could be a cop for all you know. State your business or take a walk."

He didn't like being talked down to. He raised his hand and pointed at me. "I'm here to do *you* a favor, asshole. Jumbo wanted me to—"

"Cop," Ledezma whispered harshly.

The front door opened and in walked Robby Wicks. He stopped just inside the door to take in the crowd, to assess what he was up against.

Ah, hell.

If Wicks opened his mouth, he'd burn me. With just a few simple words, he could burn down all the work we had put in at TransWorld.

CHAPTER ELEVEN

WICKS HAD HIS Western cut suit coat pulled back on his right side so everyone could see the Los Angeles County Sheriff's star clipped to his belt next to his holstered Colt .45. His eyes moved down the bar until he spotted me.

I whispered to Johnny Sin, "You better jam. I think he's here to kick my ass over a stolen car."

Ledezma heard me and said, "Karl, take it outside."

The bar went dead calm. Wicks walked over and stood behind me. I drank my beer and tried to pretend he wasn't there. I wasn't in the mood to deal with him, and if he wanted to fight, I'd mop the floor with him.

"You going to ignore me?" he asked.

I drank my beer.

"Take it outside," Ledezma said again, louder this time.

Johnny Sin slithered back to where he'd come from and watched from the mirror reflection. Nigel had talked to Jumbo like he promised, and Jumbo had sent Johnny Sin looking for me to talk guns. This was the big opportunity, and now Wicks had screwed it up.

"Hey, slick," Wicks said, "let's do what the man said and take it outside. You don't want to air your dirty laundry in front of all these fine human specimens."

I chugged down the rest of my second beer and realized Dad must've told Wicks where to find me. "Ah, man," I half whispered. I threw down a wadded-up ten and headed for the back door with Wicks close at my heels.

Outside I turned and braced for a physical attack that didn't come. Instead, Wicks stood back and stared at me. I'd worked with him too many years and could see he wasn't on edge ready to leap— or even angry for that matter. We stood under a security light meant to keep away the riffraff, the dope deals, and the quick sex acts for hire. He took out a brown cigarette and lit it with a lighter that carried the Marine Corps emblem. He'd never been in the Marines. Six years back he'd taken the lighter off Daniel D. Jacobson III, a Marine Recon, a true badass who'd flipped his nut and had gone on a killing spree. We caught up with Jacobson first when all of SoCal was looking for him. We could've bushwhacked him—shot him in the back—but this was what Wicks lived for. Instead, Wicks ordered me to stand down, told me to take him out if Wicks didn't walk away from it. Jacobson had walked through a paint store and into an alley to shake any tail that followed. We were waiting for him at the other end.

Wicks yelled. Unaware of our presence, Jacobson, quick as a snake, spun and fired. Wicks fired at the same time. The shots melded as one and echoed up and down the alley. They both went down. Wicks was hit twice, once high in the leg and once in the meaty part of his side. Jacobson was hit once in the forehead. When I got up to Wicks, he said, "Son of a bitch, did you see that? That was really something, wasn't it? God damn, that was really something."

Over the course of many years on the violent crimes team, he'd taken souvenirs from his boldest victims—three of them that I could remember—Zippo lighters.

Now he stood two feet away in the back parking lot of the Crazy Eight, smoking a thin brown cigarette, staring at me. He finally let go with a smile that cracked his tanned face.

"Robby, what are you doing here?"

"You know, that beard is a great disguise." He reached up to tug on it. I slapped his hand away. "I bet no one on the street recognizes you."

I said nothing. He wanted something from me. He'd done this before, acting as if nothing had come between us. He always came looking for me when he had an important case he couldn't crack on his own.

He squinted when he blew out a lungful of smoke and the slight breeze rolled it back into his face. He pointed at me with the lit cigarette. "You know, after I cooled down some I laughed about that Corvette in my driveway. That was a good one. I owe you though. When you least expect it, I'll get you back, you wait and see if I don't."

"I'm sorry about the car, it shouldn't have happened."

"I told you, no big deal."

"What do you want?"

He went back to staring me down. "I came looking for you because I need your help. I was going to tell you about it in the jail but . . . well, things just got out of control. That was my fault and I'm here hat in hand to apologize."

"Figured it was something like that."

"Don't come off with that tone with me." He caught himself and took a step back. He took a deep breath and let it out. "Look, you obviously don't know what's happened. The department was able to put a lid on it until tonight. It came out in the six o'clock news, and I know you never watch TV or listen to the radio."

"It can't be anything I care about." What he'd said to me in the jail—how I'd *reverted back to type*—popped back up and brought on an anger I didn't want.

He gritted his teeth. He must *really* want my help if he was putting up with my insolence.

"When I found you in the jail . . . well, it just pissed me off that you'd gone to the other side. I didn't know if it was worth trying to get that stolen car beef suppressed so you could work for me. I mean, so we could work together again."

"I didn't ask you to get me out of that beef. And I'll never work with you again. I'm done with all of that."

"Quit being a horse's ass and let me talk." He reached into his pocket and pulled out a sheriff's star. He smiled. "I had to use every favor I had in the bank to pull this off. I had to lie to the deputy chief about your arrest in the Monte Carlo. I told him you were working as a confidential informant for me. I took the heat. I told him I had signed you up as a CI."

I stood there agog. I had not expected this. I didn't take the badge from him. When the truth came out, and it would come out when the TransWorld takedown started, Wicks was going to be mad as hell that I made a chump out of him to the deputy chief.

The deputy chief must've played along and had not burned TW by telling Wicks about the sting, but at the same time the deputy chief was sending me a message that whatever Wicks was talking about had enough weight to pull me off the sting.

"What's going on?"

"I'm sorry, Bruno. Judge Connors and his wife were gunned down Friday morning. They're both dead."

CHAPTER TWELVE

My knees went weak. I put my hand on the back wall of the Crazy Eight for support. It took a couple of minutes to grasp the loss. Connors was a good friend, a great guy. Three years earlier, he'd saved my life in a shooting at 10th and Crenshaw. And his wife? Why would anyone want to kill Jean Anne? Anger took hold of me. A pure anger that begged for an outlet. I wanted to punch Wicks in the face for bringing this horrible news. "What happened? Who did it?"

Wicks shoved the Sheriff's star at me. "That's why I'm here. We're going to find out. This is a superior court judge and his wife. You cannot believe the shit storm this has caused. Everyone is howling for action, the mayor, the DA, all the way up to the governor."

"So you know who did it?"

"No. I told you, we have to figure that out." He still held his hand extended with the star.

"Hold on. We've never worked homicide. We were always the dog team that ran the guy down after homicide had the case wrapped and had a warrant in hand. We're good at chasing fugitives, not this other. We'll screw it up and it'll get thrown out of court."

"What are you talking about? We can do this, no sweat."

"Putting a case together takes expertise with an intimate knowledge of the law, interrogation, and search and seizure." My mind spun way out ahead, my own words sparking questions that spawned answers I wasn't sure I wanted.

Wicks said nothing and still held the badge for me to take.

I said, "So they agreed to allow me to work it with you? They don't want us on some thrown-together task force with a hundred other cops?"

Wicks still said nothing.

"No," I said, figuring it out as I spoke. "They probably do have that task force set up, but we're not going to be working with them, right?"

I watched Wicks' eyes and read them.

I said, "We're going to be separate because . . . because the word's come down . . . they want this handled by the great Robby Wicks. They want this handled with flash and fury. They want this guy taken off the board with blood and bone and huge press conferences afterward. They want the public to know you don't mess with our judges and their families. That's it, isn't it? This is labeled: terminate with extreme prejudice, pure and simple."

"You in?"

"Damn right I am." I snatched the badge from him and stuck it in my pocket in case someone from the Crazy Eight walked out. Now I had two of them.

He smiled. "Good. So where do we start?"

"What do you mean? You don't have any place to start?"

"Hell no, why do you think I'm here?"

"How am I supposed to know? I'm just now hearing about it."

"You worked with him for two years. You were his bailiff. You saw all the cases that came before him. You, more than anyone else, would have a better idea about who we should look at."

"If you're looking at his court cases, it could be anyone." Once a jury gave their verdict, Connors didn't hold back; he handed down the heaviest sentences he thought he could get away with. Every fifth defendant, it seemed, threatened to get even, and those were just the ones I heard in court. "Connors constantly received hate mail. It's going to take forever to ferret out his killer."

"Come on, think. You can still do that, can't you?"

"Don't talk to me that way. You're the one who dropped the investigation with Olivia."

He stepped in close, his warm and humid breath mingled with the smell of burnt tobacco. "We're going to leave that topic alone for now, until we finish this other thing. Then if you still want to discuss it, we can lump it in with the stolen car you left in my driveway and we'll have it out in the street. How's that?"

"Fine by me."

"Come on, get your ass in my car."

"I said don't talk to me like that or this isn't going to work." I followed him anyway and got in his black Dodge that he'd parked out back of the Crazy Eight. He had parked there and walked around to the front to make an entrance so everyone would see him, a grand entrance that was pure Robby Wicks.

He drove as he always drove: as if someone were chasing him. He whipped in and out of streets, neither of us talking. He accelerated out of turns hard enough to throw me back in the seat. After a few miles I figured out where he was taking us and didn't really want to go, but I knew there wasn't any way around it. I sat back, closed my eyes, and tried to relax, tried to think of who could've killed my two friends and why. There were plenty of whys for Judge Connors, but not his wife, Jean Anne; she was a kindred spirit who would never have done anything to incite someone's ire. She'd been collateral damage, wrong place at the wrong time. I didn't have to look at the crime scene to figure that much out.

Wicks made the last turn down Begonia, Connors' street. Branches from trees on both sides of the street met in the center, making a tunnel the streetlights had difficulty penetrating and making our headlights brighter. No cars or trash cans cluttered the curbs. All the homes sat quiet with warm yellow lights that spilled from the windows on large lawns and circular driveways. The well-kept houses would fit in most upscale, middle-class neighborhoods, but here at the edge of Bel Air they would cost twice as much.

Wicks pulled to the curb in front of Connors' house, where I had visited many times and fostered fond memories of dinners and long talks out on his patio in back.

Yellow police line tape marred the otherwise perfect neighborhood, strung from one tree to another, effectively marking off the house and screaming "Crime scene, stay back!" An LAPD black-and-white patrol car sat at the curb across from the house. Wicks pulled up and stopped behind it. The cop inside, a short Asian woman with short raven hair, got out and waited for us. Her nameplate said "Wu." We got out and showed her our stars. She nodded and logged our names and the time. She didn't ask why Los Angeles County Sheriff's deputies wanted to enter an LAPD crime scene. Or why one was an African American who wore a khaki shirt with a TransWorld patch. Wicks had pre-loaded the situation, knowing ahead of time that I would go along with him. I didn't like that he could read me so easily.

CHAPTER THIRTEEN

WICKS DUCKED UNDER the crime scene tape and stood on the sidewalk in front of the driveway to the house. I followed. He took a step closer and waved his hand. A motion detector mounted over the garage activated lights that flooded the driveway area and blinded us. I held up my arm as a shield.

Wicks turned toward the LAPD car and pointed up. The Asian girl had the garage door opener and pushed its button. The metal garage door came up and made a racket in the dead calm neighborhood. Wicks had been here before and knew the routine. He took a moment to light one of his thin brown cigarettes. He pointed with his lit cigarette, the white smoke filling the still air in a halo effect around his head. "Happened right in there." He pointed to the open garage. "Friday morning at 0803 Judge Connors and his wife stood by his open Mercedes car door. The judge was dressed for work, suit and tie, and his wife was still in her robe. I got the photos if you want to see them. I don't think you do."

He took another drag on his cigarette, a diversion to ponder the deadly tableau. He'd been friends with the Connorses, too, as much of a friend as Wicks allowed anyone to be. In the huge, two-car garage sat a gold Lexus sedan, Jean Anne's car, and next to it the big, heavy silver Mercedes. The front driver's door stood open. There was at least six feet between the two cars.

Wicks turned and pointed south along the sidewalk with his cigarette, the smoke trailing like a road flare. "The judge made the fatal mistake of always leaving for work at the same time. The asshole came walking down this way and stood right about here where we are. From the neighbor across the street, the suspect was medium height, medium weight, wearing a long-sleeve dark shirt and a hunter's cap, the kind that comes down over the ears and neck. The neighbor couldn't be sure of race."

"So absolutely nothing workable on the description?"

"Correct."

He still had not taken a step toward the open garage door. I wasn't in a hurry to see the bloody remnants of my friends.

Wicks turned back toward the garage and raised his hands and arms shoulder height as if pointing a rifle. Smoke came out of his mouth as he spoke. "The suspect held a pump shotgun and from this range fired twice." Wicks worked the slide on the imaginary shotgun that recoiled every time he pulled the trigger.

A shotgun—now I really didn't want to see inside that garage.

"Pumpkin balls, Bruno. The bastard used pumpkin balls."

My breath caught. Pumpkin ball was a street term used for deer slugs. Four hundred and fifty grains of lead coming out of a long-barreled shotgun generating enough foot-pounds of energy at close range to bring down an elephant. We stood thirty or forty feet from the open Mercedes door. From that range those deer slugs would have—

I shivered at the thought, how the delicate Jean Anne and poor Judge Connors faced that level of unanticipated violence, a level of evil that now needed heavy-handed assistance in leaving this mortal world.

Wicks broke into my thoughts. "Hit each one of them once, center mass. Then he dropped the shotgun on the lawn right there—" Wicks mimicked tossing the shotgun with both hands. "Then this mutt kept walking down the street like nothing happened. He rounded the corner down there where we think he had a car waiting for him.

"From this range, standing right here, it wasn't too technical of a shot." He pointed with the flat of his hand into the garage. "He left the expended shells on the sidewalk right there."

He looked at me. "Does this ring any bells?"

"What?" I shook off the fugue state I'd slipped into. "Ah, no. Should it?"

He reached up and, with a knuckle, knocked on my head. "I don't know. You were the one who worked in his courtroom."

I shoved his hand away. "Knock it off, Robby, don't treat me like that. I'm not kidding, don't do it again." I wouldn't put up with it and would slug him the next time.

I walked up to the threshold of the garage without entering, turned, and looked back down the gentle slope of the driveway to see what Judge Connors and Jean Anne must have seen of the suspect and his huge gun seconds before he shot them. A chilling prospect no one should ever have to endure.

I walked back down to the sidewalk and south. I came back walking the route the suspect took, looking at the open door of the garage. I stopped. The LAPD officer got out of her patrol car, walked to the center of the quiet street, and watched. I said loud enough for her to hear, "Can you please close the garage door and open it when I tell you to?"

She nodded, came closer to the driveway, and pushed the garage door opener. The door came down; the racket again pierced the quiet night the same as it would've Friday morning. I walked down two houses and then headed back. "Okay, now."

The garage door started up. I got to where Wicks stood just as it finished opening. "Well, boy wonder, what'd that do for you?"

I scowled at him and went back to the garage entrance. I took in a deep breath and entered. In between the cars, blood splattered and pooled the smooth concrete floor, red, turning brown. Lots of it. One of the pumpkin balls had gone through one of my friends and spattered the windshield. Body tissue and blood also littered the dashboard. I swallowed hard to keep the bile down. I'd seen plenty of crime scenes, but it came at you differently when you knew the people, were friends with them.

I walked down to where Wicks now stood with Officer Wu and said, "I'm guessing nothing came back on the shotgun or the shells, no hits on the serial number?"

"You guessed right. Got any ideas?"

I shook my head. "Not a one. From this range, the guy didn't have to be that great of a shot. He was wearing gloves?"

"Don't know, but that's the working theory. We got nothing off the shells or the gauge."

I closed my eyes. "Go through it again. Walk me through it. Talk slow and don't leave out a thing this time."

"Are you serious?"

I didn't reply but just kept my eyes closed. He started from the beginning, telling it just like he did before. I watched it play out in my mind, taking it from the suspect's point of view, then again from Connors' and Jean Anne's. The LAPD officer stood close by. I sensed her breathing.

Wicks said, ". . . then he tossed the shotgun on the lawn right here just like this. The shells were green Remingtons and were recovered right over here. The shotgun was an Ithaca Deerslayer, 12 gauge, and—"

I opened my eyes. "Say that again?"

"The blower was an Ithaca Deerslayer, 12 gauge. What? You got something?"

"Yeah, I think I do. I think I know who's involved."

CHAPTER FOURTEEN

"Son of a bitch, you're kiddin' me, right, Bruno? You really think you know?" He trailed along as I headed for his Dodge. Full dark no stars slammed down around us, making us vulnerable from all sides. I was glad to be away from that crime scene and I allowed myself to breathe freely again.

"Son of a bitch, I knew you could do it."

Wu followed. "Hey, wait. Don't you leave. My boss will want to know what you found out. Wait." She keyed the mic on her shoulder lapel and turned her chin close to it. "15 L 20, can you have a supervisor 10-87 this location, ASAP."

We both ignored her and got in. Wicks started up and chirped the tires when he pulled away from the curb. "You really came up with something, just like that? I knew you could do it. Give, who is it? Let's get after his ass."

I turned my head slowly and looked at him. "I don't know who did the shooting, but I think I know where to look."

"All right. That's not as good, but it's something no one else has. We can use it. We can work with it. Tell me."

"Just give me a couple of minutes to work it out in my head to see if all the pieces fit."

He pulled over to the curb and waited. "I'm not going to drive around in circles like some kind of circus monkey with his ass on fire while you get your thoughts together. Spit 'em out. Let me hear it. Maybe I can help talk you through it."

I ignored him and mentally traveled back three years to a time when I rode in Judge Connors' Mercedes with Deputy DA Rivers and a skinny meth tweaker named Twyla. We were after a murderer, one of three who had escaped from the jail through an elaborate and highly organized conspiracy. They had used a diversion along with electric drills to pull the bolts from the visiting window. The judge craved excitement and wanted to get involved. He put up a reward for Sammy Eugene Ray, aka Little Genie. The judge wouldn't give Twyla the money until she pointed out the location where Little Genie was hiding. A simple and benign operation: we'd drive by, she'd point it out, then we'd call in the troops and hit the house with flash bangs and shotguns. But like Dad said on many occasions, if you make a plan, God laughs. When we got close, Sammy Ray bebopped out of the apartment he'd been hiding in. He was wanted for three murders where he'd killed off his dope competition. He was death-row eligible with nothing to lose. He'd more than earned the designation "Armed and extremely dangerous." He was a major threat to public safety. I had no choice but to brace him then and there. Before I could walk up on him, two of his thugs came out of the same apartment. We went to guns. I emptied both of mine and only hit one of them. I was about to be gunned by the second one, shot point blank, when the judge intervened; he dropped him with a shotgun blast. Some of the pellets had hit me and I still carried those scars on my back.

"Let me off at the Crazy Eight. We can't do anything about this until tomorrow."

"Buuullshit, you're not gettin' off that easy."

"Okay, you want to do something tonight?"

"Damn straight I do."

"You said this goes all the way up to the governor. Well, get him outta bed and tell him to have Sammy Eugene Ray transferred down from Pelican Bay to our jail so we can have a talk with him in the morning."

"Sammy Eugene Ray?"

"That's right, from 10th and Crenshaw three years ago."

"Naw, shit, I thought you had something really good. They already looked at him and stuck a microscope up his ass. They've had two days. They didn't find a thing. They checked all his correspondence, played back all his phone calls, checked his visiting records, and ran down his girlfriends. That's a big zero."

"I want to talk to him."

"Oh, you think you can get over on him when the best guys in homicide have already had a go? I'll say it again, Bruno, buuullshit. You got anything else?" He pulled away from the curb and headed south, hopefully back to the Crazy Eight. Maybe Johnny Sin hadn't left yet and I could coax him over to TransWorld and get him to make the big gun deal. Use the concealed video to capture his every word to get that deal in the works.

I sat quiet remembering all the good times with the judge. We talked a lot in his chambers when court wasn't in session. We often took our lunches together while playing chess. I played an aggressive attack strategy that beat him cold the first three times. He figured me out, and after that, he could win whenever he wanted.

"Well?" Wicks asked.

I looked at him. The passing streetlights made his face flash bright then dark. "Well, what?"

"You didn't answer the question. Why do you think you can get Ray to talk to *you*?"

I stared at him, waiting for him to put it together all on his own. "Just tell me, asshole."

"I caught up to him in that restaurant, remember?"

Wicks' face lit up with a smile. He let loose with a smoker's raspy laugh that degenerated to a cough. He slapped his leg. "That's right. That's right, you beat that boy to a pulp, tore up that entire restaurant. I remember. I was your first phone call. It looked like a Mack truck drove through the place. And . . . oh yeah, he was still getting away and you shot him in both legs point blank. Stuck the gun right to his legs and pulled the trigger. I'll tell you what, that really raised some eyebrows. That was really something else. The news reports said it looked like an earthquake hit the joint. Yeah, you're right, maybe he will tell you something when nobody else could get dick out of him."

Wicks drove into the night, his laugh turning to a chuckle that eventually died out. He smoked his thin brown cigarette and pondered what I'd just told him. "Okay, wait. Wait. Something out at that scene tonight hit a trip wire in that big beautiful brain of yours and you thought of something else. What was it?"

"The shotgun."

"Okay, and . . . ?"

"Judge Connors used a shotgun that day on 10th and Crenshaw."

"Man, that's a real stretch even for you. There's a million shotguns out there and—"

"Not Ithaca Deerslayers. They were popular in the fifties and sixties, even into the seventies, but Remingtons and Winchesters took over. You just don't see Deerslayers anymore; they're rare."

"You mean that was a Deerslayer the judge used?"

"That's right, and for someone to use one on the judge and to throw it down in front of his house is too big of a coincidence.

Someone was making a statement. He used pumpkin balls because he was angry."

Wicks hit the steering wheel with his palm. "Son of bitch, that's good. That's really good. How did all of those homicide assholes miss this?"

"We need to look at the guy the judge shot. Relatives, friends, fellow gang members, and a good place to start is with Sammy Ray. Set it up for tomorrow morning. Now drop me at the Crazy Eight."

CHAPTER FIFTEEN

I WATCHED WICKS drive away angry that we couldn't do more
and had to wait till morning. The taillights to his Dodge flashed
red as he hit the brakes hard, made the first turn, and slid out of
view. He'd dropped me on Central, three blocks north of the
Crazy Eight. He said he'd pick me up at my place at 6:00 a.m. I,
too, more than anyone else, wanted to get after the man who killed
my friends Judge Connors and his wife, Jean Anne, but I also had
to check in on the Compton court case concerning Derek Sams,
my daughter's boyfriend. His conviction still had number-
one priority. I wanted him—needed him—to get convicted of
murdering Bumpy Spanks. But at the same time, the little voice of
my bad-self wanted Derek back out on the streets where I'd have
access to him one last time. If he walked free and I had my shot at
him, I knew my life would be irreparably changed. I had already
made the difficult decision that I could live with the guilt and
added heartache.

But for now, I needed to sit in the courtroom pews and stare at
him, give him night terrors so he couldn't sleep. I couldn't sleep,
why should he? So I told Wicks to pick me up at ten in the Compton
courthouse parking lot. He didn't like the idea. He wanted to get an
early start. He didn't want someone else to get over on him and

solve the killings before he had a fair chance at his opportunity for some blood and bone. In the end he said he'd set up the meeting with Sammy Ray at MCJ—Men's Central Jail—at 11:00 a.m.

I stepped inside the Crazy Eight to a near-packed house, thirty to thirty-five serious drinkers who left their place of employment at five and now focused on their true goal in life, trying their best to keep their glasses empty and masking the real world behind an alcohol haze.

There was no music playing, not when there was such serious business afoot, drinking. Those who talked kept the noise down to a murmur. I looked around for Johnny Sin and didn't see him, a missed opportunity I would have to rectify. A train car load of guns put on the street would equate to a serious rise in street murders and mayhem when one murder from those guns was too many.

Ledezma, the bartender, flagged me over, his wavy red hair gleaming in the low light. He set a cheap beer down on the bar at the only open spot, and I still had to nudge out of the way two factory workers who worked at a Vernon slaughterhouse. The reek of death hung on them like an aura.

Ledezma said, "I woulda bet good money you would've been spending another night in the can. How'd you dodge that bullet? That dick looked like he had a real hard-on for you."

I took a drink and shrugged. "What happened to Johnny Sin?"

"He said he'd be back here tomorrow at noon and for you not to be late. I think you're a fool for messing with the likes of him."

I nodded. "My dad says the same kind of things. You gonna be my dad now?"

I wasn't going to make noon if I had an eleven o'clock interview at MCJ with Little Genie.

"You seen Nigel?"

"Yeah, he came in, looked around, and left."

I drank half the beer, set the mug down, and tossed another crumpled ten on the bar. The Sheriff's star in my pocket radiated an unnatural heat. I became a bigger fool every minute I carried it. Undercover agents maintained their legend at all costs. I couldn't hide the badge in the car, and I couldn't take it home for Dad to find. I got in the Kadett and headed for Lakewood and TransWorld. I needed to brief Black Bart on what had happened and see how he wanted to play it. I guessed that the death of a superior court judge and his wife would trump all else. I didn't mind getting pulled from the sting. Except for the gun deal. After the sting concluded and all the warrants were served, I'd be spending many weeks in court testifying on all the marks I'd roped into TW, though having them on video would preclude the majority from fighting their cases.

I made my perfunctory cruise of the industrial complex that housed TransWorld. All the day workers from all the other businesses had cleared out and made it easier to spot anything out of the ordinary. I recognized an early-model Chevy truck backed into the yellow loading spot next to TW's front door, the tailgate down and cluttered with a couple of quilted moving blankets.

I kept going. Three tilt-up buildings down, I chose a women's clothing factory and warehouse, called Amy's Jumpers, where I parked and stayed in the shadows walking back. Now I wished I had Junior along; he could see in the dark and would alert long before I saw a threat coming.

The lights from inside TransWorld lit up the corner lot and made it easy to see Black Bart and RD at the counter dealing with a customer whose back was to the front door. That meant a deal going down. At least one other detective stood behind the one-way glass with a shotgun leveled at the mark, a trigger pull away from blending him into a rack of cheap motor oil. I knocked on the glass door framed in heavy security bars. Inside at the counter, Black Bart's hand disappeared. The door's solenoid buzzed. I pulled on the heavy door and entered.

Leo Martinez Jr. from Sparkle Plenty stood on the customer side of the counter. He turned and smiled when he saw me. Guns littered the counter willy-nilly. Black Bart grunted at me and resumed his examination of an Israeli Desert Eagle .44 Magnum.

"Hey, Karl," Leo said with a greedy gleam in his eyes. "Your boss is going to give me double what you quoted for each gun. What do you think of that?"

Black Bart looked up and scowled. I had not briefed him on the price I quoted Leo. The money didn't belong to Bart, but he sure acted like it did. The sting was scheduled to go until the money ran out. The more we paid for each deal, the sooner the job ended. And the fewer crooks we could grapple up and take off the street.

I looked at RD and suppressed my anger over his little prank, parking the stolen yellow Corvette in Wicks' driveway. "We need to talk."

Leo Martinez Jr. laughed. "You two sound like a couple of old lovers about to break it off."

RD chuckled. "I think I know the topic. How'd it go? What'd he say? Was he really pissed?"

Black Bart watched us with a supervisor's eye.

I glared at RD as I came around the corner of the counter to the employee side and started to examine the guns, acting as if I really cared about the gun deal I'd set in motion. "Did Nigel come by looking for me?"

RD nodded. "Yep, said he'd catch you tomorrow, said he was mad that you fronted off Johnny and that he'd set up another deal for noon."

"All right, thanks." I'd picked up a Saturday night special, a cheap .38 made from pot metal, real clean and new. I set it back down. Another one, an old .38 Colt Detective, caught my eye. I stiffened without meaning to. My mouth went dry and my heart raced. What the hell was that gun doing there?

CHAPTER SIXTEEN

RED RUBBER BANDS around the stock looked too familiar. I picked up the gun, opened the cylinders as if checking the functionability of the weapon when in reality I wanted to see the serial number stamped in the frame. My breath caught. I looked up. Black Bart had his eyes on me. I set the gun back down.

Bart looked at Leo. "Since I'm buying the lot, I should get a cut rate. I'll give you three thousand for all of them."

"Thirty-eight hundred?"

"Thirty-two."

"Thirty-five?"

Black Bart reached into his greasy denim pants and pulled out a wad of bills separated with rubber bands. He peeled off four sets, handed Leo three, and broke the fourth one in half and handed that one over as well. Leo's eyes opened wider than normal. He licked his lips as he counted the money. How many lives had just been saved taking this many guns off the street? Thirty-five hundred was a cheap price to pay.

I feigned interest in the whole transaction and casually slid the old Colt .38 off the counter and stuck it in my back pocket. I took up an armload of rifles and a couple of pistols and carried them back to the gun safes. RD did the same with some handguns.

RD set his down on the empty worktable alongside of mine. He'd have to run the guns to see if they'd been reported stolen, tag them as evidence, and enter each one into the SVS system as stolen/recovered. I headed back to get another load. RD started to follow along. "Come on, Karl, you're not mad over what I did, are you?"

I stopped. "You put me in a bad position. I told you, that guy is no one to mess with."

RD chuckled. "Tell me he didn't laugh after he calmed down? He had to think it was funny, right?"

I gave him a sarcastic smile. "No, he didn't, and I'm going to be eating crow for it from now until the cows come home. He'll never let me forget it."

"Really? No way. I'm sorry, Karl." His tone didn't sound like he was sorry.

"Forget about it. Just let it go and don't do me any more favors, okay?" I left him there to do his house mouse thing with the guns, busywork that would take him hours. He'd have to work through the night to get it all done. He couldn't leave it for tomorrow; that was how jobs stacked up and errors got made.

Out front, Black Bart shook Leo's hand and smiled. He turned for just a brief second toward the one-way mirror to allow the video recorder to capture the deal while he still held onto Leo's hand. Bart would have RD freeze-frame the video shot and print a color copy for the sting's trophy book, not unlike big game hunters in Africa who posed next to their kills—or Wicks with his Zippo lighter with the Marine Corps emblem.

I said, "I'll see Leo out." I moved back around the counter and gently took Leo by the arm so he understood he couldn't stand at the counter and yammer on. Bart liked to keep the marks talking after a deal; he even offered them free alcohol. Once the money changed hands, the marks relaxed and were more likely to give up other nefarious activities they were involved in, all of it also captured on video. We'd cleared many other cases besides our over-the-counter deals. Those stats helped pad the overall success of the sting.

Not tonight. I needed to talk with Leo.

Outside, Leo shrugged out of my grasp, laughing. "Hey, big man, what's the deal? You see that I got a little money and now you want to party?"

"No, come here." I moved out from under the floodlight over TW's door and into the shadows.

He lost his smile and pulled away back into the light. "What? You're not going to jack me now, are you, Karl?"

"Don't be ridiculous, you know better. I just need to ask you a couple of questions. Get your ass over here."

Leo came back, but he lost his smile. In the shadows I pulled out the Colt Detective Special and showed it to him. He pulled back like I'd just shown him a poisonous snake.

"Whoa, man, take it easy."

"Knock it off. Where'd you get this gun?"

His smile slowly returned. "Like I told you, I found it in the alley. Why? Why do you want to know about this particular gun instead of all the others?"

"Listen, my boss in there is a great guy and sometimes he's too trusting. I try to limit how much trouble he could get in. This gun stands out. It's old and beat up and it doesn't fit with all those others that are clean and hardly used at all."

"What does it matter? I thought you took all these guns down to Mexico to sell?" He just regurgitated the cover story we fed anyone who asked questions about our operation.

"We do, but what if the cops hit us and find it before we get the guns down to Mexico? You see what I'm sayin'? I'm just trying to look out for my boss, he's a good guy."

"What do you want to know about the gun?"

"I'm worried that it might've been used in a shooting, a drive-by or a murder. They can check, you know, by comparing the bullets."

He looked at me as if trying to decide. "It's cool. I'll take it back and you won't have to worry about it." He reached for it.

"No, that's not what I'm saying. Just tell me where you got it."

He again hesitated. "I like you, Karl, that's the only reason I'm going to tell you. I found it hidden in a car."

"What car?"

"A real clean '63 Ford Galaxy, high-gloss black with fifteen coats of paint. The dude came into the shop and wanted his bumpers chromed. He had the gun wrapped in a rag jammed up close to the hinge in the trunk—you know, over the wheel well, back in there."

"Whose car was it?"

"The guy's a real freak. If I tell you and it gets back to him, he'll come after me for sure."

"You know me. If I say I won't tell a soul, you know my word's good. I put this gun deal together for you, didn't I? You owe me."

"He works out of an auto parts store in Norwalk. He wants everyone to believe that he's workin' for this dweeb with these big ears named Jumbo. You can't miss him with those ears." Leo held his hands up by the sides of his head about a foot away. "Jumbo's not the main man, it's this other guy."

"What's this other guy's name?"

"Johnny. His name's Johnny Sin."

CHAPTER SEVENTEEN

I LEARNED EARLY on in life, criminals, like a lot of animals in the wild, flocked together. They also tend to frequent the same places: motels, seedy neighborhoods, and watering holes such as bars and drug houses. With TransWorld we'd created an oasis of sorts, a safe zone where skullduggery flourished. So I shouldn't have been surprised to eventually see that particular .38 Colt Detective Special appear on our counter.

Two days after Dad found my daughter, Olivia, on the floor of her bedroom with a needle stuck in her arm, I realized I could no longer stay in that apartment. The memory was like an open wound too fresh and difficult to deal with. I packed up Alonzo and all of his things, packed a bag for myself, and was about to leave when I realized I'd forgotten something.

Working with Wicks all those years, I'd come to believe that when violence sought you out it was always best, no matter what the cost, to stand at the ready rather than to be caught flat-footed. I had cut out a rectangular piece of the inside doorframe to my bedroom along with the corresponding 2x4 inside the wall. I made it like a jigsaw puzzle with a cut so fine it was hardly discernable. This created a hole between both pieces of drywall in the middle of the wall where I hid a spare gun. A gun I'd taken from a traffic stop where it had been tossed out the window. I couldn't make the case hold up in court because I didn't know which of the five crooks in the car tossed it. Rather than turn the gun in as found property, I kept it for a rainy day.

Olivia was the only other person who knew about the gun. She lived in my apartment with her two children, Albert and Alonzo, my grandsons. She was often there by herself. The way the gun was hidden, the children were far too young to get to it. Even if they did know of its presence, the puzzle piece was too difficult to remove. I showed her how to get to the gun quickly and quietly if she ever needed it. In the back of my mind, what I really wanted was for her to have protection against her nineteen-year-old dope-dealing boyfriend, Derek Sams. He'd been known to be volatile and unpredictable. Even so, my daughter had given him one more chance to walk the straight and narrow, a trial period where he lived somewhere else with only supervised visits with his sons.

That day when I was ready to leave the apartment for good, move in with Dad, I went to retrieve the gun and found it missing. I figured Olivia had told Derek about it and he had taken it to fortify his position in his drug world or he'd sold or traded it for some rock. Derek had been forbidden to enter my apartment—our apartment.

The missing gun was another circumstantial piece of evidence that pointed to Derek being involved in my daughter's overdose. And now Derek was linked to Johnny Sin. Derek had sold him the gun or traded it for dope. Not such a big stretch. Derek and Johnny ran in the same circles and Johnny dealt in guns.

The civilized part of the world has six degrees of separation. In the limited orbit of a criminal's world, that separation equated to one or two. It seemed they all knew each other or knew someone who knew that other someone.

I waited until Leo Martinez Jr. got in his truck and drove off before I reentered TW and threw the floor bolt at the bottom of the door and then the one at the top closing us down for business until the following day. I found Black Bart in his office with his size 13 EEE biker boot up on his desk as he reclined in his chair sipping a Yoo-hoo chocolate drink and munching on a bag of salted peanuts. I took the usual seat in front of his desk. He watched me with his coal-black eyes and his smile—if it was a smile—hidden behind his shaggy beard. He stroked his beard at the edges of his mouth again and again.

He finally wagged his chin. "You going to tell me about the issue you have with Stool Sample?"

"Nope." Black Bart didn't need to know how RD had misplaced the stolen yellow Corvette.

He nodded and didn't take his eyes off mine as he waited.

I leaned forward, taking the pressure off my back pocket, pulled out the beat-up Colt Detective Special, and set it on the desk in front of him.

He still waited. He knew how to interrogate, and even though I understood the concept and theory in what he was doing, I still squirmed a little and chose to wait him out.

He finally reached over, picked up the gun, and examined it. "Were you thinking about keeping this as a throw-down?"

"No."

His eyes shifted from accusatory to questioning. "Then you better tell me about it."

If I had worked with this man earlier on in my career instead of Robby Wicks, my life would have turned out differently, no doubt about it. I wouldn't have all the suspects—the victims of violent takedowns, victims of blood and bone—coming to me every evening in my night terrors.

"I did take it for a throw-down. But that was a while back, a good long while back." I let him chew on that.

"So then someone broke into your place and took this piece and it turns up here tonight, is that it?"

I nodded. "I kept it in a wall-hide and the day . . . the day my dad found my daughter, the piece of wood was displaced. Not much, just a little. I didn't think anything about it at the time and didn't think to check on the gun. With all that was going on, I wasn't thinking straight. When I got ready to move out two days later, I went to retrieve it and it was gone."

"So you're thinking whoever took the gun might be involved in the thing with your daughter?"

He called it "the thing." What he really believed was that I was the distraught father who wouldn't accept that his daughter had committed suicide, rather than my working hypothesis that she'd been held down and given a hot load of heroin. The missing gun took a big step toward proving my theory, only I couldn't tell South Gate PD about an illegal gun that had gone missing, especially after I'd crushed three of Derek Sams' fingers in the doorjamb of a sleazy motel in Victorville. In all my life I'd never made so many big mistakes.

"What did Leo tell you outside?"

Black Bart had seen me follow Leo out, something members of TW rarely did, if at all. We were too vulnerable outside the doors. They could grab one of us and come back in with a hostage to take all of our cash on hand.

I played out all the options and their possible outcomes, leaving a long pause after his question. "Leo told me some dude brought his car into Sparkle Plenty to have some chrome work done. Leo found it hidden in the trunk of that car."

"Does he know this dude?" Black Bart wasn't happy about where this conversation was headed, that his best roper was headed down the wrong path and losing focus of the job at hand to chase a dead-end lead in a make-believe case.

I nodded. "He said it came from a guy named Johnny Sin."

He brought his foot down off the desk and set down his Yoo-hoo. "Isn't that the guy you're trying to rope for the big gun deal?"

"That's right."

CHAPTER EIGHTEEN

BLACK BART SAT behind his desk staring at me as he tried to digest what I'd just told him and how to handle it, how to handle me. "Bruno, I don't want to come off sounding insensitive here, but you can't go after this Johnny Sin until the gun deal goes down. We have to get him on video and the guns have to change hands before you talk to him about this. And even then, I'd advise against it. You're too close to this thing. It's too easy to make a mistake."

Boy, did he have that part right. And there it was again, him calling my one-man crusade "a thing." He still lived in the real world where the good guys always won and Justice triumphed. I'd lost my faith long ago. As far as I was concerned, it didn't matter whether I had rock-solid evidence against Derek Sams. The way he had treated my daughter, coupled with his admission—coerced or not—about what he'd done to my grandchild Albert, was reason enough to cross that Rubicon into the no-man's land of criminality. These thoughts allowed me to remain dead calm in front of my boss. Allowed me to act as if I would follow his rules and any edicts he handed down.

I reached into my front pants pocket and pulled out the star Wicks had given me. I slid it across the desk to him.

"What's this?"

"Didn't the deputy chief from my department call you?"

"Heck no, he didn't."

"Ah, man."

"What's going on?" He opened his drawer and pulled out a plastic Ziploc baggie that contained my flat badge and the star like the one I'd put on his desk.

"Wicks found me at the Crazy Eight. He said he cleared it with the deputy chief for me to work the shooting death of Judge Phillip Connors and his wife. I just assumed the chief told you about it."

Bart sat back in his chair, his eyes never leaving mine. "I saw that killing on the news. I knew the judge; he was our favorite when it came to skinny warrants no one else would touch. That's a crying shame and the doer of that one is going to roast in hell."

"Yeah, the judge liked to sign warrants, he was a good man." That was how I'd come to know Black Bart, from Judge Connors' courtroom. That's why he'd offered me the job at TW.

"Bruno, you have a job here and you're too deeply invested in this one to pull out now. I can't spare you."

The department had signed an MOU, a Memorandum of Understanding, which said under no circumstances could I be moved from my position until the operation terminated or supervision agreed on the transfer.

I nodded. "You know, push comes to shove, we're talking a superior court judge and his wife. Wicks will get his way on this."

"What do *you* want to do?"

"I worked his courtroom for two years. He was a good friend."

Black Bart went silent thinking over the options, then he said, "You worked his court. You have any ideas who could've done this?"

"I've got a couple."

He again went silent. "Okay, how about this? You help me put this gun deal together, we take it down quick and dirty, then I'll give you all the guys on this operation and the rest of the grant money to run this killer down? We have a lot of street connections right now and we can open doors no one else can."

I smiled. "I can live with that." I didn't want those guns to get away. I also wanted a shot at Johnny Sin to find out where he'd come across my gun.

"Then you better get home and get some sleep. You look like ten miles of bad road and you're going to need to be sharp. That's an order."

I stood. "How do you want to play Wicks?"

He didn't hesitate. "Work with him on the judge's killing, but as far as TW, leave him out in the cold. I don't trust that son of a buck. He doesn't care about anyone but himself."

That wasn't true. Wicks was just difficult to get to know.

I nodded and, not breaking eye contact, reached down and re-claimed my throw-down gun. I turned and left, sticking the gun in my back pocket, waiting for Bart to say something, to order me to check it in with RD. He didn't. I'd never known him to stretch the rules and didn't understand why he'd let me this time.

Twenty minutes later, I turned down Nord, headed for Dad's house, and spotted a beat-up red BMW that I recognized: the PI. Reynolds parked three doors down. I pulled up and parked. She got out and waited in the dark by her car, her arms crossed under her breasts. Tonight, she wore a Dodgers ball cap with her ponytail pulled through the back, worn denim pants with holes in the knees, and a dark-blue windbreaker, no emblems or decals.

I came up on her and said, "That was fast." It was too dark to see her eyes. I wanted to see the exuberance in them, that lust for life I used to have. She'd left the job at LAPD before she'd lost it.

She handed me a folded piece of paper. "If you need help . . . I'd like to do this with you. With two of us as a team, it could be finessed, and they wouldn't know what happened until we got away clean."

I turned around and leaned against the car close enough to feel her body heat. "Who said I'm going be doing anything?"

She nodded at the paper in my hand. "Take a look."

I unfolded it. *1897 Laurel, Compton.* "Ah, man."

"So you know the place?"

"Yeah, it's a foster home, one of those county places that house twenty kids, too many kids to get the attention they need to keep them safe from each other."

"That's right, it's more like an overcrowded dog kennel. The place has been investigated twice and is on probation. One more violation and those people running it are going to lose their ticket; and you can bet twenty foster kids are bringing in some serious money. So I'll offer it again. You want some help springing your grandkid, Alonzo, I'm here for you."

In the world I'd slipped into—the one I currently ran in, roping criminals and coaxing them back to TW—in that world, she made absolute sense, but not in the real world where most everyone else lived. I still had one foot in the real world that used to make perfect sense and meted out the appropriate amount of justice—well, maybe not a foot, maybe one toe. I took comfort in her idea, the concept and its execution, but what then? We'd forever be on the run. No, I still needed to play the game by the rules if for no other reason than to give Alonzo a chance at having a life.

"Why do you want to help me?"

"Because sometimes the good guys need to win."

"Thank you for your kind offer, but I'm not quite there yet."

"What are you waiting for?"

"I'm waiting for Alonzo's biological father, Derek Sams, to get convicted of murder and go to the joint. Once that happens, my attorney said there's a chance we could get Alonzo placed with my father. As long as I promise to stay far away from him; it's a sacrifice I'd be willing to make."

"That's a crap shoot and you know it. Even with the conviction, they could just as easily place him with Sams' people. And the odds are that's exactly what they'll do."

"Alonzo deserves that roll of those dice. Besides, we snatch Alonzo up, then what? Where would we go? We'd be on the run."

She opened her car door. "If it were me, I'd take off south, maybe Costa Rica. That's a nice place to live. A good place to hide."

What she said made a lot of sense and made me wonder what evil event had soured her on our system and on the life we'd chosen to uphold the law.

She got in, the car door still open. "Bruno, you need anything, you have my number."

"Thanks, I do appreciate it and I'll keep your number handy as a last resort."

She closed her door, started up, and took off.

I turned to head to the house and spotted a shadow on the sidewalk. I let my hand ease under my khaki work shirt to the stock of my gun.

"Son, it's okay, it's me."

I moved out of the street and up on the sidewalk next to him. "What are you doing out here?"

"Who was that? Who were you talking to?"

"Just a friend."

He put his hand on my shoulder. "I saw it on the news, about your friend Judge Connors. I'm really sorry."

Hot emotions clogged up my words. "Hey, Dad, you want to go for a ride? I'd really like to go for a ride." When I was much younger, we used to take rides and talk things out.

"It's kind of late, where do you want to go?"

"I just want to show you something."

"All right."

CHAPTER NINETEEN

IN THE SIX months since the funeral, and after Social Services stepped in and snatched Alonzo out of our home, I had not spent a lot of time with Dad, and I regretted it. Now he sat in my Ford Ranger staring out the windshield. Hope and faith was smothered out of the both of us the same as a pot lid on a bacon-grease stove fire. When Wicks had called looking for me, Dad had told him to check the Crazy Eight. Dad had accepted my continued descent into oblivion and believed, if left unchecked, I might not ever climb out. Maybe he was right.

I stopped southbound on Wilmington at Rosecrans, waiting for the red and fought the need to tell him about TW, hand him at least some morsel of hope to cling to in a vast sea of despair.

In the close quarters of the truck, Dad smelled of baby powder, a strong reminder of the very different life we had seven months ago when we still had Olivia and the twins, Albert and Alonzo. Of how things had changed in a blink, how we had struggled to grasp at that change to stop it, and failed in the most horrible manner possible. Both of us intelligent men, experienced in the way of the ghetto, and yet we couldn't stop what happened. It was as if we stood on the tracks with a megaton freight train barreling down on us at high speed and all we had to do was take a couple of simple steps to the side to avoid certain disaster and we just couldn't do it.

Dad sitting so close in my truck also reminded me of the day of the funeral. I stood next to him at the open coffin looking down at my lovely Olivia, peaceful and at rest, my arm around Dad's shoulder as we both wept like babies. His essence of baby powder forever linked that common scent with the most devastating events in my life. No one is emotionally prepared to have their child predecease them. No one should ever have to experience it.

The light changed to green; I shifted to first and took off. "Dad, I'm okay, really. I'm getting through this. Soon I'll be through to the other side and we can start over." It would never be back to normal, but we could at least start over.

He turned his head away, stared out the passenger window, and said nothing.

I knew the address and drove right to it. I parked a few houses up the street from the foster home on Laurel and shut the truck down. Until today, the place Alonzo had gone remained an enigma, an intangible place difficult to visualize with our vulnerable grandson subject to those kinds of trials and tribulations. I wanted Dad to see the physical location in the hope it would put him at ease. And maybe I needed to see it too.

I waited for him to say something.

He finally turned to look at me and asked, "What are you thinking about?"

I couldn't see his features distinctly in the dark. I said, "I'm thinking about how, on all those special Sundays when we were just kids, you'd take me and Noble to the Thrifty's Café. We'd get three huge hot fudge sundaes, extra fudge, piled high with whipped cream and a red cherry. We'd drive to the Compton Airport and sit on the hood of the car. We'd eat our hot fudge and vanilla ice cream and watch the small planes take off and land. Those were some good times, Dad, and I never did thank you for them. I had a good life, and you were the reason for it."

His head moved in a nod, his eyes difficult to discern. "I'm worried about you, Son."

"I told you, I'm okay. I'm almost through it."

"No, you're not. Not even close. You're not acting right. The doc even said as much. He's worried too."

Dad had talked with the shrink.

"Dad, everything . . . well, it's not as it seems. You're just going to have to trust me."

"No, you're wrong, I think I do know what's going on. Vengeance is a lazy form of grief. You need to let go of it, Bruno, before it's too late. It's going to ruin the rest of your life. We can't retract the decisions we've made; we can only have an effect on the ones we're going to make from here on out."

"I know . . . I do know. I haven't stepped across that line. Not yet."

"Pish posh, don't try to use those kinds of words as an excuse—everything is not as it seems—that's just putting lipstick on a pig. Every moment you don't renounce what you have in mind, it digs in a little deeper until you won't have any choice but to act. And that's what scares me."

"No, you're wrong. I don't intend any harm to—" I couldn't finish that one. I could never lie to my dad.

"See, you can't even say the words out loud. You need to pay attention to what your conscience is telling you. Just think about it, will you, Son? Murdering Derek will cause others the same kind of pain and grief you're suffering. You don't want to do that to people you don't even know. Do you?"

His argument caught me and snatched my breath away. I had not thought about that aspect of it. I'd been selfish, wanting nothing more than to make amends for the guilt and for a pain like I'd never felt before over not protecting my family from a known threat. I'd let Olivia down, and that anger raged inside me like an unchained beast. But at the same time, I couldn't wish that kind of pain on anyone no matter how much better Derek's death would make me feel.

My voice cracked. "I'm sorry, Dad. When I wasn't looking, someone snuck into my world and changed all the locks. I haven't been thinking clearly ever since. I'm going to get through it though, I promise."

I knew my dad pretty well, yet I had no idea how he'd react if he knew what Derek had done to Albert, the satchel dropped off the San Pedro Bridge, a secret that ate at my gut every minute of every day. I needed to let it out, but I couldn't tell anyone, not with the way I'd obtained the information. And if I did expose that secret to the light of day and something did happen to Derek afterward, whether I was the one who did it or not, I'd become suspect number one. Which really didn't matter to me, but I still needed to consider Alonzo.

Dad reached over through the near dark and put his warm hand on mine. "I know. It's my fault. All of this is my fault."

"What? How's it your fault? Now you're talking foolish."

"I had the opportunity to get you boys away from here, move you to someplace nice, and I didn't. This . . . this neighborhood . . . Well, I thought if you lived a clean life and kept to your own business, it wouldn't matter where you lived. I was wrong—the biggest mistake I've ever made."

A wave of déjà vu swept over me. I'd been thinking the exact same thing about Olivia and how I'd made that same mistake. Why had I kept my family close to the place where I'd grown up? I knew better. It would've been so easy to take an apartment in a middle-class neighborhood away from all this mess, move to Downey, Lakewood, or Norwalk. Was it ego? Hubris? And to find out Dad felt the same way eased the pain just a little. Was I a bad son for thinking that way, for allowing Dad to take on some of my guilt?

"No," I said. "That's not true. This is all on me. I worked the streets. I knew better than anyone else the dangers Olivia had to deal with."

It was good we were having this talk. In its own way it relieved a little of the pressure.

"Son, I can't help thinking that you stayed around here because I stayed. We've lived in the same house in the same neighborhood for decades. That much time binds you to the place with memories of bygone years. Don't try and tell me that wasn't a factor. I stayed for selfish reasons, for sentimental reasons."

"What are you talking about?"

His voice changed. It came out filled with emotion and regret. "Olivia looked so much like your mother, it scared me. I've never talked to you about your mother. And you should have known about her early on. I was wrong to keep it from you. I'm sorry about that."

He had never said so much as one word about her, and I'd asked him enough times in my early years that I finally gave up. Now I waited, hoping tonight he'd say more about her.

Silence. Minutes ticked by.

"Dad, what was she like?"

"I guess it's time you knew."

CHAPTER TWENTY

DAD FELL IN *love with Beatrice Olivia Elliot the first time he laid eyes on her. Sure, he'd had crushes before, but nothing like this. He was twenty and she was seventeen—would be eighteen in just a couple of months. He didn't know that at the time and it didn't matter. He'd always had a difficult time talking with girls, which was the main reason why he only had one real girlfriend back in high school and none since. School and work kept him too busy to mess with something so confounding and befuddling as girls.*

Bea had come out of the theater on Crenshaw with two of her girl-friends, all of them twittering about the movie, sipping from their soda straws. They walked past Xander without giving him a look. He'd come to see a movie in one of the few theaters in Los Angeles that allowed blacks, but instead, followed along zombie-like, no longer aware the rest of the world existed. One of Bea's friends spotted him after only a short distance. They stopped, put their heads together, and twittered some more. Finally, Bea, the boldest of the three, walked back toward him. He wanted to turn heel and hightail it out of there and couldn't move. All of his muscles froze in place. Cars on Crenshaw zipped by, and the earth continued its slow-motion rotation around the sun, all without notice as he held his breath. She was absolutely beautiful, way out of his league, and here she was walking toward him and about to say something.

"Hey, you. Are you following us?"

He swallowed, his throat too dry to answer without a rasp. "No," he croaked.

"Well, I think you are."

"Okay, I am."

"What for?"

"I . . . I just saw you and . . ."

"What's the matter with you? Why can't you talk like a normal person? Do I know you?"

Talk now or she's really going to think you're an idiot. "I don't think so, my name's Xander Johnson. I'm going to junior college, taking administration of justice. I work two jobs, three really. During the day at Charlie's Liquor over off a 133rd, I stock shelves and sweep up, that sort of thing. I work security at night over to the Sands Motel on Long Beach, which isn't anything big. I'm more just a door-rattler. Oh, and I throw papers in the morning. You want to go out with me?"

He blurted out the whole thing in one long string and didn't know where all the inanity came from. His face flushed hot as he cringed waiting for the brutal rejection.

She smiled. It lit up Xander's world and he'd have done anything to keep making her smile.

"You sure talk a lot, Mr. Xander Johnson. Go out with you? Why, I hardly know you."

"That's why I just told you all about me. I don't have much of a life outside of what I told you. Oh, and I forgot, I clean a couple of pools once a week for folks in Lynwood." So the fool in him continued to spew.

"What's this college course you're taking? Is it about the law? You know the law real good?"

Down the block, her two friends yelled and waved at her to hurry up. She held up the flat of her hand, still looking at him.

"That's right," he said, "I'm studying up now so when I turn twenty-one, I can get hired and go to the police academy. I want to help the people in the community."

She moved in close, making his heart pound in his chest. She smelled of lilac, a scent he'd never forget. She pulled the ballpoint pen from his shirt pocket and reached down and took his hand, her touch electric on his skin. She wrote her phone number in the palm of his hand. Someone drove by on Crenshaw and honked at them. Someone else in the same car yelled, "Get after it, man! Go for it."

She put the pen back in his pocket and patted it. "Call me, we'll go out."

He opened his mouth to speak and couldn't.

She smiled again. "You're real cute, Xander Johnson. Call me." She turned and headed back to her two friends. They conferred with their heads together before the other two let out little squeals of excitement and looked back at him. They hurried away. He watched them get smaller and smaller until they made a turn on some unknown street. He finally looked down at the number scrolled in his palm and quickly memorized it before sweat could wash it away. With the movie forgotten, he hurried back to his small studio apartment in a regular-sized old house that had been divided into four separate apartments. He sat by the phone waiting for some time to pass so he could call. He didn't want to seem too eager and scare her off. He went over in his head the way the conversation would go, taking her side as well as his own. Hearing his replies in his head, he sounded like an absolute fool and didn't have a clue in how to avoid it.

He did eventually call and they did go out on a date. He had to borrow a friend's ratty old Ford sedan with a rust streak right down the center of the roof and ticking protruding from the seats. Bea didn't *seem to mind. He met her at the Thrifty Café, where he bought her an egg cream. They took a drive, and then a long walk on Redondo Beach at sunset. She let him hold her hand.*

He never dreamed he could be so smitten with a girl and realized after only three dates that he was wildly in love with her. He loved her so much it hurt, an ache he carried around with him every minute of the day. He couldn't sleep at night and he found himself in a daze when he should've been paying attention at work or in class.

She lived over a back-alley garage with her parents and her father's brother and wife and two kids, seven people in a small three-room apartment. Bea never complained, but he knew she wasn't happy about the arrangement and would do anything to escape the cramped accommodations. He forgot his dreams of being a cop and put in an application to work at the post office; they were hiring and paid well.

The night it all started to unravel, he took her to dinner at Stops and then to a drive-in movie. They kissed at intervals all through the first movie. Each time he kissed her, they started breathing harder and harder until she broke away. With one hand on his chest holding him at bay, she patted her hair and said, "Oh my, Xander Johnson, you really are something, aren't you?"

He didn't like to be apart from her even for a second and wanted her right next to him, close enough to touch, close enough to be sure she was real. He didn't feel whole when she moved just inches away. He didn't know what to say in response to her comment about his ability to kiss. "I applied at the post office and they called me for an interview. It's this coming Monday."

"Oh no, what happened to being a cop?"

"I can't be a cop until I'm twenty-one; that's almost two years away. I . . . I want to get a place so we can . . ."

Her eyes went wide. "Why, Xander Johnson, you mean move in together?"

He had lain awake nights wondering how he'd broach such a sensitive topic, especially since they'd only been going out a short time and here she'd just come right out and said it before he had the chance.

"Yes, that's my plan. I hope it's okay with you. I can work for the post office and save up for a place of our . . . of our own. Maybe save for a couple of years, buy a decent place."

"That all sounds wonderful. But two years, that's a long time to wait." She wiggled over to him and ran a finger down his nose.

"Really?" he said. "I mean, yeah, two years is a long time to wait."

"Yes, it is, but listen." A strange light came into her eyes. She leaned in close and took up his hand. "I know how we can do it a lot sooner. I've been working out a plan. It's foolproof, really. I just need someone big and strong, someone who knows a little bit about the law. We can pull this off, I know we can."

"What are you talking about? Pull what off?" His world started to swirl.

"Do you know that once a day a fuddy-duddy little old man goes along to all the telephone booths up and down Wilmington and Central and Avalon, lots of streets, and he takes out all the dimes and nickels and even quarters from all the pay phones?"

"What are you talking about?" What was the matter with her? She'd never talked like this before.

"This little ol' guy carries these big canvas bags bursting with dimes and nickels and he just puts them in the back of his van pretty as you please. He's got to have bags and bags of dimes in that van. Thousands of dollars."

"Bea, you're talking about armed robbery—it's a felony. The police shoot armed robbers, especially black armed robbers. That's crazy talk."

"Silly, we don't need any guns, and besides it's only bags of dimes. Nobody cares about bags of dimes. We do it right we can—"

CHAPTER TWENTY-ONE

Dad had gone into a trance-like state to tell the story of my mother, a story I had never heard before. In all my life, he'd never said one word about my mother or what had happened to her. On several occasions he got tired of my nagging and said, "Leave it alone, Son, I'm not going to talk about it." And here he sat telling me all about her from day one of their relationship. I didn't ask even one question for fear it would stop him from telling more of the story.

I had a mom.

Over the years, the mere idea of a mother had turned into an apparition, something that had, day by day, faded a little more into the sunset until there was nothing left but a ghostly wisp. Now those lost feelings from when I was a child rushed back all at once and made the world wobble on its axis. This new revelation would take days to adjust to, if at all. But why did it matter so much now? She never cared about me as a child. She had left and never looked back. At that moment I realized Sonya had done the same thing with Olivia. Sonya had knocked on my door and handed me a swaddled child, said, "Here, I can't take it anymore." Sonya never so much as sent Olivia a birthday card. Had the lack of a mother, later in life, been the key factor that sent Olivia down the path of destruction, her need to be with a sinister actor like Derek Sams? Had the lack of my own mother jaded me to the fact that Olivia had needed a mother in her life?

Dad came out of the trance in mid-sentence and looked around, suddenly aware of the street I'd parked on. He'd been a postman for decades and knew the streets better than anyone else. I was confident that if I put a mask on him, spun him in a circle, drove him around, and then took the mask off only showing him the front of one house that he'd know the street and the address and even probably name of the persons who lived there. He had a mind for that kind of thing.

"What are we doing here? Why'd you bring us here to this spot and park?"

"Dad, don't stop now, tell me the rest of it. Please? What happened with Bea, I mean, with my mom?"

He pointed. "Right down there, that house is a foster home." He turned and looked at me. "You brought me here because this is where Alonzo is, right?" His voice turned excited.

"Yes, that's right. I just wanted to give you something to put your mind at ease, a place that you could—"

He grabbed the door latch and jumped out before I could grab him. I got out and caught up to him walking down the middle of the street. "Wait. Wait, what are you doing? You can't go up there like this, not in the middle of the night, it's after ten o'clock. Wait, Dad, please. If we make any contact at all, it could ruin our chances to get custody of Alonzo." I took a firm hold of his shoulder.

He stopped and turned, his eyes alive with a fire I had not seen for the last six months. "I'm going to see my great-grandson and there is nothing you can do to stop me."

"Wait, just listen. I brought you here just so you'd know where Alonzo was, that he was safe and close by. I thought that'd give you at least a little bit of comfort."

He jerked his shoulder out of my grasp and backed up a couple of steps, moving toward his goal.

I held up my hand. "Wait. You go up there and cause a scene, it will hurt our case to get Alonzo assigned to us by the judge. We've talked about this. Don't do it, Dad."

What a tremendous mistake to bring him along. I should've learned by now that when hot emotions are involved you could never predict how someone would act.

He took a step closer and spoke with a firm confidence that almost convinced me he was right. "I know these people; I've talked to them many times in the past when I delivered their mail. It'll be all right. I promise you, don't worry. You're just going to have to trust me."

"Dad, I can't go up there. Social Services will have told them to be on the lookout for me. They think I have violent tendencies; they'll call the police for sure."

We stood under the streetlight in the middle of a gang-run residential street. He didn't reply and stared, a thing he did when he wanted me to work out the answer all on my own.

"Oh, so what you're saying is that I have to stay out here while you go in there and risk making our custody case worse than it is already?" I didn't mean to sound so calloused and selfish; it just came out that way.

He still said nothing and stared.

"Okay, I'll wait out here. But go easy, Dad, don't force it or make a scene, okay? If you meet any kind of resistance, just walk away."

This was a mistake, a big mistake. What was I thinking, "any kind of resistance?" Just knocking on the door late at night would be enough to cashier our chances.

"It'll all work out. Just go back and sit in the truck. I won't be long." He peeled my hand off his arm. I didn't realize I'd put it there or that I'd been holding on to him so tightly. He'd have bruises in the morning.

I watched him walk down the middle of the street, cross the grass parkway and the sidewalk, open the dilapidated chain-link gate, and disappear into the dark overgrown front yard. I stood there unable to move. I wanted to do what PJ Reynolds, the PI, had recommended—storm the castle and rescue my grandson. I missed him so. His absence opened a chasm in my chest that ached constantly throughout the day, a constant reminder of my inability to take affirmative action to rescue him.

I stood next to the Ford and bounced on the balls of my feet.

Dad reappeared under the porch light facing the front door as he knocked lightly. He didn't turn around and smile and wave. I could've used one of his reassuring smiles as I moved in his direction back to the middle of the street, anxiety getting the better of me.

A large black woman in a muumuu-like dress opened the door with an angry scowl.

Oh no. Dad, don't. Back away. Don't tell her your name. Just turn around and get the hell out of there.

The woman suddenly smiled, stuck both her hands out, and enveloped Dad into a hug. They stepped apart and spoke until the woman nodded. She stepped aside and allowed Dad to enter. The door closed. Dad had made it inside the impenetrable castle with nothing more than words and a big smile.

I waited a few minutes and realized I was still standing in the middle of the street, a perfect target for a gang member protecting his turf. I went back to the Ford Ranger and stood in front of it waiting, too pent up to sit.

The amazing words he'd said about my mother returned so vividly, I saw the story as a movie playing out. I could picture the whole thing. I'd never forget what he'd said or how he'd said it.

But what of the ending? What had happened to Bea? I didn't know Dad had started out with a dream of being a cop. He'd never mentioned it in all the times we sat in our living room on hot summer nights after my shift working the streets and I told him stories of the job.

A thousand other questions swirled around and around. Did my mother rob the telephone man of all his bags of dimes? What happened to her? Did she still live close by? What happened that a man like my father would banish her from his life—from my life—forever? Dad was the most forgiving man I'd ever had the honor to know.

Minutes passed. The door finally opened. No one came out right away. I held my breath.

Dad stepped out holding Alonzo. My heart soared. He came to the gate, passed through it, and stopped at the sidewalk as if he'd been ordered to go no farther. I ran across the street, tears burning my eyes. When I got close, Alonzo, with sleepy eyes, held out his hands and said, "Pop Pop." I took him from Dad and hugged my grandson.

I'd started out trying to do Dad a favor, tried to ease his mind just a smidgeon, and he ended up helping me like no one had ever helped me before. Holding Alonzo with his little arms hugging my neck and him calling out my name righted my screwed-up world and again made anything in the future possible.

"He has to stay here, Son."

"I know, Dad, I know. I don't know how you did it, but thank you for this." Dad's face was wet with tears. The front door of the house stood open and the big woman stood under the light. I waved to her. She waved back, smiling. I knew I didn't have long, and for once, wanted time to slow down, to actually stop. I memorized all the wonderful feelings of holding him, his face, his warm, soft skin, the way his chest moved as he breathed. His wonderful scent of baby powder.

Too soon, Dad was trying to pry him from my grasp. I let out a pitiful little yelp when I finally let go. Alonzo started crying and it ripped my heart out. Dad carried him down the walk and handed him to the nice woman. She waved one last time, stepped inside, and closed the door.

CHAPTER TWENTY-TWO

THE NEXT MORNING at 9:00 a.m. I pulled into the Compton Courthouse off Willowbrook Avenue. "You stay in the car, you hear me?" I pointed a loaded finger at Junior Mint. I intended to be gone all day and didn't want to leave him home, cooped up in this summer's heat. I kept a gallon jug of water on the floor of the back seat and filled a used pot I'd picked up at a thrift store. I left all the windows down and the car parked in the shade of a huge pepper tree. I'd done it before and always found Junior Mint sitting patiently waiting for my return. One time he sat on the roof of the car like he was king of the mountain. No crook would ever get close to the car. Walking away, I turned one last time and pointed at his dejected mug. "Stay."

People flowed from the two parking lots and got in the line that snaked out the front door and down the steps, everyone queuing for the metal detectors. I couldn't flash my badge and cut the line for fear one of the crooks waiting for court might be an associate and/ or principal that had done business with TW. Word would go out and that would be the end of the sting. I went to the lee of the building, looked around first, and knocked on the side door. Jenkins, an African American deputy who'd worked the street fifteen years, then the court for twenty more, opened it. He'd seen a lot of change in his time. I quickly moved past him and he got the door closed.

"Don't know why you made the trip, my friend," Jenkins said.

"What? Why?"

"Your boy didn't catch the chain from MCJ. His name wasn't on the intake list."

"The court dark today? It's a murder trial, they just don't do that; it's too hard on the jury." I said it more thinking out loud. Jenkins knew how the courts worked better than anyone. My newspaper friend had called and said there hadn't been court on Friday either. What was going on?

He shrugged. "Sorry, Bruno, not my circus, not my monkeys."

I hurried away throwing a "Thank you" at him over my shoulder. I avoided the elevator and took the stairs up to three. I peeked in the little square window in the door to the courtroom. Dark all right— the clerk wasn't even in. I moved down to Judge Connors' courtroom and peeked in the door window. Esther sat at her usual perch doing her job when there wasn't a job to do. I didn't need any more emotional soup to deal with but knocked anyway. She looked up, saw me, and smiled—a small, crooked smile where she usually beamed. She climbed down off her elevated desk and came to the door. She used her keys to unlock it. I pushed in. She immediately glommed onto me. I became a life preserver without any hope of rescue. I put my arms around her and held on tight. Her body shook as she wept for the loss of a great man and longtime friend. She spoke into my shirt. I couldn't decipher her words muffled by my chest but had a good idea what they entailed.

She finally recovered, stepped back, took her glasses off, and wiped the tears from the lens with a hanky I'd handed her. Her voice came out husky. "Do they have the pendejo who did it? Did you catch him yet, Bruno?" Esther never said words like "pendejo," which loosely translated from Spanish meant asshole. She'd always been the picture of professionalism with a smile for everyone, even the tatted-down ruthless killers who raged against the judge when a sentence was handed down.

I patted her shoulder. "No, not yet, but I'm working on it. It's not going to take me long to figure out who did it. I promise, it'll all be over soon."

Nobody close to the judge and Jean Anne could put to rest their painful emotions until the suspect was captured, the reason for the killing revealed, and the appropriate amount of justice meted out. The last part, the justice part, fell into my area of expertise, and I was glad Wicks was working with me on this one. No one ever deserved a larger dose of blood and bone than the man who'd used pumpkin balls on my friend and his wife. As a team, we rarely came away without our target captured or at least neutralized with steel or lead. One way or another, we'd put the guy down.

"Esther, can you check your computer and tell me what happened with the Derek Sams trial?"

"Sure, Bruno. Sure." She turned. I followed her over to her elevated desk and I stood below looking across at her like I had done so many times those two years I'd worked for the judge. She'd been a real pleasure to work with. The only knick-knack of a personal nature she allowed on her desk was a white porcelain vase with cerulean blue lines creating a variety of lovely flowers. The vase contained a dozen wilted red roses.

Her fingers clacked on the keys. "Says here that he's been released, 'exceptional clearance,' pending probation review and final disposition. I'm so sorry, Bruno."

My mouth dropped open. "Are you sure? That can't be right, we were in the middle of jury trial. A CI deal is never cut once a trial starts."

Those words in that sequence were a code used so everyone in law enforcement would know what had happened without letting the nosy press in on the secret. Derek Sams, the killer of my grandson, the man who had his hand in the death of my daughter, had been released from custody as an informant to work an important case.

I wanted to break something. I wanted to pick up a chair and beat the table with it and would have had Esther not been present. Someone had traded the life of my grandson away for a better case that Sams could give him.

No. No, that wasn't right either; the DA and the cops didn't know about Albert and how the cruel and brutal Derek Sams had tossed poor Albert off the San Pedro Bridge. Discarded him like so much refuse. In reality, they had traded the death of a dope dealer, Bumpy Spanks, a self-defense death at that. If for some reason that trade did hit the public eye, no one would care, an easy trade to make politically with little risk for blowback.

I took in several deep breaths, regaining control. "Does it say who? Scroll down, it'll be in the notes. The detective handling it had to have a contract with Sams, one signed off by the DA and a judge to get him out of custody." If he didn't perform what he'd promised, or if he ran, he would waive his right to a trial and would be deemed guilty and sentenced immediately upon recapture.

Sams was anything but a fool. If he said he could make a case, then he could make the case rather than risk the ire of the court. Only what case would be bigger than the murder trial he was already in the middle of, and—

Esther said the name the same time I did. "Robby Wicks."

CHAPTER TWENTY-THREE

SOMEONE HAD TAKEN a dog out of the pound to run down another dog, and in this case, I didn't know which dog was a larger threat to society. Both needed to be euthanized before they bit someone else. I retreated from the courtroom after saying my goodbyes to Esther. I promised to keep in touch, to keep her apprised of the investigation.

I took the stairs down two at a time and popped out into the bright sunlight of a beautiful day.

Someone tapped a car horn. I looked to the left and spotted the sleek black Crown Victoria with smoked windows. The car Wicks cherished almost as much as his wife, Barbara. I nodded and waved, put on a fake smile, and headed over to him. The bastard had backed into Judge Connors' reserved parking spot. Wicks knew Connors wouldn't be using it. Sometimes Wicks' lack of decorum made me want to smash him in the face. But I'd come to understand it wasn't his fault. He didn't possess the gene for tact and common social interaction. This same gene deficiency made it easy for him to pull the trigger on a dangerous criminal and afterward go home and sleep like a baby. He was better suited for a world a hundred and twenty years earlier, where in the old West, you lived and died by your gun, not your words needed to engender a circle of friends.

I walked by his open car window and casually said, "Hey, pop the trunk, would ya?"

He hit the button and the trunk deck popped open. "Why?" He said over his shoulder, as he watched in the side mirror. "Whattaya need outta there? Whattaya doin'?"

I shoved his equipment aside and found what I was looking for. I pulled out the tire iron, a long piece of black steel hooked at the end with a knob for the bolt head, and slammed the trunk. I moved to the side of the car, swung as hard as I could, and shattered the back window.

"Hey! Hey! What the hell?"

I broke out the left rear passenger window. He tried to get out. I shoved his door closed and bashed in his side mirror. Hit it several times until it hung from wires. Shards of glass tinkled to the asphalt. Then I went to work on the windshield.

He got out. "Bruno! Bruno! Son of a bitch, stop this shit right now or I'm gonna put a bullet in your ass."

I moved to the hood and banged and banged, dimpling the smooth glossy finish, exposing bright raw steel. I was finally able to let go of all the pent-up rage I'd been containing for so many months. Rage the doctor and Dad had been so worried about. I banged and kicked and moved. I broke out his headlights, stood back and kicked in the fenders and the door panels on the other side. Broke all those side windows as well.

When I came out of my fugue state, I was breathing hard like I'd just finished a marathon. Wicks had gotten out and stood back watching with his brown polyester suit jacket pulled back, his hands on his hips as he puffed his slim brown cigarette. "Well, are you finished?"

I looked over the decimated car and regretted my actions. The car had never done anything to me. "I guess so. And you'll be waiting a long time if you expect me to say I'm sorry."

People coming to court stopped to watch and a small crowd had gathered.

Wicks slid into the driver's seat. "Get in the car, Bonzo. We're going to be late for that interview at MCJ."

I tossed the tire iron in the back seat and got in. He drove us out of the parking lot and headed east. He made a right on Alameda and took it north. He smoked his brown cigarette and kept moving his head trying to see around the starred indentations in the windshield's safety glass, the opaque divots I'd inflicted. He drove no differently than he always drove, as if someone bashing in his car was an everyday occurrence. After a time, and still watching the road, he said, "I'm guessing you found out about Sams?"

I said nothing and continued to look out the missing passenger window, the summer air blowing soft against my face. His cavalier attitude about something so serious started in again on my anger.

Wicks said with a half-chuckle, "I guess I should be glad it was my car and not me, huh?"

"I know better. You'd have shot my ass and then gone for coffee and donuts."

"Yeah, I was going to get my baton out and crack you over your thick skull and realized, hey, what for? All I have to do is file a report that some thugs beat my car with ball bats while I was in court. The county will fix it up good as new. And you'll have gotten it all out of your system so we can go to work. Win-win as far as I'm concerned." His ability to shut off all emotion and not truly care about anything or anyone except the current target in his sights stunned me yet again. This unnatural ability had been one of the reasons I'd left his violent crimes team. I should have been more angry with him; instead, I felt sorry for him.

We drove on.

"Bruno, are we even now?"

"Not by a damn sight, but let's get this other thing done and then we can revisit the scoreboard."

He lost his smug smile. "Sounds good to me, buddy boy, just let me know when you're ready—I'll be happy to square off. But a small word of warning. You better bring a couple of friends to help because I'm not going to hold back."

I let it go. I was familiar with his bold talk and the way he needed it to support a cause, one he had not one chance in hell of accomplishing.

We caught a few more stoplights, still a long way from downtown.

"What did Sams offer up in trade?" I'd calmed down enough to ask the question without fighting the need to throttle him. But I already knew the answer.

"He said we put him on the street he can track down who pulled the trigger on the judge and his wife."

"I figured as much. But I know you well enough that you wouldn't give a little shitweasel like Derek the time of day unless he gave you something to make you believe he could get it done. What'd he give you?"

He held up his hand, pointing at the windshield. "Look at what you did to my car. And with my own tire iron. Why'd I open my trunk for you? That was a stupid move on my part. I should've known what you were going to do."

"Tell me."

Wicks puffed on his cigarette. The wind through the broken-out windows whisked away the swirling smoke. "Sams said he could get close to Little Genie's people on the street and they'd tell him who did the deed. He said he used to sling dope for that organization and knows the ins and outs. Says he knows who'll give it up, just like that." Wicks snapped his fingers.

"You've been had, my friend. Tell me you have him in hand and that you didn't just turn him loose on the street?"

Wicks looked from the road at me then back again.

"Ah, man," I said. "He played you."

"What the hell do you know? You don't have anything better, not right now. All you got is this talk with Little Genie who's in the can and doesn't know beans about what's happening on the streets. That's it, that's the best you got? I think maybe the great Bruno Johnson has lost his street mojo and I have to hedge my bets. If Sams doesn't perform, then based on the contract he signed, he gets slammed. And without a trial he'll get the full boat, twelve years, no good, and work time. He knows that so he's going to damn well do what I want him to or I'll pull the carrot and give him the stick."

"You don't get it, do you? He's a stone-cold sociopath without any empathy and only cares about himself. He's not going to do one damn thing for you. He'll run and gun, livin' life large until you figure out your mistake and come looking for him. But that can't happen right away because he knows your priority is finding the judge's killer. You just handed him a free pass to Disneyland until we can run him down again. And it won't be so easy this time. He's older and smarter."

Wicks looked at me again, puffing faster on his cigarette. "You don't know that."

I leaned over closer to his face. "Who do you think crushed his three fingers?"

He punched the steering wheel. "Ah, man, you never told me you were the one who did that."

"You never asked. That kid just made a buffoon out of you."

He thought about it for a minute. "Naw, we'll just see. That kid's scared to death of me. You won't mind if I reserve judgment for a couple of days, to see if he comes through. You're a little biased by my count."

I looked out the window and watched the passing landscape. I wasn't so angry about Wicks letting Sams out. I was angrier about

Sams being on the street where the Doctor Jekyll inside me could get to him. Not really angry, more scared. I didn't know how long I could put it off. I just knew very soon I'd drop everything and go on the hunt with a blood lust no one could stop.

CHAPTER TWENTY-FOUR

THE CLOSER WE drove to Men's Central Jail, the more I worried. Someone might spot me and recognize me as Karl from TW. I put on a pair of sunglasses, and when we parked, I opened the back door and grabbed a Dodger ball cap. Wicks loved that hat, kept it pristine in the back window of the Crown Vic to show team support. I shook off the shattered window glass and donned the cap low over my brow right atop the dark glasses.

"Hey! That's my—"

I took a step closer to him. "You want to do this now, right here in the parking lot?"

"Go ahead and keep the hat. It's ruined now with all your Jheri Curl."

It was a racial slur. I kept my hair shaved close to the scalp and never used Jheri Curl and he knew it. Back in the day, he'd sometimes joke with similar indirect slurs, but this was the first time it felt like he meant it, and it hurt. I unbuttoned my work shirt with the TransWorld embroidered emblem and tossed it on the seat. I pulled the bottom of my tee shirt out of my pants and let it hang to cover the .357 in my waistband.

Wicks stood by and watched. "What gives? Why are you dressin' down to go into the jail to talk to a crook?"

The entire time I worked with Wicks on the violent crimes team, I wore similar work shirts. Even after he thought I'd left the department, he'd seen me wearing it in the LAPD holding cell after the arrest for the stolen Monte. Maybe I should've changed to a different work shirt than the one with the TW emblem before meeting him at Compton Court; he wasn't a fool, not by a long stretch.

I turned to face him, lowered the sunglasses, and looked at him over the top while my mind scrambled to come up with a logical explanation, anything other than having to tell him about Trans-World. Black Bart wanted that information kept mum.

Wicks' expression shifted. "Naw, man, don't tell me you have another case pending? Do you have a warrant you're trying to dodge? That's it, isn't it? Another one besides the GTA I already took care of? What the hell's happened to you? You step away from the badge and go batshit crazy, is that it?"

I let out the breath I'd been holding and put the sunglasses back, covering my eyes. "So you're going to judge me now? Come on, let's get this over with, I got things to do, people to see." I didn't wait for an answer and headed through the parking lot up to the main entrance.

While we walked, my mind wandered to what happened the night before. After Dad and I left the foster home, after we left Alonzo where we'd found him, we rode back to the house without saying a word. The experience had been exhilarating. I had not been that happy in a very long time. Driving back in the truck with Dad, I experienced a major letdown. I hit a wallow of depression and despair so deep and dark I never wanted to be in a place like that ever again.

In the morning, Dad was gone when I woke so I didn't have a chance to talk to him about what happened, and, just as important, about how, after so many years—decades—he'd finally bared his soul about his wife and my mother. Maybe that was why he'd chosen not to be there when I woke. He'd opened up once, and now I was confident I could get him to talk about her some more. I had to know what happened. I was anxious to continue that talk.

Twenty minutes later, we entered the interview room to wait for the deputy to bring down Sammy Eugene Ray, Little Genie. Wicks sat behind a standard-issue county government table, gray with a scarred linoleum top etched with gang signs that promised hate and mayhem, a symbol far removed from an ancient maple tree in a park with a heart carved in the bark containing two names in the center promising forever love. I stood with my shoulder against the bare concrete wall, arms crossed. Ten silent minutes passed. I longed for the time when we joked and laughed and spent days on end tracking violent offenders. We'd been friends—much closer than the regular definition of friends. How had our relationship degenerated to this? I had talked to Dad about it, how with Wicks I wanted it to be like it used to be.

Dad said that maybe we weren't really friends after all. Not in the truest sense of the term. He said, "If you're truly good friends, that's forever and nothing can come between that bond." I trusted Dad more than anyone else in the world, but in this instance I either didn't understand the concept or he was just plain wrong. Wicks and I were just going through a rough patch. A rough patch made worse by Derek Sams, the young man who ruined everything he touched. He'd cut a swath through the ghetto with my family at the epicenter.

The door to the small interview room opened. Sammy Ray stood there in waist chains and leg irons. He wore the red jumpsuit of an escape risk, also the reason why he wore the chains and had to be escorted wherever he went in the jail. He'd escaped once; the sheriff wouldn't let it happen again.

He took one look at me and smiled, the exact opposite reaction I'd hoped for. I wanted him angry and at the same time scared.

"Deputy Bruno Johnson, my man, how's it goin'?" He tried to raise his hand to shake or fist bump, but the waist chain restricted him. "What an honor to be in the presence of such greatness. This must really be something important to bring out someone of your . . . of your stature."

"That's a big word coming from a puke," Wicks said.

The deputy behind him closed the door.

Wicks nodded to the chair. "Sit your ass down, inmate."

Little Genie hobbled the rest of the way in, chains rattling, pulled out the plastic chair, and sat as best he could. With the chain restrictions I couldn't tell if the bullets I'd put in the backs of his legs had caused any permanent impediment to his mobility. Did his legs ache every night and keep him awake? Did the pain remind him of the people he killed, the reason for his incarceration?

"Hey, either of you got a smoke? I'd kill me some people for a smoke right now. I'm not kiddin', a whole bunch of folks. Bam. Bam. Bam." He laughed as if that were actually funny and made a gun symbol with his hand at his hip, his index finger and thumb pointed at me. "Pow. Pow."

I didn't regret for one second the way I took him down, the bullets to the backs of his legs, nor that he had only one thing left to look forward to and it wasn't something pleasant, strapped to a table, both arms extended in a tee, with needles in them.

Sammy Ray was handsome for a criminal of his *stature*—for his chosen world: dope dealer, cold-blooded killer. If things had gone differently for him, in another life he might've been a movie star. He had a five-hundred-watt smile that lit up a room and melted women right down to their high heels. He'd had an unblemished face, smooth and perfect, until the day I'd caught up with him in that family restaurant and beat him with, among other things, a hot six-slice toaster. He now carried a little scar at the side of his right eye.

The sight of him brought back that memory hot and heavy. The smells, the pain from my burned hands, the pure, teeth-cutting violence I used in attempting to apprehend him. Wicks had been right, the battle I had with Little Genie tore up that family restaurant, overturned tables, knocked customers down, shattered the glass showcase counter that displayed all the pastries, cakes, pies, and huge chocolate chip cookies. We slipped and slid and smeared the whole mess all over the floor. I did my level best to get control of him, and, still, he almost escaped. I'd been exhausted with nothing left in the tank. Toward the end of the battle, right at the last, I had him around the leg as he dragged me along still headed for the restaurant door. He was shaking me off. I couldn't let him get away. I pulled a gun from my back pocket, a small .380, stuck it to the back of his leg and pulled the trigger. He screamed in agony and went down but got back up again. If he didn't make it through that door, he'd be on death row with every ounce of hope snatched from his grasp and gone forever. I shot him in the back of his other leg. That stopped him cold. He went down and let out a wail not of this world. Not from the pain, but more like a wolf with his paw caught in a trap with full knowledge that he would never run free again.

I'd been the one to ensure his permanent residency on the Row.

"You're not getting a cigarette," Wicks said. "And if you don't help us out, I'll make sure you get the brick for the next thirty days."

The brick was a burnt piece of protein inmates on discipline earned for jail infractions. Thirty days was the longest sentence available and a pitifully ineffective threat made by Wicks.

Sammy Ray didn't lose the smile. "Can't you at least treat me like a human and take these chains off?"

"No," Wicks said.

I reached into my pants pocket for a key to take his cuffs off. To do so, I had to get close. Sammy Ray tried not to flinch, failed, and said, "You're not taking these off so you can beat me again, are you, Deputy Johnson?"

CHAPTER TWENTY-FIVE

"I ONLY BEAT you the first time because you wouldn't stop fighting. I'm leaving the leg chains on." I pulled a pack of Red Man chewing tobacco from my back pocket that I'd brought for this purpose and tossed it on the table in front of him. All tobacco products fell under banned items in the jail, and I'd just committed a felony. I couldn't give him cigarettes because of the smell and visible smoke. He'd get caught as soon as he stepped from the room and out into the jail hallway.

"I don't use this shit."

I reached to take it away. He grabbed it. "Okay, if this is the best you can do."

Nicotine was an evil monkey to carry on your back, especially while incarcerated. He unrolled the top, took out a gob of brown leaf that smelled strongly of brown sugar, and stuck it in his mouth. He moved it around with his tongue until it bulged his cheek. He rolled up the pouch and stuck it in his red jumpsuit pocket. "Now, how can I help you gentlemens? No, wait, let me guess, you want to know something about what happened to that poor judge and his wife. Am I right? Cryin' shame, really was."

Wicks said, "You're a real smartass, aren't you?"

"I already told those other two morons in suits, the ones who drug me all the way down here from San Quentin for this mess—I told 'em I don't know a damn thing."

I said, "I don't believe you."

"I don't care what you believe or don't believe, Depuuteey, no skin off my nose one way or another."

"You've been locked down for two years, and I know you're still in contact with your people on the street."

"True that, but as you know, my peoples hung around me for two reasons: the money, and my ability to menace them if they didn't do what I asked them to. I can't do neither of those from in here. Even if I did, I won't snitch."

"Bullshit," Wicks said. "And what's with the big words? You getting educated while you wait on the Row? Won't do you any good where you're going."

Wicks wasn't helping.

I moved a resin chair around and sat closer, the way Doctor Abrams did to me in his office. "We're not here asking about what's happening out there right now."

He didn't falter with me being up so close even after what I'd done to him in our last encounter. He still carried some bold street nerve he could draw from. He smiled and chewed his tobacco. "That right?" he said. "Then what exactly you looking for, Depuuteey?"

I didn't take my eyes off his. Wicks started to speak. I held up the flat of my hand and silenced him. "What we are here for is ancient history. With ancient history you can't be labeled a snitch." That wasn't true, but it gave him an out if he wanted to hide behind it.

"You're wrong about that, but I'm listenin'."

"Tell me about Jamar Deacon."

His smile tarnished some and his eyes turned hard. "He was the homeboy the Honorable Judge Connors gunned down with a gauge on 10th Street in front of that apartment. He was workin' for me and didn't deserve what he got."

I shook my head. "He was trying to kill me. He had a gun and was shooting at me."

"I know, I was there, remember? I also know that's part of the game, but the judge messed that boy up with all dat buckshot. His mama couldn't have an open casket and that's on me. He was workin' for me at the time—that makes it my fault."

"Who ran with Jamar?"

For the first time, Little Genie broke eye contact and looked away. I let it fester some, then said, "I can't do anything for you inside. I'd be lying if I said I could, but I can do you a favor out on the street. What do you need? You have to need something."

His head whipped around, his eyes searching mine for the truth. I didn't envy what he had to look forward to: nine to ten years of appeals, the entire time the razor-sharp sword of justice perched over his head ready to swing down and snuff out his life.

"What exactly are you willin' to do? You willin' to take a dude off the board? 'Cause what you're askin' of me is pretty heavy."

He wanted us to kill someone on the street, someone he could no longer get to and still owed a bullet.

Wicks smiled. "Sure, we can do that."

Wicks was going to take Genie's information and not hold up his end of the bargain.

"No," I said emphatically. "That's not going to happen. What else can I do for you?"

He sat back and thought about it a good long time. He looked from Wicks and back to me. "Okay." He pointed at me. "I can trust you. You and I are bound by blood."

Wicks muttered, "What a bunch of street bullshit."

"What is it?" I asked.

"If I help you, I want . . . what I want is for my mama to get a dozen red roses every Monday for the rest of her life."

I sat back, stunned. In all of my years of working the street, I'd never come across such a kind request from someone in his situation, especially from a cold-blooded killer.

"Sure," Wicks said. "We can handle that."

"I'm not talkin' ta you, cracker."

"Every week is too much," I said. "Once a year?"

"Once a month?"

I stuck out my hand. He took it and shook.

"My mama didn't deserve what I put her through, the trial and then all that escape bullshit. They kicked her door in twice before you caught up to me. I can't make it up to her but I can at least—"

"Okay, okay, quit flapping your gums and tell us what you know about who ran with Jamar Deacon, back in the day."

Genie shot Wicks a hot glare that did nothing but draw deeper into Wicks' ire. Wicks had received worse and let it roll off for the moment. Genie looked back at me. "You gunned Jamar's homeboy that day on 10th and—"

"I know, forget that guy, who else? Who would be mad enough to go after the judge for killing Jamar with the shotgun? Who knows guns and knows how to handle pumpkin balls?"

A slow smile crept across Genie's face exposing white teeth. "Pumpkin balls? You're telling me that's what he used on the judge?"

"That's right."

"That wasn't in the papers."

"Homicide holds back information to keep crackpots honest who come in to claim the murder. Who is it? I can see you know something, tell me."

He pointed a finger too close to my face. I didn't like it but put up with it.

"You promise, once a month, twelve red roses?"

"You have my word."

"His name's La Vonn. He and Jamar were tight. They worked some gig together way back before they both broke bad, turned street thug, and came to work for me. He was supposed to be there that day on 10th. He is a baaadass, and if he'd have been there like he was supposed to, things would've turned out much different. I can guarantee you dat. I never ran into a dude so ruthless. He would've taken you out, Depuuteey. Just like that." He snapped his fingers.

Wicks stood and moved to the corner, his back to us, his cell phone to his ear, calling in the name to OSS, Operation Safe Streets, the Sheriff's gang detail.

"What's La Vonn's last name?" I asked.

Genie shrugged. "You want more than that, it's going to be roses once a week, Depuuteey."

I jumped from my chair, grabbed a handful of his red jumpsuit, shoved him across the short distance, and slammed him against the concrete wall. I pressed my shoulder into his chest. I got up into his face. "We had a deal and you're going to keep it."

His eyes went wide with fear. Maybe he did remember the toaster, or maybe he remembered the way I stuck that .380 against his leg, the poke of the barrel just before I pulled the trigger—the searing hot thud as it parted muscle and lodged in bone.

"I . . . I don't know his name. You know how it is on the street, no one gives their real name. Ease up on me, Deputy, step off. Come on, man."

I backed up and gave him some breathing room. "Where can we find La Vonn?"

"Don't know. He just fell out after you took me down." Genie readjusted his red jumpsuit. "I can tell you one thing though, he also ran off with my stash, couple a hundred grand. Word is he used it to open up some kinda straight shop and he's not slingin' anymore. He's an eight ta five suit now. He only does big deals. Big. Big deals. But trust me, he's just as dirty as before. That cat won't ever change his spots."

I pulled back and slapped him hard across the face.

"Hey. Hey." He cowered.

"Is La Vonn the dude you wanted us to take off the board when we first started talking? Are you playing us now? Are you giving him up just so we'll go after him?"

"No. No. I didn' know it was La Vonn you was lookin' for until you said he ran with Jamar and . . . and that he used pumpkin balls. Swear ta God, on my mother's eyes, dat's the truth."

Wicks turned around and put his cell in his pocket. "No hits on La Vonn. He's yankin' our dicks."

I looked back at Little Genie. "You have to give us something more or I'm going to start working on you."

"I don't know nothin' else, I swear."

"What was the gig Jamar and La Vonn both worked?"

"Yeah, yeah, that's right. They both worked at some kinda gym. You know, one of them body shops where all the muscle heads go and drink protein milk and slap each other's asses."

"What's the name of it?"

"I don't know, man. I don't run like that. But I know you can ask around and someone will tell ya."

I grabbed his red jumper and yanked him to his feet. He flinched away and brought his arms up to his face.

"Relax, I'm only chaining you back up. You better not have lied to me or I'll be back."

"It's the truth, every bit of it. You still gonna get the roses for my mama?"

"I'm a man of my word." I hooked his wrists to the cuffs at his waist.

"Thank you, Deputy Johnson."

I opened the door and handed him off to the escort deputy waiting outside. Wicks walked with me to the sally port that would let us back out to the freedom side of the world. He lit up a cigarette. A uniform sergeant walking by stopped. "No smoking in—"

Wicks pulled his jacket aside to show him the lieutenant's badge clipped to his belt. The sergeant shook his head and walked on, muttering.

While we waited for the sally port to open, Wicks said, "How is it that punks you beat and shoot open up to you and that never works for me?"

I didn't answer him. If he didn't already know, then it was too late for him to figure it out now.

I stood staring through the bars to the other side wondering what it would be like to be confined like an animal. I could only hope life would not kick me in the teeth and put me there. I couldn't use life as an excuse; I made my own choices.

CHAPTER TWENTY-SIX

I PUSHED THE accelerator to the floor, the engine on the little Opel Kadett winding out and threatening to blow. I wove in and around slower cars heading northbound on Wilmington. Once I hit Imperial Highway, I'd go west to Central and then go north. Junior Mint sat next to me, sensing my anxiety, and moved around from paw to paw. He was far too large for the small seat and footwell. I'd drop him at TW first, but I didn't have the time.

Wicks had let me off back at my car in the Compton court parking lot. He wanted to follow up on what Little Genie had told us. That's what Wicks said, but I knew better. What I told him about Derek Sams had been grinding on him. How Derek had used him. Wicks would page up Sams. If Sams was dumb enough to answer the summons, Wicks would have a heart-to-heart with him, one with knuckles and a blackjack employed to get the truth. Wicks would determine whether or not Sams really did have the ability to ferret out the judge and his wife's killer or if he was just feeding Wicks a line.

When Wicks asked what I intended to do, I told him I'd search for the gym where La Vonn and Jamar had worked. And I *would* do that, right after I took a run up to the Crazy Eight for the meeting with Jumbo and Nigel.

I was fifteen minutes late. Nigel had the gift of gab and would do his best to keep Johnny Sin at the bar as long as he could. I had offered Nigel two thousand dollars of TW's money if he could put together the gun deal with Jumbo. If he had to, Black Bart would go a lot higher than two grand for a deal this large, a deal that would make international news. The U.S. government had put the kibosh on the train car theft, and nothing in the media had leaked. No one knew except the government and the railroad. The government didn't want the media to find out how terribly deficient their security had been and that low-level criminals could walk away with so many guns and munitions, putting the public at great risk.

Five minutes later, I made a wide sweeping turn from Central onto 81st and into the Crazy Eight's rear parking lot. The little car bounced and banged into the driveway. I pulled up and stopped. Junior Mint barked. He sensed the excitement of something important about to happen. I checked the mirrors and looked all around. I couldn't leave Junior in the car, not in this neighborhood. Too many gangsters with guns; otherwise, I had no doubt he could hold his own against any other threat. Junior paced, moving his front paws back and forth in more of a hop, while his rear stayed put on the seat. On one pass he licked my cheek. He wanted to go in real bad. "I'm sorry, pal, this isn't the kind of place you think it is. It's not for good dogs. It's ugly inside and it smells . . . it kinda smells like ass."

"Arf."

"Okay, okay. But if I take you in with me, you have to be on your best behavior. You promise?" He licked my cheek again. I opened the door and slid out. He came out right behind me and almost knocked me down. "Hey, hey, take it easy." I grabbed his collar and clipped on a long leather leash. He about jerked my arm out of the socket heading for the back door. You'd think he was an alcoholic in desperate need of a Singapore Sling or a Greyhound. I pulled him up short to talk to him, let him calm down a little.

"Just so you know, my friend, they don't serve top-shelf liquor in here. It's strictly plastic vodka. What's plastic vodka, you ask? Well, I didn't know either until Nigel told me. It's cheap vodka poured from a plastic bottle." I patted his side. "Okay, here we go."

I tugged open the thick, heavy door reinforced with wrought-iron bars and steel. We entered the cool darkness.

Ledezma yelled from behind the bar, "No, Karl. No dogs, God damn you. Get him the hell outta here. Now."

I ignored him and pulled hard against the leash trying to control Junior. Junior wanted to belly up to the bar with all his newfound friends, but that spelled trouble with a capital T. I jockeyed him over to a large double-glass-door cooler made of stainless steel. Ledezma bought it at a fire sale and stored his overstock of cheap bottled beer where he could keep a close eye on it. He only sold two flavors, cheap and cheaper. He didn't leave the derelicts, drunks, and ne'er-do-wells who patronized his bar open to temptation and locked the double door handles together with a chain and padlock. I threaded Junior's leash through the same handles and snugged it down just as Nigel, over at the bar, yelled, "Hey, Karl, lemme buy you a beer." He held up a near-empty mug. He didn't have any money; he meant he wanted me to buy *him* a beer.

My eyes had adjusted to the dimness. I moved toward him. The bar was near capacity, half again more than normal. What was different today? Oh, *Mother's Day* in the ghetto—the day the welfare checks came out. There always came a flurry of bar activity until the money dwindled. A flash of calming behavior settled throughout the ghetto—drunks, speed freaks, and cokeheads would lie low until the money ran dry. Then, gradually, hunger would set in, malnutrition, jonesing for the next fix or pint—a hum, a vibration, would grow louder with each day until once again the eagle screamed and the welfare money hit the mailboxes. If one more person walked into the Crazy Eight, they'd have to take a seat in one of the grimy red vinyl booths where nobody ever sat, too dark and dreary in the realm of the already dark and dreary.

Over by the cooler, Junior whined.

I gently elbowed in beside Lois, a woman who spent most of her day scavenging cans and bottles with a shopping cart in order to drink her breakfast, lunch, and dinner at The Eight. She reeked of body odor and dirt and of a hopeless despair. "How's it hangin', Lois?" I slipped her a five hand-to-hand under the bar so Ledezma didn't see it in case she owed him a tab.

"Thanks, Karl," she whispered. "My kids'll 'preciate it. Now I can buy my babies some beans and rice."

Many winters ago, her three children died in a carbon monoxide accident, victims of a faulty wall heater. This while she attended the neighbor's Christmas party partaking in a nog laced heavily with rum.

If I slipped her anything more than a five, it would endanger her health with a drug overdose or alcohol poisoning.

Ledezma came over and slapped the bar with the flat of his hand. "No. I won't have it, Karl. Get that damn dog out of here now or I'm callin' the cops."

He didn't want the cops in there any more than I did.

I smiled. "Where's my beer?"

"Get him out." He pointed off into the distance with a move that looked more like a salute to Adolf.

Nigel said, "Ah, come on, man, don't be that way. Peace on earth starts at home. Give my friend a beer, I'm buyin'." He held up his clenched hand for a fist bump from the angry bartender.

Ledezma ignored the drunken Nigel and glared at me. "The health department does a surprise visit, I'll lose my ticket. They're just lookin' for a reason to close me down."

I picked up the dirty bar towel with two fingers, made a face, and dropped it on the other side onto the duckboards that hadn't been cleaned in weeks. "Seriously?"

I reached across the bar, grabbed a mug, and pulled my own draft. Ledezma watched with a scowl. I had to keep up my hardass image as part of the game of roping for TW.

Nigel leaned in close and lowered his voice to a whisper. "Johnny Sin is late, you lucked out. When he gets here and he likes what we have to say, he'll take us to Jumbo."

I sipped instead of glugged. I wanted my senses clear. "You couldn't get him to come to TransWorld? This meeting has to be here?" I wanted Johnny Sin on videotape at the TW counter talking over the deal, hard evidence for court he wouldn't be able to refute.

"Naw, man, I was lucky to get him to come here, and I'm tellin' you right now, this isn't a good idea. Johnny Sin is no one to mess with. I mean it. I'm not kidding here. Even if it's a straight deal, which from what I hear he doesn't do a lot of those, my friend. The bigger the deal, the more likely the other guy just up and disappears after the transaction. Never to be seen or heard from again. Just like that." He snapped his fingers. "Then Johnny Sin keeps the money and the merchandise."

I shrugged. "You don't know for sure. A big deal means big money—maybe they just took off for warmer climes down South."

He leaned away from me as if trying to get a better look. "You sun-stroked, son?"

The door opened. In walked a street gangster wearing an after-market football letterman's jacket, sunglasses, and a Raiders ball cap pulled down low. He wore denim pants four or five sizes too large that sagged front and back, the waist cinched up with a narrow black belt. He didn't belong in the Crazy Eight. The door behind him closed slowly, cutting off the pie-wedged light from outside.

Junior Mint stood and barked.

Ledezma, behind me, said, "Better curb your dog or you're not going to have one."

"Junior!" I yelled.

The light continued to winnow down as the door closed on its own.

The gangbanger stopped and turned his head to look at Junior, his hand going inside his jacket. He was going for a gun.

I reached under my shirt and yanked out the .357. "Junior!"

Nigel grabbed my shoulder. "Don't, Karl. It's too late."

I shrugged away.

Junior didn't like criminals. He leapt forward, jerking the tall, double-glass-door cooler and pulling it a couple of feet away from the wall. The steel-pegged feet scraped the floor. The bottles inside rattled and fell and banged. Some broke. The handles held and so did the leash.

The gangbanger pulled a chrome automatic handgun and swung his hand around.

Junior leapt again, pulling the heavy cooler filled with cheap beer along the floor a few more feet.

I jumped between my dog and the gangbanger, pointing my gun at his face ten feet away. "Back off. *Back off!*"

Everybody froze. Except Junior; he made another leap. I reached down and grabbed him by the collar, still holding my aim on the guy's head. "Put it away or I'll put you down."

The gangbanger's solemn expression didn't change. He remained cool under duress. He slowly lowered his gun, turned heel, and exited the same way he'd entered.

Nigel came over, beer in hand. He reached down and patted Junior's head. "Thanks a lot, Karl. You just ran off your gun deal and now I'm out two grand."

"What are you talking about?"

"That there was Johnny Sin."

"That wasn't the guy I saw in here before."

"Yes, it was, he just never looks the same way twice."

I said, "Here, hold my dog."

I hurried out to catch up to Johnny Sin.

CHAPTER TWENTY-SEVEN

Outside, I held up my arm to block the bright sunlight and flinched waiting for Johnny Sin's bullet to take me in the gut. In the glare, I caught movement over by the cars parked in front of the pawnshop. I brought my gun down by my leg and headed that way. Johnny Sin moved to the door of a faded light-blue VW bug and opened it. Only his head and shoulders were visible. What a perfect car to move around in. No cop would be looking for a high-powered crime figure, not one capable of negotiating a gun deal with literally a ton of guns, not driving a VW. Or maybe he really couldn't do a deal at all and he'd just hornswoggled Nigel.

"Wait."

Johnny Sin hesitated. He looked back over the roof of the VW and said, "Deal's off. Go on back to your slum bar, get blind-assed drunk, and pick the nits off each other, for all I care." He stuck his leg in, about to enter the car.

"Wait!"

I hurried down the sidewalk along the businesses in front of the cars and took a chance. I put my gun back in my waistband as a sign of good faith. I stopped at the left front fender of the VW, less than a car length away. The door to the Vee-dub between us acted as a shield for him.

Johnny Sin didn't look anything at all like I'd last seen him. He'd made a stunning transformation. I could only recognize his lips and cheekbones, and that was if I were looking for a disguise.

Johnny Sin bumped his chin up. "I said the deal's off, asswipe. Now back away or I'll pump a lead pellet into your belly."

I held up my hands. "I don't come back with this deal, my boss is going to have my head on a platter."

"Not my problem—" He lifted his sunglasses to see better and read the embroidered nameplate on my work shirt—"Karl." He said it "Karrral." Then he muttered, low and almost inaudible, "Never knew a Negro with a name like Karrral. Especially Karrral with a *K*."

He was definitely a Caucasian with a dark tan but moved and talked like an African American.

I pulled out a wad of cash, five grand I'd signed for with RD the night before at TW, money to use as flash for this deal. Black Bart didn't know about it and wouldn't have approved.

I'd just violated an important rule in an undercover deal. You never flash money without having the appropriate backup; the more the money, the more the backup. With five grand I was short about five knuckle-dragging cops. "Here. See. I can prove I'm serious about this deal. There are stacks more where this came from. I'm talkin' stacks." I raised my hand to indicate a stack four feet off the ground.

Johnny Sin let his sunglasses back down, eased the Vee-dub's door closed, and stood ready, trying to decide. He licked his lips as if hungry and looked all around checking out the parking lot for witnesses.

Now he was thinking about ripping me for the money. He pulled his chrome automatic and was about to take a step closer. I was caught if I tried to pull my gun now; he'd shoot me dead before I got the chance. I'd made a big mistake and was about to pay for it. Johnny Sin was going to shoot me and take the five grand. Why wouldn't he? I'd acted like a complete fool—too anxious to make the deal and had thrown caution to the wind in order to get all those guns off the street.

To my right, the door to the pawnshop opened. Out stepped a huge outlaw motorcycle gang member wearing a black leather jacket with too many zippers that gleamed in the sun, heavy black steel-toed boots, and a mess of black bushy hair and beard. His eyes were covered with dark sunglasses. Down by his leg he held an illegal cut-down double-barreled shotgun no more than ten inches long, a devastating weapon at close range.

Black Bart.

I wanted to kiss him.

Johnny Sin stopped. "Who's this?"

"Never mind who he is. You interested in the deal, or aren't you?"

"Not with the likes of you two."

Black Bart said nothing and just stood there.

"You change your mind," I said, "there's plenty more of this"—I held up the wad of cash—"and you're not going to find a better deal on the street for what you're selling. Ask around, but I think you already have."

He opened the Vee-dub door. "Not on your life, pal."

"You can find us at TransWorld Consolidated Freight over in Lakewood."

He got in, started up, backed out, and took off. I let go a huge sigh of relief. I turned to thank Black Bart. He'd not said a thing and had walked over to his Harley. He kick-started it and roared away. He wasn't usually so unsociable. He was mad about the money because I hadn't asked first. This after he'd just admonished me again about it the day before. And probably about doing a flash without backup. I'd hear about it for sure.

To top it off, I'd cheesed the gun deal of the century.

Terrific.

Nigel came out the back door of the Crazy Eight being towed by Junior. All Nigel could do was hold on. "Bad news," Nigel said. "When your dog here about toppled over that cooler he broke a ton of bottles and Dez is not happy."

I peeled off a hundred from the wad and handed it to him as I took the leash. "Here, go pay for it and be sure to get a receipt."

He took the proffered hundred, his eyes still on the wad in my hand. "Man, that's some load of green you got there. Whattaya say you and me go party? I know a place where—"

"I'm not in the mood. I just blew the deal with Johnny Sin. My boss is going to be mad as hell. I'm guessing he's going to fire me."

He waved his hand. "Pshaw, Johnny's a badass for sure, but he's just a flunky like you and me. I talked with Jumbo just now on the phone inside the bar, he's the main man." He hooked his thumb back over his shoulder. "He still wants to do the deal. He'll be at TW at midnight to talk price and to set up the exchange. But I'm warning you right now, he wants to see the color of your money, and you better be up front about this, because I'm tellin' you, these guys are not to be messed with."

I smiled hugely and peeled off five hundreds. I started to hand them over to Nigel and realized that, if I did, he'd disappear for days, using dope until the money ran out. "Here's a bonus for getting me out of the doghouse with my boss." He grabbed for it. I pulled it back out of his reach. "You can have it after the meeting tonight."

"Okay, okay, so this is over and above the two grand you promised me, twenty-five hundred total, right?"

"Yes."

"Cool beans." He clapped his hands and rubbed them together. "This is really working out, Karl. Man, am I glad I ran into you six months ago."

I loved to see the gleam in his eyes, the way he spoke about our friendship and yet I couldn't help thinking about the end of the sting when that friendship would come to a screeching halt. He'd hate me like no one has ever hated me before. My only consolation was that time in prison away from the dope might straighten him out, give him a chance to get his life back on track. It was a weak justification; true friends didn't betray each other.

When I first came to TW, I asked Black Bart about this unfortunate conundrum, how we worked so hard to gain the trust and friendship of people, when all along we planned to double-cross them and steal away years of their lives by putting them in concrete boxes with steel bars. He'd simply said, "That's the life we chose, as did they."

From that day forward, every time Nigel smiled at me, *as did they* echoed in my mind.

CHAPTER TWENTY-EIGHT

I HAD SOME time to kill. I didn't want to go back to TW and confront an angry Black Bart. Not right away. Let him cool down a little first. I had again left my cell phone at home. I wasn't used to carrying one and didn't know if I ever would be. With each passing day, more and more of the phone booths along the streets disappeared, and I'd eventually be squeezed into remembering to carry mine.

I needed to make a call. From the back seat of the Kadett, I took out a red banner that read "Service Dog" in white letters on the side. I strapped it around Junior's middle. It was meant for a smaller dog and looked a little ridiculous on him. I went in the back of the Crazy Eight with Junior Mint on the leash. Ledezma stood at his open cooler. He stopped what he was doing, gingerly placing broken bottles in an empty box as beer foam rolled off the ledge and onto the floor. At his feet sat a bucket with gray soapy water and a dirty rag hanging over the rim. "No, Karl. Not this time. Get that damn dog outta here. I mean it, out!"

Junior growled.

I shrugged, pointed to the red banner, and ignored Ledezma. I used the pay phone on the wall to dial TW.

While I waited and listened to the ring, I flashed back to when I attended the Sheriff's academy. The drill instructors constantly inspected our uniforms for field readiness, polished leather, razor-sharp creases. We always had to have a hard-plastic comb in our back pockets, whether we had hair to comb or not. The comb was there as a failsafe in case we were ever taken hostage and hand-cuffed with our own cuffs. We were shown how the comb could disable the cuffs. We had to practice the difficult maneuver until we got it right. We were also made to carry a spare handcuff key taped to the inside of our Sam Browne belts for the same reason. The DIs made the young and dumb me think that out on the street a whole lot of dimwitted cops were getting taken hostage. The DIs also insisted that we keep a dime in the bottom of our speed loader bullet pouch on our belt. This was in case we found ourselves away from the cop car radio and needed to make a call from a pay phone. Now all cops carried radios on their belts.

I hung up and dialed again. Listened to it ring. RD probably had his feet up on the desk watching the color television in Black Bart's office. He loved watching *CHiPs* reruns. He'd yell and scream at the outrageous scenarios, how the TV portrayed the highway patrol. "They don't do any of that shit. Can you believe this? All they do is chase taillights. They're triple A with guns. They should issue them tow trucks instead of patrol cars." And yet he continued to watch whenever he had a spare moment, which was rare.

Ring. Ring.

During my patrol days, I was glad I had that dime. More than once I had to leave the safety of my patrol car and chase a crook on foot through backyards and over fences. Twice the chase had gone several miles. When I caught the crook, I'd finally look up and realize I was deep in Indian country far from any backup and without a radio. I held the handcuffed crook in a headlock while I used the dime in my bullet pouch to call the station from a street-side pay phone.

How times had changed.

In the Crazy Eight I had to use a quarter, not a dime, to make the call to TW. With the age of cell phones, I could easily see a time when all the pay phones would disappear. I understood the need but actually liked it better the other way. With cell phones, everyone became constantly connected and people lost their sense of individuality. People became a collective of one, surging and ebbing like an ocean tide.

RD at TW finally picked up. I told him about the deal at midnight and asked him to have enough guys on hand to handle it and to brief Black Bart when he got there. RD said he would. I hung up, waved to Nigel, and yelled that I'd see him tonight. He raised his glass smiling like some kind of goof.

Nigel smiled again. *As did they* pinged off the inside walls of my brain.

* * *

Outside, I got in the Kadett and drove home, a place I'd been trying to avoid for the last six months. The bad memories there overpowered the good. Olivia and the twins used to visit Dad. I had watched him play with Alonzo and Albert on the floor as Olivia looked on with a huge smile, a memory I dearly cherished. We also met at Dad's for Christmas and Easter and Thanksgiving, warm, cheerful times. That's all I had left. Memories.

Now Olivia and Albert were both gone. We only had Alonzo left and we really didn't even have him.

I parked the Kadett in the parking lot to Martin Luther King hospital and walked back to Nord. Junior loved the outing. I talked to him the entire way, telling him stories of the street when I worked as a uniform patrol deputy. He seemed to enjoy the tales of human encounters, the good and the bad, and I started to believe maybe my dog had been a cop in another life. Hell, he might even be my partner Ned. It would be real nice if he were Ned.

We found Dad in the living room reading Dumas' *The Three Musketeers* for at least the third time that I could remember. The sight of the cover made me want to reread the book of high adventure and wonderful comradery. It was also a sign that things were getting back to normal. Dad hadn't read a book for six months. Depression could do that to a person. Throughout his life, he rarely watched television and always had a book in his hand. It would still be a while before I could sit in one place long enough to catch up on my favorite author's new books I'd let silently slip past.

Junior bounded over as Dad struggled to stand. Junior knocked him back onto the couch and licked his face. He laughed.

He actually laughed.

Music to my ears. I had not heard him laugh in I couldn't remember how long. He struggled to his feet, pushing on Junior to give him room. "Hey, Son, how are you doing?" His smile remained.

"Okay, what's going on, Dad?"

"What do you mean?"

I pointed a finger off into the distance. "Hey, I know what you did."

"What'd I do? What are you talking about?"

"You went back to Laurel and saw Alonzo again, didn't you?"

His smile tarnished some. "I might've. Is there something that says I can't?"

I exhaled. "No, Dad." I fought down the jealousy. "I'm just glad you get to see him and that Alonzo gets to see his great-grandpa." I needed to change the subject before I choked on the emotion. I went down the short hall with him following along. I got down on one knee at the threshold to my bedroom door and pulled off the piece of frame close to the bottom. The piece had a fine cut that was almost invisible unless you got right down close to look. With the piece pulled off, it gave me access to a narrow compartment behind the wall. I took the stolen/recovered Colt .38 from my back pocket, the one I'd taken from Leo in the gun deal, stashed it there, and replaced the piece of wood frame. Dad watched without saying a word. He knew about the spot; I'd told him years ago in case he ever had the need for a gun. He'd said at the time and always maintained that he could "never, ever point a gun at another man, let alone look him in the eye and pull the trigger."

"Never say never, Dad."

After I replaced the piece of doorframe, I stood and said, "Come on, let's sit down." We moved back into the living room. When I sat on the couch next to him, his smile returned in force. Junior settled close on the floor. I kicked my shoes off and removed my socks. I rubbed his chest and belly with my feet. He groaned with pleasure.

I stopped playing with Junior and turned serious. "Can you please tell me more about my mother?"

Dad lost his smile.

I put my hand on his leg. "Please, Dad?"

He nodded. "It's not something I'm proud of, Son. It's not something you need to know. I wish you'd trust me on this. It's . . . well, just trust me when I say once I tell you . . . you're . . . you're not going to be glad I did."

"Please?"

I preferred his smile, but at the same time I had a deep desire to know more about my mother, a woman I had for years been forced to create in my mind. His story the night before sparked an intrigue inside me that was difficult to quell.

Dad stared off into nothingness and started to speak.

CHAPTER TWENTY-NINE

DAD MARRIED BEATRICE *Olivia Elliot in a civil ceremony two weeks after he went to work for the U.S. postal service, the day he received his first paycheck. They took a place of their own, the rental of a run-down, one-bedroom home in the outskirts of Los Angeles amid vast empty tracts of land. The house wasn't there anymore, replaced with a park now in the city of Compton. He never remembered being so happy. Every day was a joy to come home to his new wife, who seemed to radiate love for him. They'd eat the meal she prepared, usually something boiled and flavorless, but he didn't care. Not when her eyes glowed with excitement to see him and to hear all about his day. He got in the habit of using a lot of salt and catsup.*

They'd go to bed early, make love, and then pull the covers over their heads and whisper late into the night. They'd talk about their dreams and how they'd achieve them, of how he'd move up in the post office hierarchy and they'd buy a wonderfully huge house in Baldwin Hills. In the morning, she'd get up without disturbing him and make breakfast. At the front door, he'd kiss her on the forehead and tell her, "See you tonight, beautiful."

"Not if I see you first." She said this each time and he didn't know for sure if she knew what it meant or if she just repeated a line from a movie.

Bea went to a lot of movies, this according to her. At first, she told him all about each scene with verve and élan and made him wish he'd been there with her. But as the weeks passed, her excitement started to dwindle and then fade until she took to just explaining the story arc. And finally, just the title. Life didn't move fast enough to hold the attention of his life-loving wife, and he didn't know what to do about it.

Six months to the day after they'd been married, he came home and found two strangers, a black man and woman sitting on his rented divan in the living room of his rented house. "Honey, this is Melvin Shackleford and his girl Cleo Elliott. That's Elliott with two t's, no relation. I met them at the bus stop on Long Beach, you know the one just a little south of Century Boulevard."

What the heck was she doing in that part of town catching a bus? He'd have to talk to her about it later. That part of town spelled real trouble for blacks.

He shook their hands and eyed them up and down. He didn't like at all what he saw of Shackleford, with his patched-over secondhand clothes and the scuffed and dirty shoes a bum might wear. But more than that, it was how he carried himself, with the look of a criminal on the grift.

Bea had stopped at the store and spent too much money on three cans of Chung King, the dinner with the dried noodles in a separate can taped above the chopped suey in the other can below. It was more cost effective to cook their food than to buy it already prepared. She knew that; they'd discussed it.

Over dessert of canned circle-cut pineapple, she told him that Melvin and Cleo were going to stay a couple of days on the couch. He hesitated, going over the options in his head, the cause and effect of each possible answer. He didn't want these sketchy people staying in his home. Not *for one minute more, let alone a couple of days. But he had to remember the house was half hers as well and to keep peace in his new family. He put on a fake smile and said, "How nice." The two words threatened to choke him.*

That night in bed after they'd made up a pallet of couch and chair cushions on the floor for their guests, they argued for the first time. She slept with her back to him instead of cuddled up close. The next morning, he went to work mad and at the same time hurt that she couldn't see his side of it.

All day he mulled over how he had handled the whole situation and convinced himself he'd been wrong and would apologize. When he arrived home, no dinner waited on the table. Bea sat on the couch with her arms across her chest, angry and not radiating one iota of love. She didn't have to say a word. He'd do anything to get back what he'd lost. Anything.

He sat next to her, put his arm around her, and nuzzled her neck. "I'm sorry, babe."

"Our guests left. You ran them off. You should be ashamed the way you acted."

"I'm sorry, really I am."

She glared at him a moment longer and then said, "Are you hungry? Do you want me to make you something to eat?"

"I want you not to be mad at me."

She struggled to get out of his snuggle and stood. She leaned down and kissed him on the lips. "I could never stay mad at a man as cute as you. How does warmed-up Chung King sound?"

"Wonderful."

That night in bed after they made long, slow love and he lay with his head on her hot, sweaty tummy, he joked with her. "Bea, honey?"

"Yes, dear?"

He patted her tummy. "I think you may have eaten a little too much leftover Chung King."

She whispered, "No. That's our own little Chung King."

He jumped up. "Whaaat? Do you mean what I think you mean?"

"I sure do—Daddy."

CHAPTER THIRTY

DAD SUDDENLY QUIT telling the story. I wanted more. I had to have more. He just had to tell the rest of it. *I was his little Chung King.* "What happened? You can't just stop right in the middle of the story."

Dad stared at the wall across the room, lost in a sad reminiscence, a life I knew nothing about, one he had tried hard to forget. I could see it in his face, a horrible emotion he'd always kept hidden. I'd been the one to dredge it all up.

I waited.

He said nothing.

I didn't want him to hurt anymore and asked, "Then, why don't you tell me about Alonzo? How's he doing? Does he look okay?"

The ugly emotion that filled Dad's expression shifted back to the good old Dad smile. "Don't be silly, you just saw him last night. He's fine, just fine. Better now that he gets to see his blood relatives, people who love him. You should've seen how happy he was to see me." Dad put his hand over his heart. "I stayed with him for a couple of hours. We played on the floor with his favorite toys."

Dad must've taken along Alonzo's favorite toys. What a great idea.

"That's good." I again fought down the jealousy, silly as it was. Dad was Alonzo's great-grandfather and had every right to see him. If I tried to see him more than the one time, Child Protective Services would hear about it and move Alonzo to another foster home farther away, maybe in the next county. I wouldn't push it, no matter how much I wanted to. I'd made my bed and now I had to accept the result. I'd been the one to make the conscious decision to crush Derek Sams' fingers in the door crack. I took a second to weigh the consequences of that act. I knew it was wrong to derive so much pleasure from it and didn't care. But was the act worth the cost of not seeing my grandson? No. Not by a damn sight. But I had confirmed my belief about what happened to poor little Albert. To let that kind of secret go unanswered would've eaten away at our lives and left that question forever on the forefront of our minds. No, it was something that had to be done and I didn't regret it. My mind shifted all on its own away from the heated emotion.

"Oh. Shoot, I forgot something." I stood and padded barefooted over to the phone on the wall.

"What?" Dad asked.

"Nothing big, just something about work."

I froze. Dad didn't know I'd returned to the job and that I now worked at the sting at TransWorld.

"Work?" Dad asked.

"My old boss, you remember Wicks, he asked me to talk to a guy we arrested two years ago to see if I could get him to talk about a suspect who had possibly killed the judge and his wife." No part of that statement was a lie and still blackness crowded me a little bit more.

I took a deep breath having dodged that bullet and picked up the phone as I searched for the florist's number pinned to the corkboard on the wall. I kept the number handy. In the past, I would periodically send Esther, the court clerk, flowers with an unsigned card.

She thought she had a secret admirer. The joy it brought her would last a couple of weeks. I never told her and kept sending them even after I'd gone back to the violent crimes team. The judge figured it out early on without me saying a word. He'd give me a knowing look every time the roses were delivered.

I dialed and got the owner of the florist shop. I pulled the address out of my pocket. "Hey, Lori, this is Bruno Johnson. Fine. Fine. And you? Good. Hey, I'd like to send a dozen red roses to a Mrs. Agnes Ray who lives at 1535 East 113th Street in Los Angeles. Yes, that's right, and I want you to send the roses on the first of every month. Yes, please send me the bill. No . . . okay, wait. Yes, on the card put 'From your loving son.' Yes. Yes. Thank you so much. Goodbye." I hung up.

Dad said from the couch, "What in the world was that all about?" I told him the whole story about what happened in the jail with Little Genie.

He sat back and stared.

"Don't give me that look. You'd have done the same thing if you were in my place."

"I don't know, Bruno, sometimes when I think you've crossed over to a place where I can't reach you anymore, you go and do something like this."

My face flushed hot.

He nodded to himself. "Okay." His voice came out lower and husky. "You really want to hear the rest of this?"

I hurried over to the couch and sat down. "You know I do." Even though saying that I did came with a price.

He swallowed hard. "I think it's wrong to tell you, but you're a grown man and you get to make your own choices. I don't want . . . never mind. I'll tell you what happened. Then you can judge—"

"I'd never judge you, Dad."

He took in a deep breath and held it while I waited. He finally nodded, turned his head to stare at the wall across the room, and started to tell the part of his past I so desperately needed to hear.

CHAPTER THIRTY-ONE

DAD CAME HOME *late on a chilly Tuesday night after taking half of another mail route in addition to his regular one. He needed the overtime. Heat hit him in the face when he opened the door, along with the loud racket of a crying child. His child. The house was all closed up. Bea had two burners on the stove going full blast to take the edge off the cold that permeated the house's paper-thin construction. Little Bruno, barely four months old, lay in the bassinet left alone and crying his lungs out. Bea wasn't anywhere in the house or out in the backyard. He picked Bruno up and gently bounced and shushed him, all the while whispering in his ear that everything was okay, until Bruno quieted.*

A few minutes later, he heard the muffled sound of a car pulling up to the curb out front. He parted the curtains and caught Bea slithering from the front seat of a newer Kelly-green Ford. The winter sun set early and the moonless night made it difficult to see, but he was still able to make out that scoundrel Melvin Shackleford, and his girl Cleo Elliott with two t's. Shackleford sat behind the wheel with Cleo right up beside him. How could a two-bit huckster like Shackleford afford a car like that when he didn't have a job? Bea smiled and laughed and waved as the car roared off snatching the door from her hand and closing on its own.

Xander ground his teeth, his jaw muscle working hard as he tried to quell his anger. He hurried into the bedroom and set Bruno down in the playpen and gave him a toy. He came back out just as Bea came through the door. She lost her smile when she saw him.

He kept his clenched fists down at his side. "Where have you been?"

She held up her hands. "Now, honey, don't go getting all mad. I was only gone a minute. I had to run to the store to get some . . . some milk for Bruno. He's hungry."

"You left him alone?"

"Just for a minute, honey. It's no big deal, just to run to the store. I do it all the time, but just for a minute."

"Where's the milk?"

"I . . . I got there and realized I forgot my money."

He pointed to the bassinet. "He's too big to be in that. We talked about this, remember? I brought it out here last night because I'm going to put it out in the yard this weekend and sell it." For months during the pregnancy she hounded him about having a bassinet. As if they couldn't have a baby without one. Sometimes she spent money frivolously in her desire to be somebody she wasn't. Bruno used the bassinet for four months until he grew too big and that was it, a huge waste of money.

"And it's not okay to leave him alone, not even for a minute. I have to tell you, Bea, I am not happy about this."

She gave him a wave. "Oh, what do you know." She sat on the couch.

He'd been told at work by his friends that women could act strangely right after having a child and that he should try to be understanding until it passed. He had no problem about being understanding, just not when it concerned the safety of their child. He moved to the couch and sat next to her and immediately smelled alcohol. "You've been drinking. How long were you really gone?"

She struggled to her feet. "I'm going to bed. You try watching him and see what it's like. He takes up every hour, every minute of my time."

Xander slept on the couch with Bruno in his arms. They couldn't afford it, but the next day he hired a sitter while he was at work.

For the next month, Bea would get home just before or just after he did. Six times she didn't get home until after nine p.m. He tried talking to her and she'd have none of it. All he could do was wait and hope she'd snap out of it.

One night in late April, long after midnight, he'd fallen asleep sitting on the couch with Bruno lying next to him. He was exhausted from working full-time and taking care of such a small child after he got home.

The front door burst open. Out of a dead sleep he jumped up ready to defend his home, to defend his son against this violent interloper.

His fists raised, he confronted a wild-eyed Bea. She wore a new dress he'd never seen before, made of red crepe with little fake pearls. The dress hugged her figure. It was torn at one shoulder and sagged down revealing her bra and the top of her breast. She clutched his arm. "Help me, Xander, please help me!"

"What on earth, girl? What's the matter? What's happened?" He moved around her and checked up and down the street before closing the door. In the darkness of the living room, she'd gone to the couch and sat cocked forward, her arms under her breasts as she swayed to and fro.

"How did you get here?"

She shook her head as she tried to catch her breath. His arm suddenly felt wet. He looked down and found blood. He rushed to the couch. "Are you okay? Are you hurt?" He moved his hands all over her looking for the injury and didn't find one. Thank goodness.

"What?" She checked her arms and hands. "No. It's not mine." She reached down and picked up Bruno as tears filled her eyes. "I'm scared, honey, really scared."

He didn't want her holding Bruno, getting someone else's blood on him, but let it go if holding him calmed her down.

"Tell me what happened."

Bruno roused, nuzzled her neck, and fell back to sleep. Bea still had a hard time catching her breath. Xander went to the kitchen and wet a dishtowel with warm water. He wiped down her arms and face and exposed shoulder. Her breathing calmed some.

Blood marred the sleeping Bruno's bedclothes. Xander got up again and poured her three fingers of E&J brandy in a jelly jar glass, thought about it, and poured a little more. As she gulped it down, he tried to take Bruno from her. She latched onto him and wouldn't give him up.

She calmed even more while he waited patiently on the couch for the alcohol to take effect.

Finally, she said, "Honey, I made a mistake. You're allowed one mistake in life, aren't you? Right, honey? One mistake?"

"Of course you are. Just tell me what happened."

"Okay, okay." She gulped a breath as she started to get spun out again. "We . . . we did that deal. You know the one?"

He knew immediately what she was talking about. "Oh, my dear Lord."

"No, Xander, don't say that. Please, I'm scared to death already. You have to help me, please."

"I will, just give me Bruno, okay?" She let him have the baby. He set him down on the couch and took up both of her hands. "Now tell me."

She gulped air again. "Okay, like I said, we did that job. The telephone man job. We followed the telephone man around and caught him on an empty street and conked him on the head. Easy as pie, just like I told you it would be."

"We? You mean with Shackleford and Cleo?"

"That's right."

"So all the blood . . . it belongs to the guy you hit over the head?"

"What? No. No."

Her eyes searched his, seeking comfort.

"Go on, then."

"Okay, Shackleford conked this guy on the head and . . . and you're not going to believe this. It was just like I told you it would be, but more. Much, much more. The back of that old guy's van was filled with bags and bags of coins." Her fearful demeanor shifted back to wild-eyed excitement as her eyes grew large. "So many bags, Xander . . . So many, the weight almost popped the tires to our car. We drove to a motel and waited until dark to take all those bags in the room. We counted for a long time and tried to put them in rolls. There were just too many coins. I got tired of so many coins. I never thought I'd say that. And my hands"—she looked down at her hands—"you can't believe how many times I washed the black off my hands. Money is so terribly dirty." The E&J brandy started to work. Her body gave way to too many hours of adrenaline rush and such a large dose of E&J. Her eyelids drooped and her speech slowed.

"What happened? Where'd the blood come from?"

"Whaaat?"

"Never mind." He got up and draped an afghan over her. He stood in the middle of the living room watching her sleep, torn, more torn than he'd ever been in his life. He didn't know how long he stood there.

Finally, he went to the telephone, picked it up, and dialed.

CHAPTER THIRTY-TWO

DAD SHOOK MY shoulder. I came out of a dreamworld filled with a mother who didn't have a face, just a smudged blur of brown skin. I sat with Mom in a car parked running at the curb in front of Bank of the West. She held a big Colt .45 in her small, delicate hand that rested in her lap, as she tried to explain to me that it was okay to take money from other folks as long as you spent it wisely afterward and didn't waste it. Spent it on the wonderful things she always wanted and couldn't have, a large house with regular heating, beautiful clothes, and food that filled your stomach and didn't leave you wanting.

How would Doctor Abrams interpret that one?

Dad said, "You told me to wake you at eight. I forgot to tell you there was a note on the door. Here."

"Whaaat?"

"There was a note on the door. You told me to wake you at eight."

"Yes, thank you." I got up and shook off the fatigue and the stiffness from falling asleep on the couch. I shuffle-stepped barefoot into the bathroom and turned on the shower. Back in my bedroom, I took a set of clothes from my dresser, laid them on the closed toilet in the bathroom, and stepped in the hot water. Steam roiled up all around. I let the hot water sluice over my body and ease a deep-seated tension as my mind went over the surreal story Dad told a few hours earlier. This version of his history dispelled all previous images of a mother I'd been forced to make up on my own. I could never justify any motivation as to why he would not tell me about her. Now it all made sense.

A few hours ago, he had ended his story with my mom out cold on the couch while he dialed the phone. Tears had streamed down his face as he said the last words and stopped talking. I couldn't ask him who he called back then or what had happened to her. I wanted to know but wasn't sure I could ask him to once again make that trip back to a time he would rather forget, a time that caused him so much pain.

With a refreshed mind, my thoughts quickly shifted to the obvious: poor Dad, what he had gone through. And worse, that he'd kept it bottled up for so long dealing with it all on his own.

Then another thought struck. Was I genetically predisposed to my mother's criminal behavior? Was that why I had been so good at tracking down murderers? Because I thought like them and instinctively knew what moves they'd make before they made them as the law continued to close in? Was I destined to eventually deviate and break bad like Wicks had already thought I had? Would I turn criminal and have to run from the law the rest of my life?

No. Not a chance. I was a deputy sheriff and I'd never give that up. Never. This same resolve had been challenged before and that's how I knew. I was tan and green through and through.

I dried off, dressed in my usual truck driver garb—the khaki shirt with the TW patch and denim pants—and came out into the living room carrying my shoes and socks. I sat down on the couch to put them on.

Dad stood over by the kitchen. "Where you going so late?"

I started to put on a sock and stopped. Instead I put on a shoe without the sock to see what it felt like and also as a distraction so I wouldn't have to answer his question right away.

Dad said, "What are you doing?"

"Just wanted to see what it felt like."

"Well, don't. It's uncivilized to wear shoes without socks. You can't trust anyone who wears shoes without socks."

Huh. Now at least I knew where I got some of my genes.

I put on my socks and shoes and walked closer to him. "Thank you for telling me about Mom."

He said nothing. Then, "Here's that note." He stuck it in my shirt pocket.

I said, "If you really want to know where I'm going, I'll tell you."

He raised his head a little. His eyes held mine as he thought about the offer. "All right," he said, "tell me this—are you bound to someone else, sworn not to tell me?"

My mouth sagged open. How had he figured that much out?

He said, "Never mind, I can see as much in your expression. Can you at least tell me you're not going down a bad road?"

I put my hand on his shoulder, his story of Mom still heavy on my mind. "I can promise you that I will only do what needs to be done."

"That's good enough for me. And someday you'll tell me the rest, won't you?"

"Yes, in a few days, it should all be over."

"No, not that part, the other thing." His tone had turned solemn and filled with despair.

"What?" I took a half step back, stunned. He was referring to Albert. Somehow he had figured out I knew the whole story, that I knew the why, the how, and the who of what had happened to Albert. Had Dad guessed and was he now fishing for a reaction? Or had he just known that I would not rest, that I would move heaven and earth in search of the truth regarding Olivia and Albert?

I said, "There are some things that are better kept—" I couldn't finish it. Now I knew why, after all these years—decades—that he'd broken his silence about my mother. He'd methodically and with great deliberation backed me into a corner by telling me his deepest, darkest secret. The man could always outfox me no matter how hard I tried to keep up with him. He had a brilliant mind when it came to people and how to deal with them.

My voice came out in a croak. "Yes, I'll tell you."

But I didn't know if I could ever tell him. Not because I didn't want to, but because the words were too horrific to bring out into the light of day. To say them made them too real. Just thinking about saying them took me to an edge of a cliff where I stood ready to jump.

"Soon," Dad said. "Son, I need to know soon."

I nodded and headed for the door. I needed some air; the house had turned stuffy—smothering. The conversation he wanted would be the hardest one we would ever have.

Outside, Junior Mint bounded along behind me. I'd forgotten all about him. I kept him off-leash as we walked through the dark neighborhood to MLK where I had parked the Kadett. He sensed my need for meditation and didn't run off. He stayed right at my side. He'd always been someone I could confide in, and in the last six months, when we were alone, I spoke to him nonstop. Tonight, I couldn't form the words to even talk to my dog. I had to get the words straight in my mind first. One thing I knew for sure, it wasn't smart to enter into a dangerous gun deal with a head so cluttered with emotions.

We made it to the Kadett, got in, and headed for TransWorld Freightliners, to the deal with Johnny Sin and Jumbo. We were going to try and talk them into selling a ton of stolen guns without anyone dying over it.

CHAPTER THIRTY-THREE

I KEPT CHECKING the mirrors as I drove. I couldn't see anyone tailing along behind, nothing for certain, but instinct told me someone was there. I'd learned a long time ago to listen to instinct. If no one was there, a smidgeon of paranoia was a lot better than a little bit of dead.

Who could be following? Johnny Sin? Did he want to know more about me before he fell in league with TW? A deal that could get him decades in federal prison if I turned out to be a cop? Sin acted more streetwise than your average crook, and I needed to be careful when dealing with him.

I reached over and stroked Junior's fur on his chest. He reciprocated by licking my hand.

Maybe Derek Sams was somewhere back there among all the headlights. He had every reason to come for me rather than live with the real possibility that I would again, at the most inopportune time, pop up in his life. That was if my bad-self won out and I went hunting. Wicks should never have let Sams loose. I focused my anger at Wicks rather than thinking too strongly about Sams or I might lose that battle, drop everything, and go after him.

In reality, Wicks wasn't the cause of Sams' release. The justice system had failed, letting a bad one slip through the cracks when they had him cold for a murder. You shouldn't be able to trade one murderer for a better one, like baseball cards.

Sams was a street thug and knew nothing about how to conduct a mobile surveillance. I'd spot him in an instant. It wasn't Sams back there, but it was nice to think so, to think that Sams would make a rookie play to take me off the board. That kind of amateur move would make things so much easier. Self-defense. He was too much of a spineless punk for that play. But I'd have to give it more thought. I did like the idea.

I made five passes of TransWorld before I parked farther away than normal, two long blocks down, and this time not even in the same industrial complex. I left Junior Mint off-leash and watched his reactions more than I watched the shadows as we made our way on foot back to TW. He was a good partner to have.

RD was standing behind the counter when I came through TW's front door. In the back, the soft ding in Black Bart's office would alert him to check the CCT monitor set up in his office so he'd know I'd just walked through the door. RD shook his head. "Bart wants to see you, my friend, as soon as you come in. I'd pucker up and bend over if I were you."

"Yeah, I figured as much."

"I didn't rat you out, Bruno, honest. Come here, Junior, come to Daddy." RD clapped his hands and then his chest. Junior took off, ran around the counter, and tackled RD. I sidestepped around them on the floor and headed to Black Bart's office. I entered, closed the door, and sat down in the hot seat in the chair in front of his desk.

He stared at me with those hard-black eyes. I hated to disappoint him. In a short time, I had come to respect and like him more than any other supervisor I had worked for.

I didn't wait for him to break the ice in the uncomfortable situation I'd created. With his silence he knew how to dish it, that was for sure. "Thanks for being there," I said. "I mean behind the Crazy Eight. You saved my ass."

He continued to stare and didn't move, not so much as an eyebrow or lash.

I said, "You heard what Johnny Sin said about the deal? You got a look at him?"

Nothing but crickets. Pure silence. I decided to wait on him.

He finally said, "Carl Weathers."

"What? What are you talking about? Who's Carl Weathers?" The actor from the Rocky movies? Had Black Bart finally gone over the edge? Had worrying about my unorthodox behavior, my failure to follow policy and procedure, finally pushed him too far and all his marbles now rattled around in his head the same as in an empty cigar box?

Black Bart nodded. "Johnny Sin said he'd never heard of a black guy with a name like Carl. Carl Weathers is a black actor."

"Oh." I did remember the conversation, Johnny Sin saying it when we were to the rear of the Crazy Eight, but it was weird for Bart to bring that up at that moment.

Black Bart said, "Stool Sample says the deal's going down tonight, here at the counter—is that right?"

Why wasn't Black Bart jumping up and down and yelling? Why wasn't he right up in my face dressing me down about the two errors I'd made?

"That's what Nigel told me," I replied. "Nigel said that he called Jumbo while you and I were out in the parking lot talking with Johnny."

Still with the stare he said, "That's good. If this deal goes down right, you're going to be a star with your department heads. You'll be able to pick your assignment, maybe even make sergeant out of it."

"I don't care about that; I just want to get the guns off the street. I'm sorry about the money thing and . . . the flash without backup. I didn't intend on doing the flash like that. It just happened. I felt the deal slipping away and I made a mistake. I guess I wanted it too badly. It won't happen again."

Black Bart leaned in over his desk. "I don't want you at the counter tonight. I want you behind the glass with the gauge, covering me."

"This is my deal." I said it too loudly, with too much vehemence. "I roped Jumbo on this. He wouldn't be here if—"

I sat back in my chair.

He stared and said nothing. He didn't trust me anymore and it hurt worse than if he'd yelled and screamed. I would've preferred anger and rage to the loss of his trust, the loss of my credibility and honor.

I took a deep breath. "I understand."

The soft bong sounded. We both turned to the CCT monitor. Two people entered TW through the front door. I recognized Jumbo by his big ears I'd heard so much about. The man with him wore a nice suit and tie and designer sunglasses. Jumbo had brought a lawyer to the deal. Who in the world brought a lawyer to an illegal, clandestine gun deal?

Black Bart turned back to me. "I thought you said the deal was for midnight? It's only nine o'clock."

"That's what Nigel told me."

"Then these two came early on purpose. It's a tactic to catch us with our pants down in case we had plans on taking them down. These guys are good."

"Yeah."

"The cover team for this isn't due in for another hour. We're going to have to do it without them."

"You want me at the counter?"

"No, behind the glass. RD and I will handle this."

I nodded, too angry to argue.

Black Bart opened his desk drawer, took out his cut-down shotgun, and moved around me, headed for the door. "Get ready."

"Bart?"

He turned. I said, "Just so you know, Leo—you know, Leo from Sparkle Plenty—he told me that Jumbo is only the front guy and that Johnny Sin is the main man. If you don't get a definitive answer out of Jumbo on the deal, that'll be the reason why. Sin is the shot caller."

He pointed a thick finger at me. "Damn you, Bruno. I need you on that counter with me but you're too bone-headed to follow the rules. Now get your butt on that gauge and make darn sure we all go home safe tonight."

I nodded.

"They so much as flinch the wrong way, you pull that trigger. You understand?"

"Yes, sir."

I moved as silently as I could to the room with the one-way glass window. I turned on the video camera set on the tripod and picked up the shotgun, an Ithaca Deerslayer 12 gauge, an old gun from an LACO Sheriff's patrol unit rescued from mothballs. The gun had three ancient notches in the wood stock. The notches had turned black with grime. The rest of the stock gleamed a deep polished brown. All the bluing on the steel had worn off. The gun had seen a lot of action. I eased the slide back an inch and made sure a shell was seated in the chamber. My finger automatically checked to see if the safety was off. I shouldered the shotgun and put the front barrel on the two crooks who stood at the counter talking to RD. The irony that the gun was an Ithaca Deerslayer wasn't lost on me.

Jumbo wore new designer jeans and a long-sleeve green silk shirt with a four-hundred-dollar pair of snakeskin cowboy boots. The lawyer wore a dark gray hand-tailored silk business suit that would cost more than five of my paychecks. He kept his hair shorn close to his scalp. He wore dark designer sunglasses that hid his face and—

I grabbed up the phone and dialed the internal number for the counter just as Black Bart appeared. The phone on the counter rang and rang. Neither Bart nor RD picked it up.

I held the shotgun at the ready and pinched the phone between my ear and shoulder. "Come on. Come on, pick it up."

CHAPTER THIRTY-FOUR

I LET THE phone ring. Maybe Bart would get tired of it and finally pick up. Bart had to see the lit line and know I was the one calling. He had to know I wouldn't be playing a game. Foolish spite kept him from answering. Spite that might get him killed. I lined the barrel up on Johnny Sin dressed this time as a slimy lawyer. The man was a chameleon and that made him twice as dangerous. Dangerous as long as he was out running loose, something we intended to correct.

The cover room where I stood had a speaker wired to hear what was said out front. Jumbo came up and laid his hands flat on the counter. He stared at Black Bart's sunglasses. "Where's Karl? I was dealing with a guy named Karl."

RD was smart enough to remain silent. Bart said, "He's busy, I'm the one you need to talk to. It's my money, not Karl's."

Johnny Sin sauntered over to the glass window, his face close to the one-way mirror, his back to Jumbo and Black Bart at the counter. I put the shotgun inches from Johnny Sin's nose. He raised his sunglasses, trying to peer in. He picked at his teeth as if something were stuck there and said, "My boss Jumbo only deals with the guy who set up the deal. It's a silly superstition, but it has served him well." He took a step back from the glass, turned toward Bart, and pointed back at the mirrored window with his sunglasses. "Tell your boy to put down his gun and get his black ass out here or the deal's off." He couldn't see through the glass and had made a wild assumption.

Bart hesitated, weighing his options. If I came out from behind the glass, there would be no one to cover. This violated one of Bart's hard and fast rules on safety. If Bart agreed, he'd be doing the same thing I had done earlier in the day out behind the Crazy Eight where I played fast and loose with the rules because I wanted the gun deal too badly. Bart would never do that. He'd let the deal go sour first. That was the only game Bart played, conservatively and by the book.

Over the speaker mounted in the cover room behind the one-way glass came a low growl. Junior Mint, on the other side of the counter and out of view of the two criminals, didn't like the idea either.

Jumbo put his hands to his ears. "Would you please answer that damn phone?"

Bart picked it up without taking his eyes off Jumbo. "Get your ass out here and tell Ruben to stay there and cover us."

There wasn't anyone on our team named Ruben; the name was a bluff. Once I left the glass, I was blind to what happened out front and they were without cover. I hurried around and through the warehouse. I stepped through the doorway with the Ithaca held down by my leg, not attempting to conceal it.

Johnny Sin had come back from the glass and now stood at the counter. He held open his suit coat and twisted his hips one way, then the other. "What's with all the heavy artillery—we're all friends here, aren't we? We're just here to talk. Or am I missing something?" He'd shifted to a southern accent, perfect in syntax and delivery.

Who was this guy?

The front door of TW opened. It was Nigel. RD and Black Bart startled. Bart had forgotten to bolt the door. Black Bart brought up the shorty shotgun and laid it on the counter directed at Jumbo. If he pulled the trigger, Jumbo would turn into a fine mist of tomato paste.

At the door, a drunken Nigel half-stumbled in. "Hey? Hey? What's going on? It's early. It's too early. What are you guys doing here? Are you tryin' to cut ol' Nigel outta the deal? This is my deal, remember?"

An ugly grin crept across Johnny Sin's face, exposing a sliver of straight teeth. He stepped quick, before Nigel could react, put his arm around Nigel's neck in a headlock. "Why, we'd never leave someone as important as you out of a deal like this. Would we, boys?"

Bart let his other hand drop behind the counter, where he pushed the button. The electric bolt slammed home on the front door. Everyone heard it. Now no one else could join the party. And no one could leave unless we wanted them to. Bart had violated his own rule. The bolt was always supposed to be thrown before a deal started. That was his second mistake of the evening. We didn't need any more.

At the sound of the bolt, Johnny gripped Nigel around the neck harder and turned so Nigel was a shield between him and the one-way glass. Johnny didn't know for sure if we had a guy named Ruben back there covering. He wasn't going to take any chances.

Bart raised his hand. "Okay. Okay. Let's all just calm down before things get out of hand and someone gets hurt."

Jumbo said, "Good idea, fat man. It'd be real silly for us to go to guns when all we're here to do is talk. You want to buy my product or don't you?"

"If the price is right. What do you have?"

Jumbo smiled, opened his arms. "Well, we couldn't very well bring it with us, now could we?"

"I'm not buying sight unseen."

"Didn't expect you to. I have some samples over at my shop. We came here to see if you really have the kind of money we're talkin'."

"That's not gonna happen until we see the product."

Jumbo put a card down on the counter and slid it over. "Come by this address tomorrow, say noonish, and we'll talk turkey."

Bart picked up the card. "Okay. Give me some idea of what we're talking about? How much money?"

Jumbo didn't lose his smile. "This is your home turf. I'd prefer that we talked at my place tomorrow."

Smart. He was afraid of a wire or video.

"Might be all for naught if the money you're asking is out of my league?"

"Tsk, tsk, tsk. Not my problem. There are two other . . . ah, backup buyers anxiously waiting in the wings. I'd rather keep this deal local, here in the States if you know what I mean, but if you don't have the bread, no skin off my nose. See you fellas tomorrow. And, ah, no guns allowed at my place." He lifted his hand and wiggled his fingers bye. Johnny Sin came along behind him with Nigel still in a headlock as Jumbo made for the door.

Nigel said, "Hey, hey, what's going on? Lemme go. Karl? Hey, Karl, do something. Help."

I spoke for the first time. "Let him go."

They made it to the bolted door. Jumbo said, "Unlock the door and we'll let the dipshit go."

Before I could say another word, Bart threw the bolt and unlocked the door. Johnny Sin shoved Nigel. He flew, hit the floor, and slid.

I hurried back to the office with Black Bart close on my heels. We arrived just in time to see Jumbo and Johnny Sin walk out of view and into the shadows.

I said, "They know about the cameras and where they're placed. That's how they got up on us without us seeing them."

Bart nodded. "We have to watch our step; these guys are good."

Yeah, maybe too good.

CHAPTER THIRTY-FIVE

THE NEXT MORNING at seven someone stood on the front porch of our Nord home and rang the doorbell again and again. I shuffled out of my room rubbing the sleep out of my eyes, dressed only in boxer shorts and a tee shirt. I stopped in the kitchen and grabbed my .357 from on top of the fridge. I peeked out the side window.

Wicks.

Parked at the curb was his sleek black county car, replete with tire iron pockmarks and side windows covered with cardboard and crisscrossed with gray duct tape. Behind his car sat a marked black-and-white with two uniform deputies sitting inside. What was with the deputies? What was going on?

I sighed and opened the door. Wicks didn't wait to be invited, he just shoved on past. I had Junior by the collar, restraining him. He let loose with a low growl at the unwanted intrusion and nipped at Wicks as he went by. I half-dragged Junior over to the couch and told him to sit and then to lie down. He obeyed. I didn't know why he didn't like Wicks. Wicks had never done anything to him.

"Curb your dog. He better not bite me. It'll be his last conscious act. You have any coffee? I don't smell any coffee. Hey, you just gettin' up?"

Bold talk. If he tried to hurt Junior, friend or no friend, we'd go to war.

"Oh, good morning to you too. Why are those deputies outside my house? What's going on?"

But I knew. Wicks wanted me to go with him to hit a house and he had brought the marked unit to cover the back while we hit the front. We had done it that way many times in the past; we'd just never started out from my house before.

"Take a seat," I said. "I'll put on some coffee. Why are you so hyped up?" He got this way when he was hunting a difficult target and the trail suddenly turned hot. I scooped ground coffee into Dad's old percolator, added water, and plugged it in. I came over and sat at the table. Dad came in wearing a tattered robe I gave him for Christmas eight or nine years earlier. He should've tossed it out long ago, and I should've been thoughtful enough to give him another one. Next Christmas. He saw Wicks. "Can I make you some breakfast, Lieutenant?"

Dad didn't care much for Wicks. He just didn't understand him. Even so, Dad kept up his facade of hospitality.

"No, thanks. We don't have time." He said to me, "Get dressed; we have to roll."

I took two cups down from the cupboard. "What's going on?"

He glared and said nothing. He wanted his subordinates to jump to his every command. I said, "I don't work for you anymore, remember?"

I caught Dad out of the corner of my eye. He smiled.

Wicks stood. "Is that right? Then I guess you're no longer privy to the investigation. Is that the way you want to play it?"

"Quit being a horse's ass and tell me what's going on."

He sat back down at the table and smiled. "You were right."

Dad shrugged. "Of course he was."

Wicks said, "Do you mind?" He turned back to me. "The entire investigation has shifted to this Jamar and La Vonn lead, the one we scared up at the jail yesterday."

"Good. What happened that made it heat up?"

"The Deputy Chief wants you to have twenty-four-hour protection, hence the knuckle draggers out at the curb—they've been detached from SEB. You should be honored; they're the best the department can provide."

"What? What are you talking about?"

Wicks reached into his suit coat pocket and came out with a Polaroid picture. I recognized it before I even saw what it depicted. Lead investigators took Polaroid pictures of murder victims to carry with them for the duration of the investigation to refresh the memory of a witness or suspect. This was one such photo. I didn't want to see it; I couldn't handle even one more. I'd grown tired of the senseless hate and wasted lives that photos like these represented.

Wicks set it on our table faceup.

I instantly recognized the victim, Twyla. Some evil bastard had shot her in the forehead and discarded her body on a rotting pile of Chinese food in a back-alley dumpster.

My throat went dry. "What happened?"

"Going on your theory, I remembered this girl was with you and the judge that day on 10th and Crenshaw when the judge gunned that thug Jamar. She was your unregistered informant you wouldn't reveal to anyone, not even me. You didn't tell me until later, remember? I ran her name and found out she was a victim of a 187."

"When?"

"That's where it gets good."

"Gets *good*? Really? We're talking about a senseless murder here."

"Oh, get over yourself."

Dad took a step closer. "Maybe you better leave, Lieutenant."

I waved at Dad and said to Wicks, "Tell me."

"Two weeks ago."

"So you're saying someone is taking out everyone who was out there that day? Anyone who had anything to do with the death of that gun thug Jamar?"

"Exactly. The black-and-white is at your curb for the duration. So from now until we solve this thing and get this killer grappled up, you are either with me or you're here where we can keep an eye on you."

CHAPTER THIRTY-SIX

THAT WASN'T GOING to happen, not with the big gun deal in the offing, but I wasn't going to tell him that. "What about Nicky Rivers?" She was the deputy DA who was also with us on 10th Street, the day of the shooting.

"She left the DA's office and went to work for the feds. She's an AUSA now working out of Vegas. I got Vegas Metro watching over her. Well, Metro and U.S. Marshals."

"What happened to her marriage?"

"They ended up splitting after all."

This had been a sore spot with Wicks. He was friends with Nicky's husband, John Lau, when I'd been dating her. Wicks thought that I had violated the unwritten rule about stepping out with another cop's wife. And I had, in a way. She'd never told me she was married, let alone to whom, until I'd developed a crush on her, one difficult to walk away from. She'd been separated pending divorce, but they had gotten back together to try and make a go of it. I was sorry about Nicky's marriage, that I might've had a hand in its dissolution, and needed to change the subject so I wouldn't dwell on a past misstep. "What happened with Sams?"

"Derek?" Dad asked. He came over the rest of the way and sat down at the table, his eyes anxious, pleading with Wicks to tell him.

"What about Derek?"

I shouldn't have brought it up around Dad, but he would've heard about it sooner or later.

"Yeah, you were right about that, too. He's in the wind. I put out a BOLO on him. It won't take long. I'll find his ass, and he'll wish he never crossed me."

For the first time after all the years of working with him, I heard the real meaning of Wicks' words, a tone, the manner in which he regularly spoke. The way he so cavalierly talked about running a criminal down and shooting him, how easy it was for him to put the boot to someone, to take a human life. Had I been similarly cold and callous while running with him? I didn't think so at the time but maybe now looking back . . . well, I liked myself a little less.

"BOLO?" Dad asked. "In the wind?"

I translated. "Derek was released from his trial with a promise of a lighter sentence if he helped find the person or persons responsible for the killing of the judge and his wife. He signed a contract and it was approved by the DA and a judge."

"That's wrong, Son. I can't tell you how wrong that is. It shouldn't happen that way. That boy needs to pay for what he did. One way or another, that boy needs to pay. He killed that poor man and admitted to it."

Dad said it with an edge I wasn't used to hearing from him. He had a strong understanding of how the world worked, or used to. In the last six months after the loss of Albert and Olivia, he'd stepped out of the everyday rat race and let it run him over. Not his fault. That had never happened to him before, and now he was acting out of character.

Dad said, "Bruno, how is that possible? Our justice system is broken." I cringed when he called me by name; it meant his anger had ratcheted up one more level and I had become the focus of that anger.

Wicks said, "It's called 'in the interest of justice,' old man."

"Shut up," I yelled at Wicks. "You have no right to talk to him like that."

I wanted to tell Dad it was Wicks who'd made the blunder and unleashed Derek back on the streets to prey on the unsuspecting, but I didn't. Not to save Wicks from the embarrassment but to keep peace in our little kitchen. I didn't want Dad to grab Wicks around the neck and throttle him. At that moment, the way I felt about Wicks, I might have let Dad do it. Maybe helped him.

"What else do you have on Twyla's murder? Anything linking it to La Vonn?"

"Bruno, we're talking about Derek here," Dad said. "You drop everything and go after him. I mean it. I'm not messing around here—get after him and put him back where he belongs, in a cage."

"We'll get to him." I couldn't tell Dad that if I went after Derek Sams, I wouldn't be able to stop myself, that I would catch up to him and this time the outcome would be more than three crushed fingers.

Wicks waited to see if we'd finished discussing something that was of no interest to him. He saw his opening and said, "La Vonn is off the grid. He dropped out of sight three years ago, right after the judge did that shooting on 10th. I have the entire task force looking for him, and they've come up with nothing, nada, zip. Have you checked the gyms like you said you would?"

"I got tied up. That's next on the agenda."

Without a word, Dad got up and left. I worried about him. Maybe he would get dressed, have breakfast, and go over and see Albert. That would take his mind off Sams. I had the gun deal and La Vonn to keep my mind off Derek.

My big problem would be breaking away from Wicks long enough to make the "noonish" meeting with Jumbo and Johnny Sin at his auto parts shop in Norwalk. Wicks wouldn't be fooled too easily, not this time, especially if he thought of me as bait for La Vonn. In Wicks' skewed perception of life, there was nothing more fun than a hunt that involved a staked goat. And as it turned out this time, I was the goat.

CHAPTER THIRTY-SEVEN

I SHOWERED AND dressed and found Wicks in the living room, pacing. Junior Mint sat by the couch and watched Wicks go back and forth. Junior looked on as if present at a tennis match and Wicks was the tennis ball Junior wanted to sink his teeth in.

Wicks spun around. "Took you long enough. Let's roll."

"Where are we going?"

He waved his arm. "I've been thinking about it. I got the entire task force looking for this La Vonn character. I just decided that we're going after Sams. I can't believe I was that wrong about him. I still think he can get close to Little Genie's organization, and someone in that gang will know what happened to La Vonn. If he can't, then I'll still have the pleasure of squeezing his little pin head until it pops, teach him a lesson for not answering my page."

"I don't think it's a good idea to go after Derek."

"Why?"

I couldn't tell him that I didn't trust myself, and at the same time I couldn't think of a logical reason why we couldn't go after him. Wicks didn't know what I knew about Derek, what Derek had done to my grandchild. If Wicks found out, he'd take full advantage of my rage. He'd wind me up like a little tin soldier, turn me loose, and follow along, the hunter behind the hound stepping over the carnage I'd leave in my wake. It wouldn't take much. I wanted to take up that mantle and right a wrong.

The cell phone on his belt rang. He grabbed it. "Wicks."

I watched his expression, his eyes. After a few seconds, they took on a gleam I recognized from years past. My blood ran hot and sent a tingling up my spine: this was it. The call that would put us onto La Vonn, the guy who'd brutally gunned down the judge and his wife, Jean Anne.

A smile crept across his face. He said into the phone, "Where the hell have you been, you little turd? I told you to check in every four hours no matter what. I told you what I would do to you if you didn't. And what? It's been twelve hours now?"

Derek Sams.

My excitement shifted to the pent-up rage. I didn't know how long I'd be able to suppress it without giving it a natural and obvious place to vent. Derek was no longer in jail where I couldn't reach him. He was out on the street, free as a bird and subject to all the dangers and pitfalls that same freedom allowed. He could easily die in an accident, a dislodged third-floor air conditioner, in a car crash, falling down some stairs, or from a more common form of lead poisoning that came with a great deal of satisfaction on my part.

Wicks caught the shift in my expression, turned his shoulder away, and lowered his voice. Wicks knew how I felt about Sams, but only as a disgruntled father-in-law. He knew that I blamed Sams for my daughter Olivia's death and couldn't prove it. Wicks didn't care as long as he first got the information he wanted from Sams. In fact, once Sams was no longer useful, Wicks would gladly purchase a front-row ticket to watch what I had in mind.

"No," Wicks said into the phone. "You stay right there. I'm coming to you. What?" Wicks listened then said, "You little shitass, you don't get to dictate the rules. I'll tell you how it's going work, not the other way around. You sit your ass down; I'll be there in fifteen minutes." He hung up, turned back, and smiled hugely, the same as if he had Tweety bird feathers hanging from his mouth. "I guess you know who that was?"

I nodded, unable to speak for fear of letting slip my deadly intent.

Wicks came close and put his hand on my shoulder. "Sorry, my friend. Derek said he doesn't want you anywhere near him or he won't tell us a thing. And you know me—normally I wouldn't let a lowlife like this guy dictate the game. But I still need this puke and if I take you with . . . well, you know how that scenario is going turn out, blood and bone all over the place." He held up his hand. "I'm not saying that's a bad thing, I'm just saying not right now."

Dad had been standing in the kitchen that adjoined the living room, listening to the entire exchange. "How do you live with yourself? How do you look in the mirror every morning, Lieutenant? Derek has no right being out on the street. He needs to be—"

"I'm sorry you feel that way, Mr. Johnson, but this is the life we chose. We don't make the rules. We're given the little pewter top hat, a set of dice, and we move around the board according to set rules."

What a hypocrite. Wicks rarely kept his Crayola within the lines.

Black Bart had said something similar, though, when I'd asked him about betrayal, how we could befriend someone and in the end snatch away priceless years of that person's life by putting him behind bars. I could only hope I never became so cynical and jaded.

Wicks made a quick move and headed for the front door. Junior got up, ready to take a bite out of his butt.

"Junior, sit." He turned to look at me, then back at Wicks, trying to decide if the penalty would be worth it if he disobeyed. He made the right choice and sat.

At the door, Wicks said to me, "Stay right here. I'll call you with what Sams has for us and then we'll roll on it. And, Bruno, this time answer your damn cell phone when I call. That thing is no good if you don't take it with you." He stepped out and closed the door behind him.

Dad stared, waiting for me to say something about Wicks and how I'd allowed Wicks to let Derek loose again on the public. I didn't have an answer for him. Oddly, as soon as Wicks left the house, the rage started to bleed off and I could breathe again.

The cell phone on the kitchen counter buzzed. Wicks. He was checking to see if I'd answer it. I snatched up the phone. "Yeah, yeah, see, I answered it."

It was RD from TransWorld. His words caused my knees to go weak. I eased down into the chair, too stunned to reply.

CHAPTER THIRTY-EIGHT

I DROVE AROUND and around Daniel Freeman Hospital parking lot looking for a spot. Under normal circumstances I'd have dumped the Kadett out in front of the emergency room entrance and put a Sheriff's placard on the dash. But I had to remember my cover. I couldn't risk crooks I'd dealt with at TW seeing the car. I'd made too many mistakes lately and swore I wouldn't make another.

I didn't know the extent of the injury. RD had said that he didn't know for sure and to hurry. He tended toward the dramatic. Or maybe I didn't want it to be bad and that I'd been on the receiving end of bad news too often in the last six months to let my mind accept the truth.

In order to evade the two knuckle draggers out in front of our home on Nord, I went out the back door then out through the hole in the fence at the back of the property and into the dirt alley. I'd been so focused on what RD had said, I didn't notice until it was too late that Junior had tagged along.

In the hospital parking lot, a woman in a small SUV started to back out. I stopped and backed up, waiting for her spot, nervously tapping the steering wheel. Junior sat on the seat next to me, quiet, subdued. He'd read my mood. "Hey, pal, I don't know what I was thinking. I shouldn't have brought you along. No offense, but in this situation, you're creating a real nuisance."

He let out a low whine at my unfair accusation.

Out in the middle of the parking lot, there wasn't any shade. I couldn't leave him in the car, not on a hot summer day. "All right, buddy, but I'm telling you right now, no shenanigans, you understand?" I reached behind the back seat and underneath. I pulled out a red Service Dog apron.

He barked. He liked going undercover, acting like a normal dog instead of what he really was: a misunderstood hundred-and-ten-pound half lab, half Rottweiler mix who loved most everyone in the world with the exception of crooks. The SUV lady finished making her long, slow exit from the spot as I finished tying on the apron. I parked and jumped out with Junior Mint coming from behind, shooting ahead. "Whoa there, Junior, back it up." He stopped. I clipped on the leash. We hurried to the ER entrance rather than the front door. I knew my way around Daniel Freeman but only from the ER entrance. And I didn't want to be stopped at the front desk, identified, and given a visitor badge.

The double doors whooshed open for two paramedics ahead of us who wheeled in an emaciated old woman on a gurney with an IV. She didn't look so good.

I whispered to Junior, "Okay, now I mean it this time, best behavior. Do not, I repeat, do not get us kicked out of here." He looked back over his shoulder as if the incident three months ago in the McDonald's never happened. We slid in behind the paramedics like we owned the place and stopped just inside so I could get my bearings. Junior tugged on the leash. He spotted RD before I did. RD looked different. He wasn't wearing his trademark dopey smile. He stood outside one of the glassed-in emergency rooms that had mini blinds and a solid door. A private room. Not good.

I hurried over to him. "Tell me."

He wrung his hands. "It's bad, Bruno, real bad."

All the air left me and I swallowed a couple of times. "Okay, give."

"He was driving to work today, this morning. He was on his Harley-Davidson, just like always. You know how he is. I've told him and told him to get off that bike. He was coming down Alameda, in the number-one lane all by himself, no cars around, when a truck going northbound crossed the double yellow. Bart saw him coming and pulled to the left—jerked it over, you know. But so did the truck. It was almost like it came after him, Bruno. Bart banged off the side of the truck and went down hard. It could've been a head-on if Bart hadn't pulled to the left. That would've killed him for sure. The truck just kept going. Felony hit-and-run." Tears welled in RD's eyes. "They've got him stabilized and they're waiting for a surgeon, a specialist. It's his back and neck, Bruno. They don't think he's gonna ever walk again. He's asking for you. He wants to see you."

I nodded again. All I could manage with the big lump in my throat. I handed him the leash, opened the door to the private room, and stepped in.

A short woman, slim with long red hair, stood by the bed holding Bart's hand. She looked tiny in comparison to the mound under the sheet. Her delicate hand held onto Bart's huge mitt. She turned to see who came through the door, her eyes bloodshot, her freckled face wet with tears. She wore stylish denim pants with ragged holes up and down the front of the legs, and a sleeveless blouse that displayed lean arms and an elegant neck. "Hello, Deputy Johnson?"

I'd never met her and yet she knew my name. Bart had probably told her about my behavior, how I was a nightmare to supervise. With all of Bart's black leather, his biker boots, his unruly hair and beard, this woman was nowhere near the wife I had imagined for him. I remembered what RD had said about Bart, his wife and kids, and how they attended church every Sunday, God-fearing folks who led normal lives in a crime-free neighborhood.

She let go of Bart's hand, came over slow to ease in close, put her arms around me, and rested her head on my chest. I didn't know what to do or to say. I'd never met this woman and she acted as if we were old friends. She needed someone at that moment. I put my arms around her but didn't hug. The spot where she touched my shirt turned damp with her tears.

Finally, she turned up her head. She had big emerald-green eyes. "He wants to talk to you."

I nodded. I shouldn't have had to ask her name. I should've already known, but the last six months had challenged my world, filling it first with worry and grief, and then with a depth of regret like I'd never experienced, leaving no room for decorum and manners. In another time, another place, we would've known each other from family get-togethers, dinners, and outdoor barbecues, playdates with our kids—my grandkids.

I left her where she stood and stepped over to the hospital bed where Black Bart lay. They'd shaved his beard and cut off all his head hair. A latter-day Samson. They had stolen his strength, his identity.

Now, instead of a biker, he resembled a mangled Buddhist monk. They'd secured his head with thick molded plastic and tape and a neck brace. Life-sustaining wires and tubes and beeping machines kept watch over him. I didn't recognize his face, which was bloated red with the right side an open wound of road rash where he'd skidded along the asphalt.

"Bart?" Black Bart was the nickname I used so often that his real name now escaped me. Under the circumstances, I couldn't pull it from my memory. "Bart" would have to do.

"Karl?" His voice came out weak instead of the usual Black-Bart-strong. He, too, called me by my nickname, my cover. With our fake names, we were adult children playing at cops and robbers, in a make-believe world that had suddenly turned too real.

He opened his eyes. I took his hand and leaned over so he could see me. He squeezed hard and I couldn't help thinking that at least he still had the use of his hands. "I'm right here, my friend."

"Good. Good. You came."

"Of course, I came."

Silence. After a minute or two he said, "I ruined my bike. It's totaled."

"Yeah, I heard. Did you get a look at the driver? Will you be able to identify him?" I didn't know what to say and reverted to my training, asking him a cop question. That question made me finally comprehend what had really happened. This had not been an accident; this had been done with malice and forethought; this was attempted murder. Johnny Sin wanted to deal only with me. He'd said as much the night before. Once denied, his ego now required it. This was his way of making that happen. I gripped Bart's hand harder as my mind shot out ahead figuring how I'd take down Johnny Sin. I'd rent the largest dump truck I could find and drive it right through the front window of his auto parts store in Norwalk. I'd get out, hook a chain to Johnny Sin's feet, and drag him down the street. Blood and bone.

I stood in the same spot by the hospital bed and didn't know how much time had slipped by. Bart was still holding on tight to my hand when he said, "I gotta ask you a big favor."

"Sure."

"It's a big ask."

"I'm here for you."

CHAPTER THIRTY-NINE

STANDING AT BART'S bedside, his hand clutched in mine, he said, "I don't want you to go through with the gun deal."

I tried to let go. He held on tighter than ever. "Bruno, I want you to promise me you won't go through with it."

"But . . . wait . . . That's not right. We can't let those guns hit the street. Too many people will—"

"Turn it over to ATF—the feds are better equipped for a deal like this. These guys we're into, they play for keeps. I couldn't live with myself if any of my guys got hurt over this and I wasn't there."

I knew how to play for keeps.

Bart had no idea what I was capable of, and now the gloves were off and we were going to knuckles. I wouldn't let Johnny Sin score even one more point. I was going to put him down *for keeps*.

Blood and bone, that's what life always came back to, and over the years I'd learned the hard way in how to play that game.

"Bruno, promise me you won't go through with the gun deal."

I could not lie to this man, not while he was on his back critically injured waiting for surgery, the outcome unknown, not with his only concern being for the welfare of his men. All of a sudden, his true name bubbled up in my brain, *James Barlow*. "Jim, that's an unfair ask, and you know it."

"I know it is and I know you better than you think. Let the law have this guy. He's not worth a career. He's not worth a prison sentence."

I guess he did know me, that or he could read minds. He wouldn't release my hand. He'd hold on until I relented, he'd hold on even after the docs put him under, hold on until he got what he wanted.

"Promise," he said. "You're a man of your word. Promise."

I could let ATF have the guns and Jumbo, but I'd give Johnny Sin the personal touch. "I promise I won't go through with the exchange."

He eased up on his grip. Under the sheet and light-blue cotton blanket the tension in his body eased as if a great load lifted off him. He closed his eyes to rest.

I turned to leave. His wife stood in front of the door and held out her hand, her jaw set firm. I headed over and took her hand in mine, cool and delicate.

Her tone came out in a low whisper so Bart couldn't hear. "My name is Greta, we have two sons, Jason and Sonny, one little girl, Darlene; she's four years old."

"Nice to meet you, Greta. I'm sorry for all of this." Why was she telling me about her family?

This time it was Greta Barlow who wouldn't let go of my hand and held on tight. Through clenched teeth she said, "Darlene and Jason are never going to play with their father again, not on the swings, not in the sandbox, not in the tree house Jim just finished. If he's real lucky he's going to be in a wheelchair for the rest of his life. That's a life sentence for something he didn't deserve."

I didn't know what to say.

Tears welled in her eyes. "Do you know the man who did this?" Her husband had told her what had happened. They had a relationship where they kept nothing from each other.

I nodded.

She stepped closer, went up on tiptoes. "Then wreck him. You hear what I'm saying? I want you to wreck him."

My mouth sagged open. I had not expected this kind of personal request, not with such vehemence, not from a thirty-five-year-old woman who looked more like a high school senior. For a moment her demeanor and her words shook me to the core, how she could so easily step from her world into mine and ask for blood and bone. Demand it. I leaned down closer to her ear and whispered, "It'll be my pleasure."

She'd not expected the coldness in my response. Her eyes grew large and her lips parted as she shifted from messenger to my world back to hers. Her other hand came up to her mouth. She stepped back and let go of my hand. She stared at me as if I were a monster. And in the case of blood and bone, maybe I was.

I stepped out of the room and eased the door closed.

RD sat on the floor, his back to the wall under the window with the closed blinds. Junior Mint sat next to him, watching all the activity in the ER.

RD struggled to his feet and handed me the leash. "Well? What do you think? What'd he say?"

"He wants to put down the gun deal."

RD waved his hand. "Of course. Why in the world would he think we'd go through with that now? Not after all this . . . I mean with what we got going on here." He paused, as if his mind had just caught up with the words coming out of his mouth. "Why would he ask you to stand down on that deal . . . unless . . . unless . . ." The sorrow in his expression shifted to pure predator, something I'd never seen in him. He'd always been the House Mouse at TW doing the busy work. He shook his finger at me. "He thinks this"—he pointed the same finger at the window to Jim Barlow's room— "that this is related to the gun deal."

I stared at him.

His mind continued to put it together. "He didn't make you *promise* not to do this gun deal, did he? That'd be just like him to do something like that. You're still going to do the deal, aren't you, Bruno? Aren't you? I want in. I want a piece of this guy."

I held out my hand. "Give me the business card those two left on our counter last night."

He reached into his pocket and pulled out the business card and held it close to his chest. "You're taking me with you."

I said nothing and glared at him. If I took him along, he'd be more a hindrance than a help. He gave in, slapped the business card in my hand, and said, "I checked out the location—it's a professional center. I was in the middle of a background check on it when all of this came down. What are you going to do?"

"I don't know yet." I put the card in my shirt pocket. I'd caught a glimpse of the address the night before. I had lived in LA all my life and knew that area by feel, not by the named businesses.

"You're not going to do the gun deal?"

"I promised him I wouldn't do the exchange. I didn't say anything about a little *reconnaissance*."

"What do you want me to do? You're the default supervisor, that's the way the org chart is set up. You're in charge."

I'd forgotten that part. "What do you have on the truck that ran him down?"

RD fumbled to get the notebook out of his back pocket and opened it. "Forest-green Ford F150, earlier model but real clean. Except now it has right-side damage from Bart's bike. Witnesses said they thought a woman was driving." He stopped and looked up. "That's why I didn't think to link this incident with what we had going at TW, the fact that a woman was seen driving."

"Johnny Sin wore a wig."

"No shit. How do you know that?"

"Trust me on this. I want you to make up a flyer on the truck and personally take it around to every police station in the area. Tell them the truck is wanted in connection with an attempted murder on a police officer. Put a 'stop and hold' on it for prints. It's going to be abandoned somewhere, and I don't want some half-assed job on the recovery. Then I want you to contact the agency handling this crash and tell them we have motive and intent and that this isn't a felony hit-and-run. You understand? Tell them that we are taking the lead on the investigation and get everything they have on it. If they balk, refer them to me."

"I got it. What are you going to do?"

I checked my watch. "I'm going to keep our meeting with our friends, Jumbo and Johnny Sin."

A crooked smile filled his face. "Are you taking a cover team?"

"Don't need it. Remember what Jumbo said, we're still in the talking stage. And he said no guns."

Black Bart would never let me take a meeting of that magnitude without three or four guys close by backing me up. Maybe I wanted Johnny Sin to make a move. I wouldn't let him get the jump on me again. This time I wouldn't come begging for a gun deal. This time I would be on the offensive and that would make all the difference.

I walked away, stopped, and looked back at the closed door that RD stood next to holding Junior's leash. Greta's unforgiving words continued to echo in my head. *Wreck him. I want you to wreck him.*

Out of the mouths of babes.

CHAPTER FORTY

I LEFT JUNIOR Mint with RD, who needed the company. I told RD I'd pick up Junior at TransWorld a little later. As the new supervisor, I didn't have to tell the other members on the TW team what to do. Black Bart had the place running on automatic pilot. Bart had only controlled the money and the actual meetings at the TW counter. He was also there to hand out stern reproaches if we wandered too far afield from safe practices. I'd get the team together later on and we'd discuss what to do: shut TW down and make all the arrests, or let it run as planned until the money ran out. At the moment, I really didn't care one way or the other.

The address on the card was a couple of miles or so on the other side of the Los Angeles River in Downey, right at the edge of Norwalk. I knew the area, or at least I thought I did. I drove by in the ratty Kadett and double-checked the address on the plain white card—no business name, just an address scrolled in pencil: 9539 Firestone Blvd. Avenue Suite #A. Downey. Above the address in pen was written "Bruno Johnson," probably put there by RD.

I'd been expecting an auto parts store, and in its place, found a high-end office structure with Mercedes and Audis and Lexuses in the secured parking lot with a guard shack. I made another pass. I had the address correct and thought about calling RD to make sure he'd given me the right card. Instead, I decided to check the location first. I made two more passes in a widening grid search of the surrounding neighborhood, just like I would have if this had been the right address. I wouldn't make another mistake.

It was only ten o'clock in the morning, two hours early for the meeting. Johnny Sin and Jumbo came early last evening to Trans-World. Turnabout was fair play.

In the upscale neighborhood, the Opel Kadett stood out like a piece of coal on a snowbank. I found an alley posted No Parking Any Time and drove down to a wide spot and parked. I got out and left it unlocked. The immaculate alley didn't have graffiti or visible trash cans. What self-respecting alley didn't have trash cans? All the outfacing garage doors and buildings were recently painted, the grounds well-groomed and -maintained. My Opel wouldn't last long before someone called it in to the police as suspicious. I hurried. I came out of the alley on Hasty Avenue, three or four blocks north of the location, and headed west on a tree-lined street where sixty-year-old houses had been converted to professional offices. I froze. My subconscious caught something I'd missed.

I turned around. Parked at the curb half a block down the street sat an early-model forest-green Ford F150 truck. It had not been there minutes ago when I cruised the area. No way could I have missed it.

The truck's presence meant only one thing: that Johnny Sin *had* been involved in running over Black Bart. Ol' Johnny had been following me. The best way to vet someone you're about to sell a bunch of military-grade guns to is to follow him around. He had to be really good at it for me to miss him. He'd seen me go by the office a couple of times, saw me park, and strategically parked the truck where I'd see it. A little in-your-face kind of thing to put me off my game. Mission accomplished. Or maybe he thought I'd be a softer touch with a little taste of violence perpetrated upon my boss.

I stepped over to a poplar tree with a thick trunk for cover, put my back to it, and looked around. He had to be close by watching what I'd do. People came and went from the offices, cars drove on the street, and the birds sang under the bright summer sun. I stuck my hand under my work shirt to the stock of the .357 and walked to the truck. I touched the radiator grill. Yep, still warm, almost hot. I peered in the cab. Wires hung from the ignition. The inside was spotless, the carpets vacuumed, the dash without a speck of dust and gleaming, no fast-food wrappers or any extraneous personal items like a dream catcher hanging from the mirror. Showroom clean. Except one item. A cheap blond wig sat in disarray on the seat. The wig also left there on purpose. Why wouldn't Johnny Sin dispose of the wig unless he wanted me to see it, to thumb his nose at us? To thumb his nose at me.

Long striations marred the right side of the truck, exposing silver metal dented from impact. Curled bits of paint still hung from the fresh damage. I moved to the rear of the truck, looked around, then knelt and pulled a switchblade from my boot. I sliced the rear tire. It hissed. The back of the truck tilted down. I put the blade back and walked to the meeting.

I came out onto Firestone Avenue and checked up and down the busy street as I made my way to the address and to Suite A. Less than two blocks away, the 605 Freeway crossed over Firestone Boulevard, the boundary between Downey and Norwalk.

I found the right office and entered the expansive, well-appointed lobby. Four white leather couches in the center and large contemporary paintings on two walls set off all the dark wood everywhere else. I stopped. What the hell was going on? This wasn't an auto parts store. I spotted the building legend and went over to check the name on Suite A: "Manfred and Manfred Attorneys at Law." This was a law office? Was Johnny Sin really an attorney? Was his real name Manfred? He sure made the right moves at the right times like someone well versed in the law. Why would he give up his true identity without good reason? He hadn't made a wrong move yet—why now? I wanted to back out and give this new twist some thought.

He'd left the card the night before to set up the meeting. He said no guns for good reason. No ambush would occur in digs like these. Curiosity got the better of me. I walked deeper into the lobby to the double mahogany doors with the brass plaque to the side that simply stated "Suite A." I took a breath, turned the knob, and entered.

I'd been in many law offices over the years for various depositions and other legal matters, and this one was no different. Yet, I still couldn't shake the feeling of being out of my element. I dealt strictly with street thugs. I knew how they acted, knew how they walked and talked, how they thought, and most important, which way they would jump before they knew themselves. I knew nothing about this world and how to survive in it. This was exactly how Johnny Sin would want his opponent, set back on his heels and made to wonder which way was up.

The receptionist sat behind a desk, a fiftyish woman dressed in subdued business attire and stylish glasses. She glanced away from her computer screen and looked me up and down, assessing.

"Mr. Bruno Johnson?"

CHAPTER FORTY-ONE

IN THE LAW offices of Manfred and Manfred, I stood before the receptionist in denim pants and my khaki truck driver shirt, underdressed and two hours early to the meeting. "Yes, that's me."

She picked up the phone and spoke in low tones. She hung up. "Ms. Franklin will be right out."

"May I use your phone, please? It's a local call."

She eyed me suspiciously, as if I may have crapped the bed. "Dial nine and please make it brief."

I turned my back to the woman and dialed TransWorld. When RD picked up, I told him where to find the forest-green Ford F150.

"Jesus, Karl, how the hell did you find it so fast? This is great."

"Get forensics on it right away. I would really rather that you drive out here and handle it yourself to make sure it gets done right."

"I'm on it. Where are you going to be?"

"On a follow-up. Stay close to the phone. I'm going to be calling soon for backup. Put the team on alert."

"Roger that."

I hung up before he could ask any more questions.

A light-skinned African American woman in a charcoal-gray suit with a matching pencil skirt and medium black heels came from the hallway. In a past life, before she went to law school, she could've been Ms. Hometown USA or fifth or sixth runner-up in the Ms. Universe contest.

She extended a delicate-boned hand while displaying a pasted-on lipstick smile. "I'm Marjory Franklin, it's so nice that you could join us."

She somehow managed to say it without a hint of sarcasm.

I took her hand. "I think I'm in the wrong place."

"No, you're not. This way, please." She turned and headed back from whence she came. I followed in her perfumed wake, an essence of lilac that quickened my step to get more.

"Is Johnny Sin already here?"

She stopped. Pulled her shoulders back. She turned and said, "Excuse me?"

"Johnny Sin, that's why I came, you know, for the meeting."

"Is that a real name?"

"Uh-oh. I think I'm in the wrong place." I turned to get the hell out of there. Nothing good can come from being in a law office when you have no idea why. The kind of law this office practiced could strip a person naked just as fast as the IRS.

"Excuse me."

I turned back. She'd again offered me her hand, and this time the thrown-on smile came with a hint of promise like to a sailor from a siren on the rocks. I didn't take her hand and stood there conflicted, not by her feminine wiles, but by curiosity to find out exactly what was going on.

"We have some light refreshment, and I promise this will only take a minute of your time."

I smiled. "So this isn't going to hurt?"

She winked. "Not a bit." Confident she again had me hooked, she turned and continued. I followed along, the perfect wayward puppy looking for his mother.

Something wasn't right: the business card with the address, the forest-green Ford truck parked three blocks away, and Johnny Sin and Jumbo asking for this meeting. She opened an office door with her name on the wall next to it and stepped aside to allow me to pass.

I stepped inside.

I could have played a half-court basketball game in her office, with its high ceiling and abundant square footage. The room had been decorated to impress and accomplished the mission with a spartan taste in furniture. She moved behind her all-glass desk and sat down, her back to a tinted window that ran the entire wall. Outside, the sun shone on an exterior quad that contained a Japanese rock garden, a small waterfall that gurgled, and perfectly trimmed topiary animals. She held out her hand. "Please have a seat."

"Thank you, but I'd prefer to stand. Now that you got me in here, please, tell me what's going on."

She opened a manila file on her desk as a tease. "First, would you please show me some identification?"

I took out my wallet and handed over my driver's license. Her smile disappeared. "Why, this says your name is Karl Higgins."

"That's right—who did you think I was?" I had a complete legend made up to work the sting.

"I . . . ah . . . my receptionist said you were Bruno Johnson."

"Who?"

"There's been a terrible mistake." She stood. "What are you doing here?"

I put on a dumb expression and pointed in the direction of the wall. "My car broke down, and I just came in to use the phone. Johnny Sin doesn't work here? I thought he worked here."

"Oh, I'm so sorry for the confusion."

The interior door opened. Out came a voice. "No. No. No, that's him. That's Bruno Johnson. He's yanking on your dick, lady."

And in came Derek Sams.

My breath caught. What was he doing there? A miasma of emotion made the world spin and the floor tilt.

Sams said, "Told ya, you left a note on his door with just the address he'd get curious and come lookin'. He's always stickin' that fat nose where it doesn't belong."

I recovered from the shock, gritted my teeth, and took a step toward him. He lost his smile and jumped back. Ms. Franklin hurried round her desk, the flat of her hands pushed outward. "Hold it. Hold it." She spun on Derek. "I told you to stay in the other room, that was the deal."

"I didn't want to just hear this," he said. "I wanted to see it. I wanted to see the look on the big man's face when I finally took him to his knees. I wanted him to see that I outgunned him but good."

She reached down to her desk and into the file.

Seeing Sams, hearing his worthless words, dumped me into a fugue state. I hadn't stopped moving toward him, instinct telling me what needed to be done.

Ms. Franklin slapped a paper to my chest. "You're officially served with a protection order. You cannot come within a thousand feet of my client. And while under this order you are not allowed to carry a firearm. You're not allowed to call or contact my client in any manner or you will be in violation of this court order and arrested."

Derek smiled again. He sucked his teeth the disrespectful way hoods did on the street that said "fuck you." "Good thing you're not with the pooolease anymore, Johnson, or they'd have ta give you a rubber gun and put you on the desk. What do you think of that, Mister Big Assed Bruno Johnson? I kin just see you ridin' a desk. Too bad, huh?"

I looked down at the paper she held to my chest and relieved her of it. "A protective order? What are you talking about?" I read the single sheet of paper. I knew all about protective orders. I wrote plenty of them while working patrol on calls for service for domestic violence. I wrote them for battered women who needed relief from abusive husbands. Derek Sams was an ignorant street thug too stupid to make a smart play like this. What the hell was going on?

"Hah, look at the big man. Looks like I got him good. I stumped him for sure. Same as if I pulled the gunny sack over his big head and beat him with a club."

His words helped pull me out of my funk. I crumpled the pink sheet and tossed it. "This is just a piece of paper and if you think that it's going to—"

Ms. Franklin picked up the file folder from her desk. "We took a full deposition from our client in case something happens to him. We are filing a lawsuit for punitive damages, cruelty, duress, torture, kidnap, false imprisonment, and emotional and physical abuse. I'd advise you to seek legal counsel before you say another word."

I took a step back, again stunned. "A lawsuit?" Sams had managed to get out of custody and out from underneath a slam-dunk manslaughter charge. Now he had found a way to pull *me* into court? He'd turned the tables, gone on the offensive, and caught me flat-footed.

"Yes, a lawsuit to recover damages. And again, I'm advising you right now that if anything happens to my client, I will personally seek criminal charges against you. Now, please leave this office."

CHAPTER FORTY-TWO

I DIDN'T MOVE from where I stood in Ms. Franklin's office. I just stared at Derek Sams. How could he be standing there? How did he get there?

Three years earlier, with dark intent, I grabbed him up from the street in front of a pager store on Central Avenue and took him for a ride. He was dating my daughter, Olivia, at the time and had put her in jeopardy twice. Due to his nefarious ways, crazed cokeheads with guns held her against her will in a rock house. The second time, he took her to dinner while carrying a gun. Like any concerned father, I wanted to protect my daughter. I just wasn't sure how. That night I had set out to permanently solve the problem with a little blood and bone.

But I erred. My mistake. A simple one really: I'd spoken to him when I shouldn't have. I should've put a piece of tape over his mouth. At the time he came off as nothing more than a soft, vulnerable kid, the kind of victim I worked hard to champion my entire career. In the end, I couldn't do it. I put him on a bus to Barstow to go live with his father. I gave him a stern admonishment never to return and what the consequences would be if he did. My lack of the proper corrective action that night was one of the biggest mistakes of my life. Had I carried through with what I intended, my daughter and grandson Albert would still be alive. We'd still be a family. I was ashamed of my lack of fortitude, at my inability to protect my family. I never told anyone what I had done.

Except Dad. When I told him, he reassured me that I'd made the right choice. But the right choice for whom? Surely not for Olivia and Albert.

Now, in the office, Derek appeared different somehow, older, mature. He'd filled out, even since the night I'd caught up with him at the Green Spot Motel in Victorville and crushed his fingers in the doorjamb until he told me the truth about what he'd done to grandson, little Albert. Derek stood six feet tall, a hundred and sixty pounds, and he'd let his Afro grow long while in jail fighting his manslaughter case. He had not cut it after his release. He had pale green eyes behind light black skin sprinkled with freckles. People in the ghetto labeled this common look as a "strawberry."

In those sparse few seconds, I stared him down. What struck me odd and would forever change my view of him was his five o'clock shadow. I had not noticed it before. In my mind I had always seen him as a kid, a misguided child.

Olivia had been nothing more than a kid trying to get by in an adult world, so I had equated the same for him. She worked hard to raise her two twin boys and this . . . this creature had ruined all of that. But the light beard now made Derek Sams a man, it brought him firmly into my world, it made him subject to all the penalties the real world afforded people who violated the law, who violated the sanctity of family.

I let loose a lazy grin.

"What are you smiling at, big man? You got nothin' to smile about. You lose big-time. I'm going to own you. You understand? Own you. I'm gonna take your car, your house, everything you got. Even that dumbass ratty shirt on your back."

"Did Johnny Sin help you out with this? I know *you* don't have the brain power or the funds to pull it off."

"Who? What are you trying to say? I thought this up all on my own. Me. And I got money. I got a crew on the street slingin' rock for me."

Ms. Franklin put a restraining hand on Derek's chest. "Take it easy. He's just trying to antagonize you. Don't say another word." She turned back toward me. "Get out."

"Tell Johnny, when you see him, I'm coming for him."

Derek said, "I don't know no Johnny Sin. What the hell are you talking about?"

I'd regained control of my emotions. I'd said it to check his reaction in search of the truth. I couldn't read him, though. He seemed genuine in his response. But that couldn't be. To have the forest-green Ford F150 parked three blocks away was too big of a coincidence, and I learned the hard way to never believe in coincidences.

Unless Johnny Sin had just been following me.

Ms. Franklin kept one hand on Derek's chest and pushed a button on her desk phone. "Call the police."

The receptionist replied, "Right away."

"Why are you working for this guy?" I asked her. "Do you know what he's done? He's a despicable lowlife who doesn't care about anything but his own skin." I wanted to say that he killed children, but those words proved too dark to bring into the light of day.

She removed her hand from Derek's chest and spun around, her eyes flashing angrily. "I do know who I'm working for. I'm doing it because every person needs access to a voice." She reached down and took up Derek's left hand. His three crushed fingers had not healed properly and had turned into gnarled tree roots. Thinking he knew more than the doctor, he probably took the splints off too soon. "I do it because of this. Because people like you run roughshod over the victims of this world who can't defend themselves. You, sir, are nothing more than a street thug who exploits the weak."

My breath caught. For a brief moment her description fit me like a glove. During my entire career, I had worked hard to champion the rights of children and of those who could not defend themselves. Her accusation cut me down and challenged my core beliefs. But the sight of Derek's smug expression snapped me out of it.

"He's anything but a victim. Do you know what this man did to my family? Or do you even care?"

Her anger faded a little. "We're not here to debate the issue. You'll get your chance in court."

I smirked.

"What?" she asked.

"Nothing. I just realized it's his left hand. If I had thought it through that night, and played it smart, I would've done his trigger finger on his right hand." I held up my hand and worked the index finger and thumb to mimic firing a gun at him. I winked.

Her mouth sagged open in shock.

I turned and walked out.

CHAPTER FORTY-THREE

I CAME OUT of the building into the bright sunlight. I'd let the moment in Ms. Franklin's office get away from me. In front of Derek's attorney, I had as much as admitted to crushing Derek's fingers. Now they would have an easy path to winning their civil judgment. Another error. Proof positive that when emotionally involved in a situation it is always a good practice to back out and let someone else handle it.

A horn honked. And honked again. I held my arm up to shield the glare until my eyes adjusted. A dark gray Taurus with smoked windows pulled a U-turn in the middle of the street and parked at the curb three feet away. The side window whirred down. "Get in the car, asshole."

Wicks.

I hesitated, going over the pros and cons. I made my choice and got in the passenger side ready for his barrage of epithets. Instead he closed the window and stared at me.

"What?" I said too harshly.

He stared some more, anger apparent in his expression.

He hadn't driven by the attorney's office out of coincidence. This had been the location of the meet with Sams, and in his mind, I'd followed Wicks there for no other reason than to screw up his case. To stomp Sams into the dirt, put him in the hospital so he couldn't work the street for Wicks.

"What are you doing here?" Wicks asked. "How did you follow me? I was real careful."

"Take it easy, it was an accident."

"An accident that you're sitting here in my car in front of this office, really? That's what you're going to go with?" He waved his arms. "A county of ten million people and you want me to believe you just happened in here?"

"Take it easy."

He pointed a finger. "Don't you tell me to take it easy."

I took the plain white business card out of my shirt pocket. With it came a second card that fell into my lap. I picked it up. Here was the source of all the confusion. The card read, "Harry and Sons Oil to Nuts Auto Supply, 11050 Firestone Blvd., Norwalk." The real card Jumbo and Johnny Sin had put on the counter at TW the night before. Harry and Sons was just down the street a few blocks in Norwalk. It wasn't a huge coincidence; Johnny Sin *had* been following me. Crooks tend to swirl in one large vortex, bumping into each other in their travels, using the same dope dealers, the same fences, same attorneys, the same hidey-holes. All of them connected by two degrees of separation instead of six like regular folks.

Seeing both cards, I remembered Dad had found a card stuck in our front door, the one Ms. Franklin had put there. The one to lure me over to her office to serve me with the TRO and make the service so Derek could be present to gloat. Dad had put that card in my shirt pocket, and with all that had been going on, I'd forgotten about it. I hadn't even taken time to look at it. Muddled emotions over a family lost could do that to a person.

"Don't you tell me to take it easy," Wicks yelled. "You're not a cop anymore, so I can arrest you for obstruction. Is Sams okay? What did you do in there?" He grabbed my right hand and checked my knuckles for injuries and didn't find any.

Then the full impact of what had happened in the law office hit me. What that little punk had pulled off. I punched the dash. Punched it again and again.

"Hey! Hey! Are you outta your mind? You're not going to take out another one of my cars. What the hell's the matter with you? You got a thing against my cars? Get out. Get the hell out, now." He shoved hard on my shoulder. "I'll pistol-whip you if you don't get out of my car right now."

I stopped punching his dash. I had developed an anger issue, but only where it concerned Derek Sams. I took in several long breaths. "I'm okay now. It's not about your cars, really. It's Sams."

He took in several deep breaths and settled down some. "Yeah, I figured as much. You need help, pal. You need to get your head shrunk. And don't waste any time doing it. I'll drive you to a doc right now."

"No, I'm okay." I needed time to think.

"The hell you are. When I drove by you were standing out there on the sidewalk, big as you please with a huge bull's-eye on your chest." He leaned over and knocked on my head with his knuckles. "Remember La Vonn, the guy who gunned down the judge and his wife with deer slugs? He killed that coke whore. He's still out there gunning for you. You weren't supposed to leave your house. Buddy boy, you gotta get your head on straight or end up on a slab in the morgue. I'm not kiddin' here. You get serious or La Vonn is going to pump a pumpkin ball right up your ass."

"I know, I'm sorry. I promise I'm going to play it smart from here on out. What are you doing here, at this address? Did you drive Derek to this office?"

He squirmed a little. "That's right. He said he wanted to see his attorney before he'd tell me a thing. So I said, what the hell could it hurt? What were *you* doing in there?"

I handed him the plain white business card with the Firestone address Ms. Franklin had left at my house.

"What's this?"

"Your informant Sams put it on my front door. He wanted me to come here."

"For what?"

"His attorney just served me with a TRO."

Wicks sat back in his seat. "You have got to be kiddin' me? Why that little shit." He smiled and shook his head. "You know, if you think about it, that's really a smart move. He's locked you out. Now if something happens to him, you're suspect numero uno. Somebody bangs him in a drive-by, and they're coming for you."

"I don't think it's so funny."

"Oh, this is ironic. With his lifestyle, you might want to hire him a bodyguard."

"Stop it."

"Listen, you've had plenty of chances to cancel that puke's ticket and you haven't. I know you. If you haven't done it, you're not going to. For some reason, you don't have the stomach for it. I'm guessing it's because he's your daughter's fiancé, the father of your grandkids. I get it, I do. But if all your lookin' to do is to kick the bejesus out of him, wait. Lay low for a few months, let him think he's safe. He'll let his guard down. That TRO is temporary. Let it expire. Then if you still feel the same, wait for your shot and waylay him in some dark alley. Hell, I'll even help you. But for right now, leave him be until we track down this La Vonn. Okay? Just put it on the back burner. It's the smart thing to do. I'm the one thinking clearly here, you're not. You hear what I'm saying?"

I stared at him, wanting to tell him the rest, the part about Derek's fingers, the part about Albert's body in a valise and how Sams threw him off the San Pedro Bridge. Discarded him like so much trash. And couldn't. Shame for allowing all of it to happen wouldn't let the words materialize. How could I tell Wicks? He wouldn't understand why I hadn't already disappeared Derek. Why I had allowed him still to be breathing the same air as all the other nice humans. Had Wicks been in my place, he would not have hesitated. Wicks looked at it as if it was our responsibility to protect the herd from this kind of threat. He was a sheepdog with a Colt .45.

I nodded. "They also said . . . the attorney took a depo from Derek. He's suing me."

"Big deal. If I had a nickel for every time I got sued, I'd be a rich man."

"He's going to win."

"What? Of course he's not. He doesn't have a—"

"Remember, I'm the one who crushed his fingers. I admitted as much in front of his attorney."

Wicks' mouth dropped open. He broke into a smile. "I forgot about that part." Wicks smiled and held up his hand, his fingers imitating a claw. "Ouch." He shook his head and chuckled. "As far as winning the lawsuit, they can't get blood from a turnip, right? You said you're broke from fighting for custody of your grandson. This is an easy one. Have your attorney make a deal to pay him, make it ten million if that's what it takes, then file for bankruptcy. Start over. See, no problem."

A lump rose in my throat as it always did when I tried to talk about what happened to little Albert. I couldn't get the words out to tell him the rest, and let it go. Tears blurred my vision. "Can you drive me around to my car?"

CHAPTER FORTY-FOUR

I COULDN'T GO to the meeting at the auto parts store, not with my thoughts all in a jumble. I got in the Kadett and drove. I stopped at signals not fully aware of the colors green or red. My foot knew what to do and made the changes on the pedals all on their own.

Telling Wicks that I had caused the injury to Sams' fingers made me realize the source of all my recent mistakes, the reason for them. The most recent, letting Johnny Sin follow me around in a truck, a truck I was looking for. I had a black cloud hanging over me, one so real it tinted the sunlight and followed me wherever I went. I couldn't get rid of it until I unburdened what had happened to Albert. I'd kept the incident all bottled up since the night at The Green Spot motel in Victorville when Sams admitted what he'd done. His words created horrible unwanted images that floated just above my head and leapt into my brain whenever I tried to close my eyes. Perpetual sleep deprivation had caused me to commit too many errors. Telling Wicks the part about the fingers relieved some of that pressure. I could see that now. I needed to tell someone all of it.

I left the Kadett in the parking lot of Martin Luther King hospital and walked home. I couldn't tell Dad, but I needed to tell someone. Doc Abrams was the logical choice. But he was a contract doctor for the sheriff's department, and normally he was restricted from relaying any information generated from his sessions. Unless what I told him was a threat to public safety. Putting Derek's fingers in the doorjamb one at a time to solicit a confession certainly qualified.

I took the three steps up our stoop and hesitated. I moved my ear closer to the door. I tried to recognize the noises coming from inside and refused to believe what I heard . . . a child giggling and laughing. Was it a hallucination?

I opened the door and rushed in.

Dad sat on the floor with bright-colored building blocks, playing with Alonzo. At the sight of my happy grandson, all the worries of the world melted away. I wilted to my knees and crawled over. He saw me, smiled even broader, and scuttled quickly to me. I stopped and scooped him up, tears in my eyes, my heart filled with joy. He laughed and patted my face. "Pop. Pop."

I hugged him and kissed his fat cheeks. I laughed with him and bounced him and cried.

I didn't realize until that moment how much he looked like Olivia.

"Dad, what's going on? What's he doing here? This isn't for real, is it?"

"No. No, he can't stay. It's just a visit. I told you I know those folks at that foster home. Ms. Kinder is one of the nicest people. You have to meet her. She let me take him to get some ice cream. I thought it would cheer you up to see him."

"You have no idea how much I needed this."

"He can't stay much longer. I've had him here for a while already. I was hoping you'd come home a little sooner. You need to keep that cell phone with you."

"Thank you, Dad."

He beamed and held out his hands.

I closed my eyes and took in a big whiff of Alonzo. He smelled of everything right in the world; he smelled of the way everything used to be when Olivia and Albert were still there in the house.

Dad tugged on Alonzo. "I'm sorry, Son, I have to go. We don't want to ruin what we have going with those folks at the foster home."

"Of course, you're right." I reluctantly released my grandson. Dad stood with Alonzo in his arms. "I'll run him back and then make you some dinner. How's that sound?"

I nodded and thought evil thoughts. *We could take Alonzo and make a run for it. I didn't have anything holding me in Los Angeles, not anymore. It would be so easy.*

But I couldn't disappear forever, not without taking Dad along, and he wouldn't go; his strong ethics and morals wouldn't allow it. And running wasn't the right thing to do.

Dad left with Alonzo in his arms. When the front door closed, the strange dark tint that covered my world returned. I sat on the couch and stared at the wall as depression closed in and made me want to curl up on the floor of the clothes closet with the door shut tight. I tried to bring back the memories of happier times that Alonzo carried with him wherever he went, and couldn't. The expression on Derek's ugly mug, his mocking words in the law office, pushed out everything else. I wanted to crush him more than ever.

Dad came back seconds later, or at least it seemed like it. He set a warm pizza box on the kitchen table and got out two plates. "Come. Sit. Eat something."

I did as he asked.

For those brief moments, Alonzo had brought light back into my life, but when he left, it somehow made the darkness worse, taking it right to the edge of unbearable.

The pizza tasted like cardboard and warm tomato paste.

Dad reached over and put his hand on mine. "It's going to work out, you'll see."

Only he didn't know what I knew. He didn't know that I had to tell someone or risk never climbing out of the dark hole I'd fallen into.

Misery loves company, and I didn't like myself for it, but I asked anyway. "Tell me what happened that night?"

He pulled his hand away. The residual joy in his eyes from his time with Alonzo turned to flint. He knew what night I meant. He stared at me.

"Dad, when Mom came in with someone else's blood on her, who did you call that night? Was it the police? Is my mother in prison?"

"You really want to know the rest of it?"

"I don't want to know—I have to know."

He nodded and started talking in a low monotone, his eyes staring off into the distance.

CHAPTER FORTY-FIVE

THE NIGHT DAD'S *wife, Bea, came home covered in blood, he called Agnes Reyes, the regular sitter, and asked a big favor: Could she take Bruno overnight, just this one time? He'd pay her extra. Fifteen minutes later, when Bruno was safe on his way, Xander could think clearly, well, a little better, anyway. He filled a deep soup pot halfway with warm water and used the softest bath cloth he could find to give his sleeping Bea a sponge bath. He gently stripped off her damaged red crepe dress with the fake white pearls and soaked it in the kitchen sink to get the dark maroon blood stains out.*

Afterward, she lay sleeping on the couch in bra and panties with an afghan cover. He held the back of her hand up to his cheek and stared at her angelic expression. She smelled of E&J brandy and Ivory hand soap. He was more scared than he'd ever been in his life. What the heck was he going to do? More important, what had she done? Had she killed someone? Was there, this minute, a police dragnet out for his gentle little flower that he loved so dearly? Would they batter down the door and drag her away screaming? Would she be housed in San Quentin for the rest of her life? These thoughts darkened his world.

When he couldn't wait any longer, he nudged her awake. "Baby. Babe, come on, wake up."

She jumped and scrambled away from him, her eyes wide with terror. For her to be so scared caused an ache in his chest. His number one job was to protect her, and he'd failed horribly.

He held up his hands. "It's okay. It's okay, it's me, Xander." Fear left her. She crawled over to him. He hugged her like it was the last time he'd ever have the chance. She held on tight and spoke into his chest. "Honey, tell me it was just a dream. Please tell me it was all just a bad dream and I'm awake now."

Life hadn't been fast enough for his naïve young wife, naïve in the ways of the world, in the ways of the ghetto. Now she'd had her taste of the life she'd desired and found it too bitter to handle. She wanted to go back to the way it had been. But that wasn't how it worked. The true price was yet to be paid. He believed in law and order, but for the first time, he thought that price too high.

With an effort, he pulled her away from him. "I can't tell you that it wasn't a nightmare."

He waited for her to respond.

She said nothing more.

"I wasn't there with you in the motel. Tell me what happened. You have to tell me."

Her chin quivered as tears filled her eyes and wet her cheeks. She stared at him, her eyes begging for relief from her anguish. It ripped his guts out.

"Bea, tell me what happened. What did you do?" He held onto her shoulders and kept her at arm's length even though she wanted back into the hug, a place of comfort and safety.

She finally nodded. Her knees collapsed. He caught her and picked her up the same as he had the night he carried her over the threshold, a little more than two years before. He set her back on the couch that still held a bit of warmth from where she'd been sleeping.

He waited for her to speak, the silence unbearable as she gripped both of his hands.

She nodded at nothing and gulped. "It was awful, honey. Absolutely awful."

He waited for more.

"I never . . ." she said . . . "I never thought two people could be . . . I mean, the greed; it was like a beast let loose from inside both of them. Ugly and violent. Their . . . their eyes were wild like animals. Baby, there was money enough for all of us, bags and bags of coins. More money than I have ever seen in one place, and it was ours. Had to be a couple thousand dollars . . . more, even three or four thousand." She looked down at her cupped hands as if she still held a mound of the precious coins she worshipped. She looked back up at him. "We hadn't even finished counting it.

"They didn't have to fight over that much money, right? There was plenty for all of us. We'd done it. We got away with it. But that wasn't enough for either one of them. They had to have it all and . . . and went at each other."

Bea stopped talking. Her eyes no longer saw him and jetted back and forth in a nervous tick, as she must've relived the violence that got her dress torn and her hands and arms covered in someone else's blood.

"Tell me," he whispered.

She again nodded, not looking at him, staring off at the wall. "They were both so happy. Or they played like they were. When we got to two thousand dollars in the count and still had half the bags left to go, she . . ."

"Cleo?" he asked.

"Yes. And Melvin. They both stood up. Held hands and danced around and around in that small motel room, laughing and yelling. I clapped and laughed with them. Cleo turned toward me with this

huge smile; she said, 'Come on, Bea, join us. Get up and join us.' Then
. . . Then she lost her smile. It turned to . . . shock. Her eyes went wide
as saucers and her mouth . . . her mouth became a little 'O.'"

Bea clutched Xander's hands tighter. "While Cleo still faced me,
Melvin had pulled a knife and stuck her in the back. I didn't know
that's what happened until she let out this screech like some kinda alley
cat. She spun around and . . . and pulled a straight razor she kept
under her dress on a garter belt. She went at Melvin in a flurry. That
razor flitted through the air like a bee. She did it with Melvin's knife
sticking from her back.

"Melvin held up his arms and backed away, but she went at him. It
was the most horrible thing I have ever seen. Blood went everywhere.
His arms in shreds, he finally turned his back to her to open the door.
She got him there, too, long deep slices in his back right through his
shirt. He ran out into the night howling. Cleo slammed the door and
turned. She had a knife stuck all the way in her back clear up to the
hilt. She just stood there like it was nothing. Like she wasn't human.
Melvin's blood dripped down her hand and ran down her arm. I
thought she was coming for me. I backed up to the wall.

"Then all of a sudden, she must've realized she was stabbed. She
dropped the straight razor. She said, 'He's done gone and killed me,
Bea.'

"I'll never forget those words. I'll never forget the look on her face as
she wilted to the floor. She died right there in front of me."

Safe in the living room on Nord, Bea turned to Xander. "Her body
was so hot. I remember it was so hot and slick when I picked her up
and put her on her side on the bed. I didn't know what to do about
the knife in her back. I wanted to pull it out but I couldn't bring
myself to do it. I couldn't even touch it." Bea shuddered. "Hold me,
honey, please hold me."

* * *

Dad came out of his trance, his eyes sad. His words had created a flash-brand photo of my mother, one I'd never forget. An image, a persona of her I wished he had not created. He'd been right all along in keeping it a secret.

He said, "I didn't tell you because . . . well, you can see it wasn't something a child should hear. And when you got older, you never asked again, or I would've told you. You believe me when I say I would have told you, don't you, Son?"

"Yes." My voice cracked. "You still haven't said what happened to her."

He again turned his head away, unable to look me in the eye. "First and foremost, I had you to consider, your well-being. That's what I tell myself. I loved her, Son, so much words can't describe." He turned his attention to his own hands, as if they held the answer to the secrets of the past. "She not only violated the law, she put you in jeopardy. I didn't know if Melvin Shackleford survived. If he did, would he come for Bea? Would he come to this house with you here? Would the cops come busting down the door with guns and batons looking for my beautiful Bea?

"The worst part about all of it . . . she . . . she wasn't the girl I'd married. Not anymore, she wasn't. I know that isn't fair, but it was true. I couldn't control her and that might've been all right if it were just me, but I had you to worry about.

"So when she fell back to sleep, I called the sheriff. I always believed there should be justice with mercy. I just never thought I'd be the one not to practice it.

"They came and took her away; they had to drag her out. It tore me up inside. The look of betrayal in her eyes . . . well, it's something I'll have to live with the rest of my life." He turned his attention back to me. "It was the single most difficult thing I have ever had to do. I never saw her again. Never heard from her, not so much as a letter."

"I'm sorry you had to go through that. I think you made the right choice."

He gave me a wounded smile. "Thank you; you don't know how much that means to me."

Dad believed so strongly in law and order, he turned in his wife whom he loved more than life itself. How could I ever admit to him what I did to Derek's fingers? Admit to Dad what I had in mind to finish the issue with Derek? Not to protect my family like Dad did. I had already failed in that respect, failed to bring a full measure of justice to Derek.

The shame of it shrank me to two feet tall. I hugged Dad much longer than a normal hug. I hugged him like it might be the last.

CHAPTER FORTY-SIX

I DROVE AROUND the Crazy Eight three times checking out the cars parked in the area and watching the pedestrians for a furtive movement that might be a cloaked threat.

No more mistakes.

I parked five blocks away instead of the usual two or three and moved along the sides of the buildings on full alert. I had missed the meeting with Johnny Sin and Jumbo and they knew I frequented the Crazy Eight. This would be the first place they checked. I had too many problems swimming around in my head. I needed to pare them down one at a time to make them manageable. I'd take on the biggest threat first: find the man who had killed my friends—Judge Conners and his wife, and Twyla. The man who might, at that very moment, be targeting me. I had to dig this La Vonn character out of his hole with a little blood and bone. After that, I'd take care of Johnny Sin for running down Black Bart and at the same time take his guns off the street.

And then I'd finally deal with Derek Sams. I had to constantly fight the urge to move Sams higher on the to-do list. But I knew once I took care of Sams my life would be irrevocably changed, and not for the better. He had me locked in a box with the restraining order and the lawsuit. I'd need time to think that one through.

Maybe Wicks was right when he said to let time muddle the issue, cool it out.

I stepped inside the Crazy Eight and I let my eyes adjust to the dark. Nigel stood at the bar, his arms and shoulders a protective shroud over a half-empty mug of cheap beer, a hungry dog protecting his food bowl. His body had the gentle sway of a skilled drunk settled in to finish his main goal in life: to drink the world dry.

I grabbed him by the scruff and yanked him along. He yelped. His hand in the mug handle jerked beer on the bar and onto the man sitting on the stool next to him.

I headed to the back door with my bellowing package. "What's going on? Let me go. Who are you? What the—"

Ralph Ledezma, in his purple satin bowling shirt and red wiry hair, yelled from behind the bar, "Hey, Karl, he hasn't paid his tab."

Blurry eyed, Nigel's wobbly head came around to look up at me. "Oh, it's you. Sweet Jesus, Karl, you scared the livin' piss right out of me." He looked down, to a widening wet spot on his crotch. He'd peed his pants the same as a scared puppy does when you raise your voice at him.

I shook my head. "Ah, man." He was going to smell up my car.

Ledezma was lying; he never let a drunk like Nigel run a tab. Ledezma would go broke if he did. But I didn't have time to deal with it. I dragged Nigel back to the bar as I reached into my pocket. I threw a crumpled twenty on the bar. Ledezma snatched it up. "Hey, he drank more than this. He's been here for hours." Another lie.

"Tough, live with it."

Outside in the bright light of day, Nigel withered. "Hey, hey, what's going on?"

I shoved him up against the wall. He didn't fight it. "Hey, Karl, my man, take it easy, would ya? These are my best duds."

Best duds? He looked like he'd been sleeping in an alley for a month.

"How much have you had to drink?" A useless question. He had not been acquainted with any part of the truth for two decades.

He brought his hand up with an accusatory finger. "You missed the meeting with Jumbo. I worked hard to get that set up. I have a reputation to protect, you know. And you—"

"Shut up and listen to me."

He shook his head. "No, sir. No. We're no longer friends, you and me. You cheated me out of twenty-five hundred—"

"Sorry, my friend, I hate to do this to you." I slugged him low in the soft part of his stomach. I held onto his scruff and stood back. He threw up several mugs of beer. Maybe Ledezma had been telling the truth about how long Nigel sat at his bar.

I held onto him and walked us around to Central Ave. where cars zipped by. He coughed and choked and sputtered and finally recovered his breath. He smelled of urine and soured eggs.

We walked on.

"Why you doin' this to me? I thought we were friends."

"Your buddies Jumbo and Johnny Sin ran over my boss with a truck. He's in the hospital fighting for life."

"Whaaaa?" He tried to stop but I dragged him along.

"Keep walking. I need you sober."

"I'm sorry, I didn't know." All of a sudden, he sounded more alert. Adrenaline could have that effect on drunks.

"Karl, I told you to be careful around these guys. I told you they play for keeps. I did. You can't say I didn't warn you."

Cars drove by on the street in the noonday rush. Pedestrians on the sidewalk gave us a wide berth.

"You're not sobering me up just to throw me out in the street under a car, are you? You know, like to get even for what Johnny did to your boss?"

"Don't be ridiculous." I stopped and pushed his back against the wall of a defunct thrift store with soaped-over windows. "Look, I need your help on another matter."

"I'm here for you, my friend. You know that." I moved my head back away from his words that carried the sour scent of fermented hops and stomach acid.

"Little Genie, you know him?"

"Yeah, sure I do. Who doesn't?"

Addicts and alcoholics lie, even ones who call you friend. It's the biggest part of their psychological makeup. They lie even when they don't have to. "No bullshit here, Nigel, this is serious business."

"I don't know what you want with him, but as of right now, right this minute, he's doin' time in the big house. He's never gettin' out. So I don't know how he can help you with this problem."

A kernel of the truth. "That's right," I said. "Good. Are you familiar with his organization? I'm looking for a gun thug who used to work for him."

He turned sheepish.

"What?" I asked.

"Is there money in it for me?"

I shoved him hard against the wall.

He brought up his hands in surrender. "Okay, okay. Sure, I can help you with this. Sure, I can."

"How do you know Little Genie's organization?" I checked over my shoulder to make sure no one came up on us. All clear.

Nobody cared if a black truck driver accosted a drunken vagrant. People went about their everyday business and diverted their attention as they passed by. I didn't recognize any threat and turned back to him.

"He was slingin' rock, that's what he was all about, that and women. He liked the ladies, kept three or four wives and a few girlfriends. He had that kind of money. I've copped from his boys before, lots of times. But he lost it all, his whole network. Poof. He tried to run it from prison, but since he's never getting out . . . well, there's just not much threat there anymore, if you know what I mean."

"Who's running it now?" I eased off him and let him stand on his own wobbly legs. He moved a little to the left and put his palm out flat on the plate-glass window for support.

"Guy over in Fruit Town, on Peach, or maybe it's Plum, I think."

"What's his name?"

"Doesn't matter, he's in jail too, pending a case. Who are you looking for? It can't be him."

"A guy named La Vonn. He was—"

"Yeah, yeah. He was close friends with Jamar Deacon when that judge gunned Deacon over in the Jungle off Crenshaw. I know, I've heard all the stories." He waved his arm. "All of a sudden all the cops on the street are askin' about this dude La Vonn."

"Yes. That's right, that's the guy. You know La Vonn?"

"No. But I heard about what happened on Crenshaw a few years back. Everyone heard about it, it's a damn legend. You hear about it? That was the day this big ape of a cop named Johnson caught up to Little Genie in this little restaurant on Crenshaw. Kicked his ass and shot him in both legs. You believe that? Shot him in both legs. They about tore the whole restaurant down doin' it, too. It was really something, man. That Johnson is some kind of knuckle-draggin' thug, I can tell you that much." He stiffened, checked the street out both ways, then said, "You can bet I'd never let him do that kinda thing to me, no sir." He made a fist. "I'd put him down with this if he ever got within a mile of me. I swear I would. Damn cops. Right, Karl?"

"Yeah, I did hear something about that fight in the restaurant. Do you know someone who can track down this La Vonn?"

"Why? What's he done?"

"He brought a stolen car into TransWorld and—hey, never mind what he's done. Can you find him or not?"

"You and me, we're friends and all, but come on, Karl, a guy's gotta eat."

"How much?"

"A grand?"

"You get this guy La Vonn fast and I'll give you five hundred. You get me a name in the next hour and I'll give you a thousand. You get the address for the place where he's laying his head in the next hour, and I get him, I'll give you two thousand. You starting to get the idea how bad I want this guy?"

With each amount I mentioned, Nigel's back straightened a little more as he continued to sober. "Okay, if you got that kind of money, are you willing to pay the guy I take you to and pay me at the same time for hooking you up to him?"

It wasn't my money. I now had control of the TransWorld bank, all the federal grant funds we had left to use for the sting. What did I care if I didn't use it to buy stolen property and instead took a dangerous felon off the street? When money talks, criminals go to jail.

"Yes, whatever it takes. I want this guy La Vonn and I want him now."

"Then what are we waiting for, come on." He took off walking in a half-stagger. I again grabbed him by the scruff and turned him around. "The car's this way, my friend."

CHAPTER FORTY-SEVEN

"Who's this guy again?" I asked Nigel. We sat in the Opel Kadett out in front of the La Sierra apartment building in Lakewood.

"His name's Turk, or Big Turk or something like that. Supposed to be a big fat dude who likes the young stuff. Midlevel dealer sells o-zees of rock. He's the guy picking up most of Little Genie's network and putting them back to work. He started out as a runner for Genie, so he'll know all the players past and present. He'll know all about Jamar Deacon, the guy the judge shot on 10th."

"I don't need to know about Jamar, I need La Vonn."

"Since this guy Turk knew Jamar, he'll know about La Vonn. But from what I hear, he's not gonna want to help you with anything. He's a real hardass. In fact, he's probably going to cause you a big problem. You might have to slap him around a little. You might want to get a few friends before you go in and brace this guy."

"I can handle him."

Nigel smirked and leaned over closer in the small confines of the Opel. "Karl, bless your little heart, you're no Bruno Johnson. I'd get a couple of friends if I were you."

This was the third place we'd tried in the last two hours, and I wasn't feeling hopeful Nigel knew what he was talking about.

"How come you didn't bring me here in the first place? Why'd we mess around with those other poobutts at those other places?"

"I just told you, this guy is a badass. He's the last resort. You go in there, the odds are he's gonna make you wish you hadn't. He'll mop the floor with you, I'm not kiddin'. It's gonna take four or five guys to get this guy to talk."

"Then you better stay here."

"Karl, trust me on this, you're outta your league."

I got out and checked up and down the street for anything out of place. Nigel got out and stood on the sidewalk. He hitched up his pants as he looked to the entrance gate.

I adjusted the .357 in my waistband under my shirt. Something wasn't right and I tried to figure out what it was.

He said again, "Hey, are you—"

I held up my hand to silence him as I stood in the street by the closed door of the Kadett. A car on Lakewood Boulevard zipped by. The street was empty now without another car coming for at least a mile, leaving the street and neighborhood semi-quiet.

That was it. The quiet. In the jungle, when an apex predator stalks its prey, the other animals/victims turn quiet. That same kind of quiet now emanated from the apartment complex.

I moved from the street up to the sidewalk. "When was the last time you were here?"

"Buddy boy, I've never been here. I got it from a guy on the street a while back who was bumpin' his gums about this place sayin' it's some kinda safe house or something like that and no one dared come close or risk getting their asses shot off. This guy told me it was the La Sierra Apartments on Lakewood Avenue number 102, that's all I know."

Nigel must've been a helluva aerospace engineer before he took the dive into crystal meth and rock cocaine. He had a memory for details when he wanted to.

"You stay out here and watch the car."

"That's okay by me. You don't have to tell me twice. No, sir, I'll stick right here, thank you very much."

I hurried through the open wrought-iron gate and noticed as I passed that the lock had been compromised. I entered the quad area of the upper-middle-class apartment complex. The quiet grew more conspicuous. All the doors to the apartments were closed and the curtains pulled. It was the middle of the day and the place was empty. Not so much as a breath of air moved in the quad filled with small shrubs and dwarf trees and flowers in tall pots.

The door to number 102 stood ajar an inch or two. Fresh bloody fingerprints from one hand marred the outside edge as if someone tried to close it in a hurry. I pulled the .357 and eased the door open.

Most everything in the small apartment was overturned or smashed. There had been a fight. A big one.

A fat naked black man wearing only a pair of white briefs lay on his back, half in the small kitchen and half in the living room. Someone had battered his face, his eyes were swollen shut, and his lips were fat as inner tubes for a small bike. His chest rose and fell like a bellows, making his lips spatter a fine mist of blood. Punctured lung maybe.

I followed my Smith and Wesson in and checked the only bedroom and bathroom before I put the gun back in my waistband and returned to the main room. My adrenaline leveled out and allowed me to view the scene as a professional cop. The furniture was overturned, some of it broken.

In the kitchen, everything on the one granite counter—dirty dishes, water glasses, a box of cereal, pizza boxes, and beer bottles—had all been swept off to the floor. Streaks of smeared blood led from the counter edge to the sink.

I looked closer at the unconscious owner to see if I recognized him, but didn't. Bad luck. But I did recognize a familiar injury. Imprinted high on his cheek under his left eye, he carried a mark only I might recognize.

Wicks.

Wicks had been here. He was running hard without me. Good. It didn't matter who got to La Vonn first, as long as someone got him.

The mark on the guy's cheek came from a custom-design LAPD SWAT ring, the one Robby Wicks always wore on his right hand. Wicks worked Los Angeles County Sheriffs, not LAPD. The ring was yet another souvenir from a previous hunt he wanted to remember.

* * *

Wicks and I had hunted down an ex-LAPD SWAT member who'd gone on a killing spree. A guy named John Singly, a sergeant upset over a recent divorce and child custody. He killed his wife and then went to his in-laws and killed them for having the nerve to produce the daughter that did him wrong. As we followed Singly's trail, getting closer by each hour, Wicks' anxiety grew. This killer was highly trained in the same art that Wicks practiced. The killer would be difficult to take down. In the quiet moments, Wicks talked about a prolonged firefight once we caught up to him.

We'd been on Singly for five days straight, gaining on him with each contact. We stopped to get gas and went inside for snacks. We stood in line, me with corn nuts and a Jolt Cola for the sugar and caffeine, and Wicks with his Tallboy beer and two Slim Jims. John Singly, as it turned out, stood in line in front of us. Singly had shaved his head. Wicks was too tired to recognize him.

I simply said, "Excuse me, sir." Singly turned. I said, "Would you please hold this?" Before he could answer, I handed him my Jolt Cola. When he took it, I yanked out my .357 and chunked him over the head. Wicks thought I'd lost my mind until I fell onto Singly's back and handcuffed him.

Not all the criminals we chased ended in blood and bone.

*   *   *

Back in the apartment, I turned to the kitchen. The cleared-off sink confirmed that it had been Wicks. When he wanted information from an obstinate witness, he'd punch the guy in the face with his LAPD SWAT ring and then drag him and his hand over to the garbage disposal. Wicks would turn on the disposal and tell the guy he'd grind his hand down to his wrist if he didn't talk. It worked every time.

I took a pitcher down from the cupboard, filled it with water, and tossed it on the fat man's face.

CHAPTER FORTY-EIGHT

THE FAT BLACK guy, flat on his back with too-tight white briefs, sputtered and coughed but didn't come around. Not good. Concussion. Probably a skull fracture.

"Sweet Baby Jesus, Karl." Nigel came into the apartment. "What did you do to him?"

"Don't be ridiculous, he was like this when I came in."

Nigel came closer. "Geez, would you look how big this guy is? Where's the harpoon?"

"Stay back. It's better if you wait outside so you don't leave any evidence."

"Who did it?"

"Doesn't matter. You know this guy?"

He moved closer, with short steps as if approaching a sleeping bear. "Nope."

A noise came from the only closet in the living room area, a muffled clunk, like shoes being shoved around. I yanked out the .357.

Nigel's eyes widened as he stumbled backward to the front door. I moved over to the closet and didn't hesitate.

"Karl, I don't like guns. I told you, I don't like guns." He put his hands over his ears, closed his eyes, and hunched over like a cartoon character waiting for the dynamite to explode. He'd be a real asset in a gunfight.

"Next time you'll do what I tell you and stay with the car."

I jerked open the door. A young black girl not more than fifteen huddled under the hanging coats. She yelped and tried to crawl deeper into the shallow closet, clawing at the back wall.

I put the gun away and got down on one knee, extending my hand. "It's okay, sweetie, it's all over. You can come out. No one's going to hurt you."

She didn't move.

"Really, it's safe now," I said. "Those bad guys are gone."

I flashed on a memory from three years ago, when Olivia huddled scared in the clothes closet of a rock house and called me for help. That was really when all the problems had started. She'd gone to the rock house with Derek Sams to pay his dope debt. Later I found it to be at the behest of a murderer I was chasing named Borkow, who wanted me distracted and used Derek and my daughter to get it done.

"I promise I'm not going to hurt you."

"We have to go, Karl, the police are going to be here any minute."

I turned and scowled at him. "Get on the phone and call 911—tell them a man is down and needs paramedics. Tell them what the guy looks like."

"That'll bring the police for sure."

"Do it, Nigel."

He jumped.

The girl heard the part about 911 and must've realized I was telling the truth. She ventured out.

"Here, give me your hand." She crawled on hands and knees. She wore only a sheer see-through red negligee. I reached up behind her and pulled down a black and gray Pendleton shirt-coat that belonged to the child molester unconscious on the floor. It was big enough for five girls her size. Tears streaked her pretty face. She wore too much makeup. It made her into a life-size Barbie doll.

I wanted to console her with a hug, but that's not what she needed at the moment, especially not from a male. She tried to walk by me, headed for the door. "Wait." I put a hand on her shoulder. "The police are coming. They'll take care of you. They'll need to talk to you, get your statement."

"No. I can't be here for the police."

She lived on the street, a runaway, probably wanted for property crimes committed to support her rock coke habit.

Nigel finished talking and hung up the phone. "They're on their way. Now we really have to skedaddle."

The young girl needed to stay so the deputies from Lakewood Sheriff station could hang a child molest case on the fat slob on the floor. But she wouldn't stay unless I did, and I couldn't afford to have Nigel hear me tell the deputies that I was an undercover detective. It would risk the viability of the TransWorld sting and ruin the roundup of all the criminals already in our net, a great loss of man-hours and money. It would also tip off the Johnny Sin and Jumbo gun deal.

"Where are your clothes? Did you come here on your own or did he force you to come here?"

She didn't answer and moved to the couch, where she grabbed up some clothes mingled among other discarded ones and again headed for the door. The Pendleton came down to her knees and wouldn't draw too much attention out in the public eye.

Nigel hurried past. "Come on, my friend, we gotta roll."

In the quad area, the apartment complex started to come back to life. Doors opened a crack, and people peeked out curtains. They would have our description, a broken-down white guy with a black truck driver escorting a half-naked black girl from the premises.

Outside at the sidewalk, she didn't say a word when I opened the door to the Opel. She got in the back and Nigel got in the front. We took off, headed west on Lakewood Boulevard. Five blocks down, a black-and-white sheriff's car whipped by with his overhead rotating red lights, no siren. Silent running, shark-like.

I missed working in a black-and-white responding to calls, not knowing what I'd find when I arrived on scene. The threat of the unknown was a huge adrenaline rush. This time they'd find no action in apartment 102. Only cleanup. And a go-nowhere assault investigation on a victim who really wasn't a victim, with a description of three people they'd never be able to track down.

I caught movement in the rearview as the girl, unabashed, took off the shirt coat and negligee and put on her clothes. Nigel leered at her over the seat. He didn't do it on purpose; he couldn't help himself in his drunken state. I shoved his face around.

"Oh, yeah, sorry. I didn't realize. Geez, what's the matter with me? Thanks, Karl."

He meant it.

She finally sat back and watched my eyes. I asked, "Where can we drop you?"

"You know Greenleaf and Atlantic?"

"Sure."

"That would be fine, thank you."

"When's the last time you ate something?"

She shrugged.

"We'll go to Lucy's first on Long Beach if that's okay with you?"

She shrugged again.

Nigel said, "Can't we go someplace that serves a libation with a little kick, or, you know, at least beer?"

"No."

"Okay, take it easy. For a minute there I thought we were friends."

CHAPTER FORTY-NINE

TEN MINUTES LATER, I pulled into Lucy's parking lot. We ordered at the walk-up window and took our food to an outdoor picnic table among others under a patio awning. The other patrons continued to talk and eat and paid us no mind.

Until the girl dug into her beef enchilada plate shoveling down the food. People at other tables whispered and threw sideways glances, pretending not to notice the spectacle.

"Careful," Nigel said. "Don't get your hands near her mouth, you'll lose a finger."

Nigel, all skin and bone, was the one who needed to eat, but he only nibbled at his bean-and-cheese burrito.

"What's your name?"

She paused in her food shoveling. "Why?"

I held out my hand. "My name's Karl."

She stared at me for a moment. "No it's not."

My heart rate shot up. "Nigel, go wait in the car. No arguments."

"But I—"

"I said no arguments."

He stood, leaving his burrito on the table. "You know, you treat your dog better than me."

I waited until Nigel closed the Opel's door, then turned back to her. "Do I know you?"

"Who really knows anybody? All of us swirl around and around in our own lives doing our own thing not giving a damn about anyone else. We come into this world alone and that's the way we go out."

She'd been on the street longer than I thought.

"That's an awfully pessimistic point of view for someone so young. Please answer the question—what's your name?"

She put down her plastic fork. "You really don't recognize me? I went to school with Olivia. You're her father, Bruno Johnson, the deputy."

Oh my God, how could that be?

"I'm sorry, I don't remember your name."

"Jessica."

I sat back on my bench seat, stunned. "Jessica Lowe?"

She nodded.

She used to be one of Olivia's best friends and had been over to our apartment in South Gate many times hanging out and doing homework. She always had a bright expression, a light in her eyes that nothing could extinguish. At least that's what I thought at the time. I hadn't seen her in a good long while. When Derek came on the scene, he pushed away all of Olivia's friends. Then with the twins, Albert and Alonzo, our lives sped up and they filled every available minute with happiness and joy that blurred the lines between hours and days and months. Those two boys left little time to ponder the past. I had not thought to even ask Olivia what had happened to her best friend.

Jessica stirred her beans and rice around. "I'm sorry about O. I only just heard about it the other day. She had so much going for her. Those wonderful kids. You know, she never used drugs. Never. It was an accident, wasn't it?"

Jessica was asking if Olivia did it on purpose. That's what the establishment had determined.

A lump rose in my throat. But it wasn't a suicide, and when I had the chance, I'd sweet-talk Derek Sams the same way I had the last time. I'd get him to tell me that he had a hand in it. That he'd done it to get even for what I'd done to his fingers. First he'd hurt Albert, then Olivia.

I reached over and lifted Jessica's chin for a better look. Tears filled her eyes. She wore too much makeup now, kept her hair long when I had always seen it short. Still, I should've recognized her. She wasn't fifteen like I thought back at the Lakewood apartment. She had to be a youthful nineteen. She had one of those childlike faces that never aged. But that wouldn't be true much longer. On the street, every dope year equals five regular ones.

"Where are your parents?"

She shrugged and went back to eating, her face hovering over the paper plate, tears dropping into her enchilada sauce.

I didn't ask her how she came to be in the apartment. I knew how easy it was to fall prey to the glass pipe. It happened to a lot of good people. Even so, I wanted to go back and kick that fat slob a few more times.

"I'd like to help you if you'll let me."

"If you have a few dollars you could spare, that would be great."

To give an addict money is the same as handing them another nail for their coffin. Until they hit rock bottom and were ready to call it quits, there wasn't much anyone could do. I took out all the folding money I had and handed it to her. She grabbed at it. I pulled it back. "Where are you staying? For real, don't lie to me."

"At the Jacaranda."

"On El Segundo off of Willowbrook?"

"Yes."

I handed her the money.

"Thanks, Mr. Johnson."

"Now tell me, who came into the apartment and did that to . . . What's his name?"

"Turk. I just know him as Turk. I think you already know who came there and did that. You're just testing me."

"Please tell me."

"It was Derek. There's something wrong with that boy. He wanted to take me right there, said he wanted to bend me over the couch and yank down my panties. But the cop with him wouldn't let it happen. The cop shoved me in the closet, closed the door, and told me not to come out."

"Then what happened?"

"You saw. They tore the place up fighting. Took both of them to take down Turk. I really didn't think they'd be able to do it."

"Did you hear anything they were saying?"

"They were yelling. The cop wanted to know where to find a guy named La Vonn."

"Did Turk tell them where to find La Vonn?"

"I don't think he knew or after all of that he would've told them. I . . . I heard the garbage disposal running. I didn't look before we left. Did they use the disposal on him?"

"No."

"Too bad. Why does everyone want La Vonn?"

"You know him?"

She shrugged. "Yeah, sure."

CHAPTER FIFTY

I SWIVELED MY head, checking out the environment yet again in the patio of Lucy's restaurant. Nobody looked out of place. Nobody could hear our conversation, at least not enough of it to matter. Nigel got out of the Kadett and walked over to a pay phone. With all the traffic on Long Beach Boulevard, he wouldn't be able to hear us either.

I turned back to Jessica. "How do you know La Vonn?"

She'd gone back to eating and paused to swallow. "Couple of years ago—that's when I got hooked on rock—I used to go down to this place on El Segundo. He hung out there."

"Where?"

"You know those burnt-out apartments? They've been there forever. Nobody ever does anything with them."

"I know the place."

"Okay, right down from there on the same side of the street is this auto body shop, the kind that specializes in crashed cars."

"What's it called?"

She shrugged. "They didn't put a whole lot of time or imagination into the name. It's called The Body Shop."

That was the place. It all fit now. When I'd talked to Little Genie in the jail, he had it wrong. He must've gotten bits and pieces of the info from someone else. When that someone told Genie the *Body*

Shop, Genie assumed, since two guys hung out there—La Vonn and Jamar Deacon—that it had to be a gym. I would have been wasting my time looking for the gym Genie described.

"This Body Shop, is it still open for business?"

She took a bite of rolled-up corn tortilla dipped in refried beans, and shrugged.

"Do you know La Vonn's first name?"

"That is his first name."

"What's his last name?"

"The one that goes with La Vonn, or his real name?"

"Please, tell me both."

"La Vonn Lofton."

"That's an aka he goes by?"

"If you mean his fake name, then yes."

"And his real name?"

She let out a half smile. "That's the reason he changed it. His real name wasn't serious enough for his image on the streets. It didn't have a hard edge like he wanted. Folks would've laughed at him. He only told me because I promised I wouldn't tell anyone. His real name's Billy Butterworth. Can you imagine a hard-core thug named Billy Butterworth?" She used the tortilla to mop up the rest of the enchilada sauce on the plate as she smiled. It was good to see her smile. She muttered again, "Huh, Billy Butterworth."

Without asking, she reached over and took my plate and slid it in front of her. I hadn't touched it. I'd lost my appetite seeing how far this beautiful girl had backslid. She talked and acted like an experienced street person when she should've been in college having fun, dating, and enjoying everything life had to offer.

She started to unwrap the yellow paper around the gargantuan burrito.

"Why did he tell you his real name?"

She broke eye contact and shrugged.

But I knew. She didn't have to say the words. Shame burned my face for even asking such an inane question.

"What's this Lofton look like?"

She stopped eating, pulled the burrito down from her mouth, and stared off in the distance as she tried to conjure him up. She turned back to me. "Average, I guess."

"Does he have any scars, marks, or tattoos?"

"That's another thing different about him. One time I asked him why he didn't have any tattoos. Every gangster has tattoos. He said, 'If you're in the life, why in the world would you want to make it easy for the cops to identify you? It's the same as a brand on a steer.'" Jessica shrugged. "To me, he made a lot of sense."

"So how tall is he?"

"Average."

"Weight?"

"Average. I'm telling you if I saw him on the street today, I don't think I could recognize him. He just blends in. That's why at first no one took him serious. That's why he went out and shot up some folks, just gunned them down for no reason at all. After he did that, you can bet people took him serious."

"Where was this? When did it happen?"

"The way the story goes, he made his bones in a bar called the La Fiesta on Compton Avenue, the one by White Street. He walked in and killed six Mexicans drinking in there. Just shot them and walked out."

I had heard about that shooting—they called it the La Fiesta Massacre. It was never solved and was an open cold case.

"Oh," she said. "You asked about scars. He's got one." She reached down and pointed to her bottom. "It's on his left butt cheek. Looks ugly like someone shot him with a big gun."

The location of that scar wouldn't help to identify him until we had him in custody, and if we had him in custody, we could check him through fingerprints.

"Can you draw the scar for me?" I took a pen out of my shirt pocket and handed it to her.

She moved aside the plastic food basket and drew on the white butcher paper covering the entire table. What she drew depicted a blob with ragged edges. I'd seen something similar before but couldn't place it.

"I'm not a very good artist but that looks a lot like it."

"Thank you."

Jessica handed the pen back, took a bite of burrito, and chewed. "I also heard he was mad as hell when that judge killed his running buddy. I know you know about that one. That judge shot Jamar Deacon up there in the Jungle off Crenshaw?"

I would never had guessed that incident on 10th would have such far-reaching repercussions. Violence is like dropping a stone in a still pond: each ripple continues on and on, ruining more lives.

"Yeah, I heard. Where does Lofton lay his head?"

"He moves around. Never stays in one place more than three nights. He said that's another part of being in the life. All he ever wanted was to be a badass street thug. Looks like he got his wish if you ask me. If you're smart, you'll stay far away from him, Mr. Johnson. He's pure poison."

"Jessica, I really appreciate you telling me all of this. One more question. If *you* were going to look for Lofton, where would you start?"

She stood abruptly, anxious to get on with running her young life full-speed into the ground. I'd crossed the line into dangerous territory. If she told me and it got back to La Vonn Lofton, he would hunt her down and make her wish she hadn't.

CHAPTER FIFTY-ONE

I SAT AT the picnic table at Lucy's restaurant, reached over, and put my hand on Jessica's. "Please?"

I was a grade A heel for putting her on the cross and asking her a question that put her at risk.

She nodded. "From what I heard he moved on, and I don't know where. Honest. That's the truth."

"Thank you, Jessica. If you ever need anything, look me up. I've moved back into the house on Nord in the Corner Pocket with my dad. You've been there before. Stop by anytime. I mean it."

Her expression shifted to neutral. "Why do you still live down here in this sewer when you don't have to? You made it out. Why come back if you don't have to?"

"This is where I grew up. This is where I belong."

"I can take care of myself. You're the one who needs to watch out. If you keep going after Billy Bee, it won't matter whether you made it out and came back, 'cause you won't be around much longer. I'm serious, he is one bad white dude."

"Wait. He's white?"

"Yeah, I thought you knew that. He's a white dude who wants to be black in the worst way. Walks and talks like a black dude."

She turned and headed down Long Beach Boulevard. She stepped to the curb, held her thumb out, and seconds later a car pulled over. In a couple more years, after the last of her youth faded, she wouldn't be able to do that anymore. Well, at least not as quickly.

La Vonn Lofton was a white dude. Probably the single most important piece of information I'd gotten out of Jessica, and I'd almost missed it.

Nigel hung up the pay phone and came back to the Kadett where I stood watching the car Jessica got into grow smaller and disappear. I wished there was more I could do for her. And I would, after things settled down. I'd take her off the street even if I had to use force. I'd put her up in a seedy motel and keep her there until she could detox.

I moved around and stood by the open car door of the Kadett on the street side. Nigel stopped on the sidewalk by the passenger door, looking over the roof.

"Are you getting in?" I asked.

"Don't think so, my friend. That scene at the La Sierra scared the water out of me. I'm afraid my nervous system now requires that I seek the closest locale that serves carbonated libations. I'd appreciate it if you could see your way to fund such an endeavor."

I kept an emergency hundred-dollar bill folded up behind my fake driver's license in my wallet. I eased the car door closed and came around to the sidewalk as I dug out the bill. With undue fervor, Nigel watched every move of my hands.

"I guess I owe you for taking me around."

"Yes. Yes, that is correct, young sir." He continued to watch my hands. "Did you glean any information of value from the girl? As we agreed, you said if I took you to anyone who gave you good information, I would be owed quite . . . a lot." Nigel unconsciously shifted to a different language and syntax when begging for money.

"I'm a man of my word. I'm leaving here to check out another place she gave me. If it pans out, I'll come find you with your money."

"I know you're honest, Karl, and that I can trust your integrity."

I started to unfold the hundred. It had been in the wallet a long time, the creases sharp and flat. If I gave him the entire hundred, I wouldn't see him for a few days, until the dope the money bought ran out. He knew it as well.

He couldn't wait for me to finish unfolding and snatched it out of my hands. He must've thought it was a twenty. When he opened it all the way, his eyes turned wet with joy as he fought back tears.

"Thank you, my friend, you are truly generous to a fault when dealing with this bedraggled old man." He started to turn to leave and took a couple of steps in what would be a beeline to the nearest meth dealer and a date with a glass pipe.

He checked himself and turned back. He pointed to the phone. "That was Jumbo. He still wants to do the deal. He said now it's just you and him. He called it 'Mano y Mano,' or some bullcrap like that. He's a real wingnut. Be real careful, Karl. I don't like the idea of dealing with guns in the first place, but making a deal with the likes of that guy isn't smart. I hope you know what you're doing. He'll be at his auto parts store whenever you're ready. Sooner is better than later, according to him."

"What about Johnny Sin?"

"I asked him about Johnny, and he wouldn't come right out and say it, but I think Jumbo's afraid of him. That's a good thing, my friend." He took a step back toward me. "You going to Jumbo's? You want me to go with you?"

"I have this other thing with La Vonn Lofton I need to deal with first. Where can I find you later?"

He opened his hand to make sure the hundred was still there and he'd not dreamt it. Ben Franklin stared up at him as he tried to decide. He came back to me and held out his hand with the bill. "Here. Hold this for me."

"You sure?"

"Just take it before I change my mind."

I took back the bill.

He said, "I'll go to the auto parts store and talk with Jumbo in person, make sure he's on the level, and set a time and place for the deal. Come by there when you get this other thing cleared up. If I'm not at Jumbo's, I'll go hang out at TransWorld and wait for you there. Check TransWorld first."

"Thanks, Nigel, I know this is hard for you"—I held up the hundred— "but it's the right decision."

He ran a shaking hand through his greasy hair. "Please. Please just take your leave. Get out of here before I change my mind."

CHAPTER FIFTY-TWO

I STARTED TO make my first pass of The Body Shop on El Segundo to check for furtive bad guys or lookouts and spotted Wicks' Ford Taurus out front. I pulled in behind it. He'd beat me to yet another location. It sparked a hard pang to be with him on this hunt instead of trailing in his wake of carnage. If I'd been with him now, as in the past with these types of situations, we would have had a chance to glean the information without violence. I tended to use words instead of force, but at the same time realized the need for both. Something Wicks didn't understand. In his world, he was a hammer and everyone else was a nail.

I still craved his comradery.

We were far more effective working together. During this manhunt, for reasons I couldn't fathom, Wicks was more out of control. He had never taken an informant along while making contact. It was wrong for two reasons. First, the informant was burned, because the contact would know who ratted him out. And second, he had no one watching his back. He had to watch the informant—Derek Sams in this case, whom he couldn't trust—and the contact. Tactically it came out all kinds of wrong.

I got out and eased the car door shut as a muffled shriek came from inside the office. I pulled the .357 and held it by my leg. The front glass door had mini blinds, so I couldn't see in. I pulled the door open and entered fast.

Wicks yelled, "I said leave her alone."

Derek Sams had his back to me as he forced a woman up against the customer counter. He had a hand full of the woman's dress and bunched-up bra underneath tugging hard at her breasts. The woman was pale as white paint and about to collapse under the onslaught of the sexual battery. Sams didn't see or hear me come in; his sexual depravity had him by the throat.

I stepped over and pistol-whipped him across the back of the head. Maybe a little too hard. He collapsed to the floor the same as if I flipped off a light switch. The frightened woman slid down the front of the counter to the floor and scrambled away on all fours, tearing up her pantyhose on the rough tile grout. She reached up to the doorknob to a side exit, opened it, and crawled out into the shop. I should've consoled her, but rage ruled the day.

Three men in dark blue work jumpsuits stood out in the bays. All of them were scared and ready to bolt. When they saw the woman crawl out, they fled out to the sidewalk and down the street.

Back in the office, Wicks stood on the other side of the counter with a hand filled with the dress shirt and tie of the manager, who had a nameplate pinned to his shirt that said, "Manager/Owner Joseph Morgan."

Wicks, looking over his shoulder, had seen me neutralize Sams. "Ah, man, why'd you go and do that? Now I'm gonna have to kiss his ass all over again. I hate tellin' that little puke I'm sorry. Good to see you, Bruno."

I leaned over and patted Sams down for weapons.

"You're wastin' your time," Wicks said. "He's not strapped."

I found a Raven .25 auto in his sock and held it up for Wicks to see.

"That little son of a bitch. I patted him down, I swear I did, Bruno." Wicks still had not let go of Manager Joe.

I tossed Wicks the Raven. He caught it with one hand and shoved it in his suit coat pocket. "Mr. Body Shop here was about to tell me where to find La Vonn. Weren't you?" He turned his attention back to Manager Joe.

"I already told you everything I know."

I said, "You mean about La Vonn Lofton?"

"His last name is *Lofton*?" Wicks said. He shook Manager Joe some more. "How come you didn't tell me his last name?"

"Robby, ease up on him, he's just a businessman trying to get along."

Wicks shifted his grip and grabbed onto the man's tie. "That right?" he said to me. "Come and have a look-see." He led his captive into the back office, dragging him along by the tie.

I stepped over an unconscious Sams spread out on the floor like a rag doll. The memory of that chunk I gave to his head, the way it vibrated through my hand and up my arm, gave me a twinge of satisfaction. I fought the urge to expand on that wonderful sensation with a boot to his face, something I'd regret not doing later. Instead, I followed my ex-boss, partner, and friend into the back room. I passed the door to the work area where the woman had fled, and closed it. The woman had recovered her running legs and was no longer in sight. Someone was going to call the police. We didn't have much time. If we stayed, we'd be stuck for hours explaining and filling out reports.

In the back office, Wicks stood by a large polished desk, still holding Manager Joe by the tie, his face going red and bloating.

"You better ease off him or he's going choke out."

"Never mind him; come on over here and take a gander at this."

I came around the desk. A small safe stood open and held a couple stacks of cash and some Ziploc bags that had to contain several ounces of rock coke. Maybe nobody *would* call the police.

"What we got here," Wicks said, "is a midlevel operation. That's why Deacon and Lofton hung out at this place as muscle. I was just discussing a trade with John Q." He shook Joe Manager by the tie again. "He gives me La Vonn Lofton and I give him a walk on all that's happened today inside his fine establishment. You think that's a fair deal, Bruno?"

"More than fair. The dope alone is five to seven in the joint, and if you throw in the money laundering, which I'm sure he's doing through this less-than-legitimate Chamber of Commerce–awarded business, well, I think he's gonna get another ten years from the feds."

Wicks shook Manager Joe. "See? Didn't I tell you almost exactly the same thing word for word?"

The man tried to talk and couldn't; the tie was cinched too tight. "You better ease up or this whole thing is going to get real difficult to explain."

Wicks let go. The man struggled to get his tie loosened. He put both hands on the desk to support his shaking knees and took in large chest-fulls of air. The red in his face started to fade.

Wicks' tone turned serious. "Now, tell me where to find Lofton."

I said, "You mean *Billy Butterworth*."

The man's head whipped around.

Wicks punched him in the stomach. "What's this you say? Did you lie to me about Lofton's real name, again?" Wicks pulled his cuffs from his belt and cuffed the man behind his back.

The man sputtered and coughed. "Wait. Don't, please don't. I'll tell you everything I know; I promise I will."

Wicks grabbed him by the arm and started to haul him out.

"No. No, please don't. I'll tell you the truth this time, I swear."

"Wait," I said. "Give him one more chance."

"Yes. Yes, like he said, one more chance, please?"

Wicks stopped. "Spill it."

"Okay. The last address I had for Lofton—"

Wicks jerked the man's arm.

"Okay, okay, it's apparently Butterworth," Manager Joe said. "I swear I didn't know his real name was Butterworth. Lofton, Butterworth, or whatever his real name is—he lives at the La Sierra Apartments on Lakewood Boulevard, number 102. He's got some rock there, more than I got, and a lot of money, a lot more than I have. He's the guy *I* cop from."

Wicks grabbed the man by the throat and shoved him up against the wall. "We just came from there, and guess what?"

"That's the only address I have, I swear. That's all I got on him is that address. You have to believe me."

"You haven't told the truth since I walked in here, so why should I believe you?"

"Wait. Okay, okay, there is something else. It's not much, but I heard something on the street. I don't know if it's true or not."

"What? This better be good."

"I heard from someone that Lofton was seen going into a high-dollar fence over in Lakewood, a place called TransWorld Logistics."

"So?"

"This TransWorld is buying up anything and everything on the street and paying top dollar. Everybody from miles around has gone to this place one time or another. Everybody's talking about it. All the other fences are getting mad as hell about it. Check there for Lofton. Check out this TransWorld place. You won't regret it. If he's not there, they can tell you where to find him. Those guys are a much bigger fish than I am."

My heart took off at a run. The man just fed Wicks a giant bone, one Wicks would never let go. He'd go to TransWorld with the intent of tearing it down to the ground. He'd screw everything up for sure.

Wicks turned to me. "What do you think, Bruno? You think he's telling it straight this time?"

"No, but do we have a choice? Let him go. Let's get out of here."

CHAPTER FIFTY-THREE

WICKS SAID, "YEAH, you're right."

I took hold of Joe Manager and escorted him through the side door that led into the shop area and the three repair bays.

Wicks followed along. "Hey, what are you doing?"

The manager was a midlevel dealer responsible for putting a lot of dope out on the street. He'd been doing it for a while. I had never gone back on my word with a crook. I never dealt away something I wasn't willing to give up. Times change. Olivia had died of an overdose, and the sight of Jessica Lowe sitting across from me at the picnic table at Lucy's was too fresh in my mind. Her ruined life and what the rock had turned her into. Rock had forced her to sell herself to the likes of that fat slob Turk.

I didn't answer Wicks and pulled the owner along. Out in the closest bay, I unlocked the handcuff on one hand and cuffed him to a steel loop on the hydraulic lift that held a crunched Toyota sedan high in the air. While Wicks watched, I moved to the phone on the wall and dialed the Lynwood Sheriff station's Watch Deputy number.

"Lynwood Sheriff's Station, Deputy Baldwin."

"Listen, Baldwin, take this down. This is Detective Bruno Johnson. Get a unit out to The Body Shop. It's a business on El Segundo about a mile west of Wilmington. There's a man down, and another one handcuffed out in the shop. There's three ounces of rock coke in the office and cash in the open safe." I hung up.

"What the hell?" Wicks said. "You know you just impersonated a law enforcement officer, right?"

I shrugged. "We can't keep leaving a trail of blood and bone behind us; the brass will figure us out." I hadn't used a heavy hand except with Sams, and he didn't count—he never saw what hit him. I wanted to let Wicks know I was with him all the way on this one, but he had to know there was a line I wouldn't cross. "I'm headed to TransWorld. You coming with me?"

A large smile broke across his face. He punched me in the arm. "Now we'll get this son of bitch Lofton for sure."

"Yep."

He hooked his thumb over his shoulder to the open office door. "What about dipshit? He's going to be madder than a hatter after what you did. I'll never be able to walk him back from that ledge."

"You don't need him anymore, you got me. We got the final piece to the puzzle with this TransWorld lead."

And we did, too. We could check RD's meticulous bookkeeping, the black three-ring binders, and find the deal Lofton made with TransWorld, his photo, his RAP sheet, the whole thing.

Wicks shrugged. "You really think so?"

"I'm sure of it."

"Then we might as well make his day, huh?" He took the Raven .25 from his pocket and tossed it through the open door. It landed on the prostrate Derek Sams' back.

I smiled and held out my hand. Wicks shook it. We hurried out to our cars. I yelled, "Let's drop mine in the parking lot of MLK."

Wicks gave a salute, got in, and took off with me close behind.

The entire drive, I tried to visualized Wicks' face when I told him about TransWorld—when I told him I had lied to him about resigning from the Sheriff's Department and how I had failed to bring him into my confidence when he came to bail me out for the stolen Monte Carlo arrest. I squirmed in the seat as stomach acid rose up in my throat. He'd falsely assume I'd played him for a fool and nothing more. Something you didn't do with Wicks. Not without making him a permanent enemy.

Ten minutes later, he pulled in and stopped at the far outer perimeter to the clustered cars in the parking lot of Martin Luther King Hospital. I parked the Opel in a slot without any other cars around. The only people present that we could see over the tops of cars stood by the emergency entrance fifty yards away, milling around, little steam engines puffing cigarettes, hoping for a favorable outcome for their loved ones who suffered inside the meat market.

I got out and stood in front of Wicks' Taurus. He stuck his head out the driver's window. "What the hell's the matter with you? Are you going to get in?"

"Come out here a minute. I need to tell you something."

He opened his door. "God damnit, Bruno, we're burning daylight." He got out and slammed his door. "We don't need any touchy-feely shit right now. We're gaining on this asshole, and I got a good feeling about this. It's going to be like the good old days. You and me are going to catch this guy before that whole task force that's after him even has a clue."

"That's what I need to talk to you about."

"Okay, talk."

I gave him a half-kidding smile. "Can you first lock your gun in your trunk?"

"What? Quit messing around and tell me what's going on."

I held up both my hands. "Take it easy and don't get mad."

"Quit dickin' around or I will get mad."

"Okay, here's the deal." The words fled my brain without leaving a note when they'd be back.

"You going to tell me, or are we going to get in the car and get back to work?"

"I was sworn to secrecy. I want you to know that up front."

Wicks put his foot up on the bumper. "Now I know I'm not going to like this. We're supposed to be friends, and friends don't keep secrets. Tell me."

I cringed. "I never resigned. I've been a deputy all this time working undercover."

His back stiffened and he stared at me with his foot still up on the bumper. "That's your big revelation?"

"Yeah."

"Sure, I'm hurt that you didn't tell me, but I'm not some kind of ogre. If they swore you to secrecy then what's the big deal here, huh? Wait, you're not investigating me, are you?"

"What? No, not at all. Man, am I glad you're not ripping my head off right now. You can't know how it tore me up not being able to tell you."

"Your dad know?"

"No. No one except the Deputy Chief and the guys I'm working with."

"Well, if your dad doesn't even know, then I have no right to be mad, now do I? You tell your dad everything."

"Good."

"Why are you telling me this now?"

"I've been working at TransWorld. It's a federally funded grant sting that—"

Wicks punched me in the mouth. The blow staggered me backward and for a second made lights flicker behind my eyes. He followed it up swinging low, giving me body shots that thudded into my abdomen and knocked the wind out of me.

I put a hand on his face and violently shoved him away. I followed in close and gave him my best haymaker. It caught him high on the cheek.

That shut him down.

He staggered back and swayed on his feet, almost going to his knees. His hand went to his face and came away. He examined it for blood.

Breathing hard, I shifted my stance, with raised fists as I lowered my center of gravity preparing for him to come in again.

He'd used his left for the sucker punch to the face or I'd have had the LAPD SWAT ring imprinted on my cheek. "What was that for?" I yelled. "What's the matter with you?"

He took two angry steps toward me. His right elbow, out of instinct, swept back his suit coat to clear the stock to his Colt .45 for a quick draw. He pointed his finger at me. "You should've told me about working for LAPD. They're the enemy. You're working for the enemy."

"Don't be ridiculous. Sure, there's always been some friendly competition going on, but they're not the enemy."

"That gig, that sting, it's being run by Jim Barlow, Black Bart."

"That's right. How do you know who's running it? It's supposed to be a secret."

"Yeah, well, it's not as big of a secret as you think, bucko. The Deputy Chief told me all about it; he just neglected to tell me you'd been sent there TDY. And the Chief not telling me is chickenshit. He knows about you and me, that we only work together."

"What difference does it make? Who's Jim Barlow to you?"

"That's none of your damn business."

I flashed on a memory standing in front of Black Bart's desk with him being insistent that I not tell Wicks about the sting. He made me promise. I thought it odd at the time. I knew Wicks would keep it quiet—he'd take it to his grave if asked. I thought Bart just didn't know Wicks. Out of loyalty, I complied with Bart's demand of complete secrecy. Now it looked like Bart had been using me as a pawn to get back at Wicks. That's why Bart had chosen me for the sting in the first place. I liked Bart a little less for it.

"Tell me. What's it about?"

"If you wanna know, we were friends once. Just like you and me *used to be*. Not anymore, buddy boy. Not after this."

I waited for him to tell the rest. I could see he wanted to get it all out.

Some tension finally left his body. "We were real tight. 'Used to be' are the operative words here for the both of you now."

"What happened?"

"What happened? What always happens, a girl got in the way. And leave it at that."

"Who, Greta?"

His expression shifted to shock that I would've guessed her name, but he recovered quickly. "Yeah, *Greta*." When he said her name, his expression shifted yet again from anger to dazed and confused. I'd never seen this one on him before. I hadn't worked with him for a while, though, and people change, sometimes rapidly.

"So I guess you haven't heard," I said.

"What?" He quickly came toward me. "Tell me."

"We . . . I mean me and Black Bart had this gun deal set to go, a big one. It was with a punk named Johnny Sin. Sin didn't like the look of Black Bart and wanted to work with me exclusive."

"Yeah, and?"

"This morning Black Bart was coming to work on his Harley. Johnny Sin ran him off the road. Bart's in Daniel Freeman in critical condition."

Wicks ran for his car door. I hurried and got in the passenger seat just in time, dragging my foot to get the door closed as he took off spinning the tires and slewing the Taurus' rear end.

CHAPTER FIFTY-FOUR

I PULLED THE review mirror around and checked out the swelling on my cheekbone under my left eye, gingerly touching the painful, puffy spot. Wicks put his hand on my head and shoved me away, still angry. He moved the mirror back in place. He worked his jaw with his hand. "You really got me good with that one, pal o'mine. I think some of my teeth are loose."

"You going to tell me the rest of it?" I asked.

"I told you, it's none of your damn business."

I waited it out and stared him down.

"There's nothing to tell, so quit giving me the evil eye."

I didn't let up.

He drove, weaving too fast in and out of traffic, periodically checking to see if I'd eased off the stare. Twice he pulled into opposing traffic to get around a slow car.

"Okay," he said. "Way back, me and Barlow, we were friends. We worked a narcotics task force together . . . that was when I first made detective."

He said nothing else, his eyes making rapid movements as he mentally returned to an era long past. His foot eased up on the accelerator.

"That's all you're going to give me?"

"Ah, hell. We got along better than good. We were like brothers. We tore up the street. We drank hard and played hard and worked harder. We were lovin' life."

"He's pretty religious."

His head whipped around. "He wasn't back then. When the task force ended . . . well, it wasn't really ending as much as the bosses wanted to separate us. That's what it really came down to. We were too proactive, and because of it, we got into some real action."

In all the years we worked together, he'd never talked about this, the genesis of the job that made him into what he was, a man chasing violence.

"Me and Jim took down a lot of hard-core assholes who didn't want to go to jail. You of all people know how that goes; it creates a lot of paperwork for the brass and fodder for the media hyenas."

He turned silent and watched the road.

"What about Greta?"

"He met . . . we met her during a surveillance. Her daddy owned an apartment building she managed on the side while she attended school. We wanted to use an empty apartment to watch a target across the street. She was going to UCLA and had the apartment down the hall from where we'd set up. We saw a lot of her in those two weeks. She liked to hang around. You know, the Double-O-Seven syndrome."

He again turned silent, lost in reminiscence.

Greta was older than I first thought, and it didn't make sense her having two young children. Earlier at the hospital when Greta came close, took hold of my arm, and made her demand for vengeance, her youthful appearance threw me off. I had naturally thought she was much younger than her husband, Black Bart, and that they'd gotten a late start on their family.

"And?"

"And, nothing. Like I said, me and Barlow, we were tight when the brass tried to break us up as a team. They reassigned me and left him working dope on that same team. I . . . I went as far as applying to LAPD, a lateral transfer from the Sheriff's so we could work together again, that's how tight we were. When we worked together, I knew every move he was going to make before he did. We were like twin brothers."

I knew what he meant. Ned and I were like that before Ned was shot and killed by a teenage rock dealer during the service of a narcotics search warrant. His absence led to a huge void that had finally begun to fade, but it would never fully dissipate. And I didn't want it to.

Wicks had tried to steer the conversation away from Greta.

"Then what happened?"

"What do you mean then what happened?"

I said nothing and waited.

He turned up Alameda, gunning the Taurus.

"Greta," I said. "What happened with Greta?"

He slowed his words and lowered his tone. "Greta ruined him. She was going to school studying theology. She wanted to be a minister." He took his eyes off the road to glance over at me. "She was the one who really split us up, not the brass."

"Did she finish her degree? Did she become a minister?"

I thought about her last words to me, her request for vengeance: *Wreck 'em.* I didn't think I'd ever forget her expression. She said it with such hate, such vehemence, without one iota of forgiveness.

"How should I know? We had this big row . . . over . . ."

"Over what?"

"Never mind what it was over. We split and I never talked to either one of them again. That was twenty-five years ago."

I didn't want to push him any harder.

I had plenty enough to think about with my own issues, so I let Wicks brood for the rest of the trip. Twenty minutes later, we pulled into the parking lot of Daniel Freeman Hospital.

Ten minutes after that we got off the elevator in ICU. A slim nurse with brown hair dressed in blue and pink flowery scrubs at the nursing station tried to stop us. "I'm sorry, you can't come in here." Wicks kept walking, not even glancing at her.

I grabbed his arm. "Show her your badge or she's going to call security." I would've shown her mine but I wasn't carrying one.

He grunted, reached inside his suit coat, pulled out his flat badge wallet, flashed it, and kept going.

"Please excuse his manners," I said. "James Barlow is a good friend of his. We're here to talk to him about what happened."

"Oh, I'm sorry. James Barlow is in room 610. I don't know if he's awake; he's just down from surgery. His family is in there now."

"Thank you." I hurried to catch up. Wicks slowed at each open door and peered in, being a rude dog violating each occupant's privacy. I passed him. He followed. I entered 610 to find Greta sitting by Black Bart's bed holding his hand. Two young children about seven years old sat in chairs busy coloring in Bugs Bunny and the Road Runner. Both were Asian, probably Chinese. Jason and Darlene. They had to be adopted, and it answered a lot of questions. The Barlows had started a family late.

Wicks stepped around me and froze. Greta stood and stared at him. She let go of her husband's hand, gently replaced it on the bed, and slowly walked toward Wicks. He opened his arms. She put her head against his chest, her eyes closed with tears leaking out. Wicks, with his eyes closed tight, rested his head on the top of hers. He took in a deep breath through his nose, taking in her scent.

I stood there, an alien from a distant planet, trespassing in a place where I had no business. I took two steps backing up, turned, and exited. Down the hall came a well-built, uniformed LAPD officer who had two stripes on his arms, a P-2. This had to be the department liaison checking up on their downed officer.

From afar, the officer's eyes locked on me, again making me the intruder. Somehow even more so. Ten feet away and still coming, my jaw dropped all on its own. The officer's mannerisms, his forehead, his eyes, made me flash on a Robby Wicks from days of old, a much younger Robby Wicks. A clone.

He stopped in front of me, his hands down at his sides, loose at the ready. "Excuse me," he said. "I saw you come out of this room. What business do you have here?"

The nameplate on his uniform read "J. Barlow."

CHAPTER FIFTY-FIVE

OUTSIDE JAMES BARLOW's room I extended my hand to LAPD officer J. Barlow. "Bruno Johnson. I'm real sorry about all of this. How is your father doing? He is your father, right?"

His expression shifted, from solemn to a hint of a smile. And out peeked Wicks again. Unmistakable. I tried hard not to stare. Same color eyes. This had to be the source of the big row Wicks spoke of, the one that broke up the partnership.

"Yes, he is. My mother told me about you. Dad was in surgery for four hours. We won't know how much mobility will be lost for a couple of days. Is there any news on who did this?"

"I have a few leads on the driver."

"Excellent. Are they good ones?"

"I think so."

He reached up, unbuttoned his pocket, took out his business card, and handed it to me. I read it. He was assigned to the elite Metro Division, the place SWAT worked from. SWAT chooses their team members exclusively out of Metro. You had to have your game wrapped tight just to get in Metro. Most everyone in the division waited their turn for a shot at being on the teams.

"I'd like to ask a big favor," he said.

I held up my hand to stop him. "I know what you're going to ask—and it's not a good idea for you to be in on the takedown. I think you know why."

He lost his smile and moved in closer. "Wouldn't you want to be in on taking this guy off the street if it was your father lying in there?"

I had become close friends with the kind of emotions he described. I'd gone after Derek Sams, caught him, and crushed his fingers getting him to admit the worst, the most heinous crime he could have perpetrated upon my family. I now lived with the aftermath of that decision that tore me up inside and went against the strong moral values my father worked so hard to instill. I had trampled all over them.

And yet, all I could think about was going back and finishing the job. That desire got in the way of all logical thinking.

"A P-2 in Metro," I said. "Black Bar . . . I mean, your father must be real proud."

That backed him off and took away the sheen of the vengeance in his eyes. "I know what you're trying to do," he said. "I still want in."

I wouldn't be able to stop Wicks from doing what Wicks did best. He was going to drop the La Vonn manhunt and go after Johnny Sin. I would have done the same—deal with Johnny first.

"I'm having the truck held for forensics and—"

"You've recovered the truck? That's great. My dad speaks highly of you, and I can see why. Who's the suspect?"

"I'm not going to tell you his name. There was a blond wig on the front seat that matches with what happened. I know who did this, and as soon as the fingerprints come back from the truck, I'll be able to get an arrest warrant."

"If you know who, then you have to have enough for a probable cause arrest."

"Aah, maybe, but if I arrest him now, I won't have any evidence, and the case will have to depend on a confession until the fingerprints come back. I know this guy; he's not going to give it up. After an arrest, I'd have to have the fingerprints back in forty-eight hours or he's going to skate right out the same door he came in. You know how all this works."

If there were any fingerprints to be found in the truck. Johnny Sin could've been wearing gloves. And so far, Johnny Sin had not made one wrong move.

"We take him down, I'll walk the prints through myself. I have a friend in Cal ID."

I took him by the arm and glanced over my shoulder as I pulled him aside. "Okay, look, if I bring you into this thing, you have to promise me you'll do exactly as I say, when I say it."

This was a bad idea, but I understood what he was feeling. If I let him in, I'd at least have a chance of controlling what happened. If I didn't, he'd go out on his own and that would definitely screw everything up.

He nodded. "No problem, I'll do whatever you say. Thank you for this."

"I'm making a big mistake here and—" I just realized why Black Bart had made me promise not to do the gun deal. It wasn't to protect me. He didn't want his son to be in on the takedown; he knew hot emotions during violent confrontations ruined careers.

"What?"

"This guy I'm talking about is very, very good. There might not be any fingerprints in that truck. I haven't had the time to check, and now that I think about it, my guess is the truck's going to be clean."

"But you do know who it is? You're sure?"

"I'm sure."

"Then we can—"

"Just hold it a minute. Before your dad went into surgery, he made me promise I wouldn't do this gun deal and—"

"You have a gun deal in place with this puke?"

"Yes, and if we can't make him on what he did to your dad, then we can put him away for a long time on these guns, twenty or thirty years."

The only problem was that I gave my word to Black Bart that I wouldn't do it. But the situation had changed. I had to do the gun deal to control his son. That's what Bart would want if he were conscious and I had a chance to talk to him. At least that's what I wanted to believe.

James Barlow Jr.'s jaw muscle knitted and he spoke through clenched teeth even though he tried not to. "Don't worry about making the case on what he did to Dad. We get him in custody for the guns, he'll cop out to what he did. I promise you that."

"This is a bad plan."

He took hold of my arm and squeezed, his eyes looking down into my soul.

"Okay, I get it." I peeled his hand off my arm. "Can you have six members from your team on standby, and I mean on a moment's notice?"

He smiled. "I can have as many people as you need suited up and waiting for the phone call."

"They need to be heavily armed. This is a gun deal for military-grade weapons. A lot of them."

"You don't have to worry about that."

"I know this guy. Once the deal's set, he's not going to give me any time to set a trap, so there's not going to be any preplanning. This is going to be a run-and-gun takedown."

"I understand."

And I did too. One of LAPD's finest went down under the truck of a bad guy and they'd move heaven and earth to make it right. As much as I despised Johnny Sin, I wouldn't want to be him in the next twenty-four hours.

"I'm leaving here right now and going to set the deal."

He nodded, took a cell phone from his pocket, and stepped away.

"Wait, he might not set it up for a day or two. I don't know what he has in mind. I'll push to get it done though, tonight."

He held up his hand as he spoke quietly into the phone. He understood and didn't care. He'd have his people in place even if it took standing ready in shifts and sleeping in their cars on their own time.

I turned back to look into room 610. Wicks had moved over close to the hospital bed and stood next to the unconscious Black Bart, holding his hand. Wicks wasn't one to show his emotions.

CHAPTER FIFTY-SIX

WICKS CAME OUT of the hospital room in a rush headed for the door. He didn't give James Barlow Jr. a second look. He grunted an acknowledgment more at the uniform than the man in it. Did Wicks even know? Couldn't he see the resemblance? I skip-stepped to keep up with him. "Where are you going?"

He didn't answer in his headlong mission to burn down the man who dared cross the line into his world. Halfway to the nurses' command and control area, I grabbed his arm and spun him around. "Wait."

He shrugged out of it. "What?"

"Where are you going?"

Nurses and doctors froze at our raised voices.

"I'm going to TransWorld to get the information on this punk and then I'm going to hunt him down. What did you think I was going to do? You're welcome to come as long as you stay out of my way and don't give me any holier-than-thou crap about policy and procedure."

"No, you're not. No cops are allowed on-site at TW. You know how stings work. Someone sees you, you'll burn the whole operation."

He stepped in close, his breath hot with the burnt scent of the little brown cigarettes he constantly smoked. He pointed back to the room. "You think that matters now? You think a sting is more important than what happened to that cop in there?"

"No, of course not. But you're not thinking straight."

"Oh, is that right, buddy boy? Well, enlighten me. But you got about five seconds, then I'm gone."

I lowered my voice. "What? Are you planning to just run him down and gun him?"

"I can't believe you're even asking me that."

"Do you trust me?"

He hesitated, then broke eye contact, uncomfortable with the question.

I said, "Not an hour ago, I told you I've been working this sting. I'm the one who told you about all this, remember? I'm the one dealing with this guy, Johnny Sin, and I'm here to tell you right now we got dick on him. No intel. You running out to the sting site will burn it to the ground. Johnny Sin gets wind of it and he'll disappear. We won't have any clue where to look for him."

Wicks' expression shifted as he realized what I said made a lot of sense. "All right, you talk like you have a plan. What is it?"

"I'll go and talk to Jumbo. Johnny Sin works for him. I'll set up this gun deal. I'll make sure Johnny is at the deal. We take the guns down and get Johnny Sin at the same time."

"Oh, so that way you get to protect your precious sting program."

"Don't talk like that. You know better."

"How long?"

"I won't know until I talk to Jumbo, but if you go off half-cocked, it's going to screw up everything."

"What am I supposed to do in the meantime, sit on my thumbs?"

"If you want to keep busy, you can chase down La Vonn Lofton, take some of your pent-up aggression out on that case while I get this other thing set up."

He thought about it for a second. "Okay, I'll give you twenty-four hours. But the last lead on Lofton is at the sting, remember? The Body Shop guy said word on the street was that Lofton was doing deals there. That's all we got."

"Give me your cell phone."

He handed it over. I dialed RD at TransWorld.

Rodney Davis picked up.

"It's Karl," I said. "Talk to me."

"We got the truck. I went out there myself and stood by while it was processed. The interior was wiped clean. I had them tow it back to their shop to check the entire exterior in case this guy didn't glove-up until he got in. I know it's a long shot. I'm also backtracking where the truck was stolen in case someone saw something when the guy took it. I got LAPD all over that. They really want a piece of this investigation. If they get anything, I'll call you direct. Are you carrying your cell? Probably not."

I ignored his last comment. "Okay, write this down, it's something different. Do you remember a deal at the counter of TW with a guy named La Vonn Lofton?"

"Why? Does this Lofton have something to do with what happened to Black Bart? Shouldn't we be—"

"No, stay focused here. Yes or no on Lofton?"

"No, doesn't ring any bells. Hold on, let me get my criminal index." Background noise came over the phone as he moved to the long table he used for a desk and where he kept the three-ring binders listing all the TW customers.

"Nope, not here."

"What about William Butterworth?"

"Nope. I know I'd recognize *that* name. This guy could be one of the John Does that we haven't been able to identify, thirty-six at last count. What's with this guy Lofton or Butterworth? Why aren't you working on Johnny Sin? He's our main focus."

I ignored the question. "Do a full workup on the Lofton and Butterworth names, then call back on this phone and give all the information to Lieutenant Wicks. You got it?"

"Yeah, I got it. I guess it's better than doing nothing. Where are you going to be?"

"I'm going over to Harry—" I'd almost made a huge mistake and said the name of the auto parts store in Norwalk in front of Wicks. "I'm going to meet Jumbo."

"You're taking someone with you, right? A cover team? You're not going alone, Karl."

I turned to look at Wicks. "No, you're right. I'm taking someone to cover. Get back to us as soon as you can."

"I'm on it."

I closed Wicks' flip phone and handed it to him. "I'm going to meet Jumbo to set the gun deal. You want to stand by as cover?"

"Hell yes."

CHAPTER FIFTY-SEVEN

I DROVE THE circuit around Harry and Sons Oil to Nuts three times, scoping it out. Wicks sat in his car next to a gas station market five blocks away, chain-smoking his little brown cigarettes. If he didn't see my car drive out of the mixed-use light industrial area in twenty minutes, he was to roll in. He'd come to the counter, flash his badge, and ask a mundane question unrelated to Jumbo, Johnny Sin, or the guns.

With the sun low on the horizon headed for dusk, I didn't clock anything out of the ordinary in the area, and parked the Opel in the slot right in front of the store's double doors. No other cars in the parking lot meant they didn't get a lot of legitimate business. Old posters advertising car parts and supplies from several manufacturers plastered the windows, making it impossible to see inside. I got out and spotted three cameras under the eaves that covered the entire parking lot and the street approach.

Inside was similar to the false front at TransWorld: four aisles filled with cheap car accessories, oil, tools from China, air fresheners, floor carpets, and the like. Dust covered everything. The place smelled of burnt marijuana and body odor.

Jumbo stood at the counter, smiling. He had a long face that made his ears look bigger. He had age lines in his cheeks and at the corner of his mouth from smiling too often, a million false smiles meant to fool his opposition. "Good to see you, Karl. I didn't think we'd ever get this thing done." He waved his arm. "Welcome to my humble establishment. Come on around back. I got some twenty-year-old scotch."

I stopped at the counter. "There's no one else in the store, so let's do this here."

Behind him a wide opening revealed part of the big warehouse room in the back where lots of eight-foot-tall shelves were filled with parts in boxes open at the top.

He still smiled and casually let his hand drag off the counter out of view. I stuck my hand under my work shirt and tapped the counter with my other finger. "Put it back. Keep them where I can see them."

His smile broadened. He complied and put his hands flat. "Hey, hey, what's with all the hostility? We're friends, ain't we? Friends just tryin' to do a little business. We don't need any kind of threats, do we?" He lifted his hands and held them wide from his body.

I glanced up at the clock with a camera mounted in the wall next to it and then back at him. "Where's Johnny?"

"He and I, we don't, ah . . . get along anymore."

"That's not what I heard. I heard you're just the mouth and he's really the shot caller."

He lost his smile and leaned forward, putting his hands back flat on the counter. "I don't know who you been talking to, but you got your information all wrong. Now, are we going to talk turkey or are you going to get the hell outta my store?"

"I think I'd feel more comfortable if Johnny was out here where I can keep an eye on him. I know he's back there watching."

"He's not—"

I yanked my .357 and rested it on the counter, the barrel pointed at his chest. If you didn't want them to think you were a cop, you couldn't act like one.

He slowly raised his hands. "We don't need to do it this way."

"So you're saying you don't know anything about what Johnny did this morning?"

He shook his head, doing a good imitation of an ignorant fool. A cunning fool.

"Johnny ran down my boss with a stolen truck."

He pretended to be surprised.

"Don't," I said. "I'm not buying it."

His smile shifted, this time to a grin, no teeth. "You don't look like you're all broke up over your boss going down."

"Maybe I'm not. But I'm worried that if you'd do that to him, what do you have in mind for me?"

"You're who we really wanted to work with. Your boss was—"

Johnny Sin stepped out from the other room. He wore a security guard's outfit, a light-blue uniform shirt with dark blue pockets and a cheap tin badge. The shoulder patches said "Olympia Security." He wore the matching bus driver–type hat low over eyes concealed with green aviator sunglasses. I'd come to recognize him now by his cheekbones and mouth, the line of his jaw. He rested his hand on the stock of a black automatic pistol in his holster. "For the record, I had nothing to do with any kind of hit-and-run."

I fought the urge to reach across the counter, grab him by the throat, and throttle him for what he'd done to my friend. He held all the cards. I had to play it smart.

I said, "I don't trust either one of you fools. I'm only here because I think we'd both make a lot of money if the price is right on those guns. Now let's get to it or I'm walking out of here." I glanced up at the clock: six minutes left before Wicks made an entrance and ruined everything.

Jumbo said, "How do we know you have the kind of money we're talking about?"

"Back to the same question as before? I got the money. If it's not enough, I can get the rest. You saw the size of our operation. But one of us is going to have to show our hand or we're not going to get anywhere. So I'll show you mine. I got five hundred thousand cash, twenties, fifties, and hundreds." I reached behind my back waistband and pulled out a wrinkled brown paper bag wrapped with two red rubber bands. I held it up. "This is a show of good faith, ten percent, fifty grand."

Jumbo's grin widened. "Fifty is a long way from five hundred thousand."

Johnny Sin dropped his chin and eased his sunglasses down to look over the top. "Not to mention that our price is at least three times what you say you got."

"Then let me buy it by the piece, one-third of your load. It'll work better that way. Then we can start to trust each other. I'll get the rest of the money and come back."

Jumbo looked at Johnny. The poker tell. Confirmation Johnny was calling the shots.

"Okay, big man," Jumbo said, "you can have some of the M-4s for three grand a piece."

"Naw, too much. You're not going to play me for a fool. Wholesale street price is two thousand and you know it."

"Twenty-five hundred."

"Two thousand."

"Twenty-four," Jumbo said. "And that's as low as I'm going to go."

"Nice doing business with you." I backed up, keeping the gun down at my side. I almost made it to the door.

Johnny whispered something, his lips barely moving. Jumbo said, "Okay, two thousand, but that's only one mag each and you have to leave the fifty thousand here as good faith."

I came back to the counter.

No deputy sheriff had ever let fifty thousand in buy money walk. But this wasn't a typical deal. I tossed Jumbo the brown paper bag. All the serial numbers were registered. "Where we going to do this?"

Jumbo opened the bag and thumbed the bills, checking to make sure there wasn't cut newspaper in between. He looked up. "Tomorrow night at—"

"No, tonight. You got my money. I get to call the time, midnight tonight. You get to call the location."

"Fine. Give me a number. I'll call you one hour before, at eleven, and tell you where. I ring the phone number once, you're not there the deal's off and you lose your deposit."

"Do I need to bring a truck?"

"We'll have the truck and it won't even cost you extra. Just don't drive it around too long."

Jumbo stuck out his hand to shake.

"I'll be waiting for your call." I left his hand hanging in midair, backed out to the double doors, turned, and hurried away.

CHAPTER FIFTY-EIGHT

I NEEDED SOMETHING to do until the phone call from Jumbo. I stopped at TW to pick up Junior Mint. RD was all over me about what was happening with the investigation. At the same time, Junior Mint jumped around and grabbed my hand loose in his mouth like he always did when he was happy to see me. His undaunted devotion allowed a spark of joy to enter my life. I told RD as little as possible and left in a hurry. I needed some time to think.

In the car on the drive home, Junior sat tall on the seat next to me and periodically leaned over and licked my cheek. "Yeah, I know. I said I was sorry for leaving you there so long." He licked my cheek again. "Yeah, you can only take so much of RD, I get that. I'm the same way. I promise it won't happen again." He gave me the big eyes. "I said I promise."

I parked two blocks away from our house instead of all the way over in the parking lot of MLK. After tonight it wouldn't matter anymore; I was going to close the sting down and do the roundup. With the gun deal, whether successful or not, word would hit the street and the cover would be blown. TW clients would scatter in the wind.

Dusk settled, coloring the horizon in dark grays and varying shades of blue. Venus burned bright.

From a few houses away, I could see that the front windows of our house on Nord were dark. Odd. Dad should've been home. Junior stayed at my side until we hit the yard. He bounded up the three steps of the porch and waited. The door wasn't locked. Something wasn't right.

Inside, Dad sat on the couch in the darkened room. My heart sank. This had been the same way I'd found him the night I came home and he told me about Olivia's overdose. Told me she was gone forever. He'd been the one to find her, a huge burden to bear. I didn't know how I would've handled it. Not well.

I turned on the light and went to him. "What's wrong? What's happened?" He stared off into space, his hands clasped in his lap, fingers gripped tight. He didn't answer.

I put my hand on his shoulder. "Dad, what's the matter? What's happened?"

His head slowly turned toward me, his eyes sad.

"Is it Alonzo?" I asked. "What's happened to Alonzo? Dad?"

"They got him." His voice came out in a whimper. He'd always been so strong and firm, I'd never heard him whimper, not once. Life had beaten down this wonderful man.

"Who's got him?"

"Margaret came by to tell me."

"Margaret?" The woman from the foster home on Laurel, where Social Services had placed Alonzo.

"And?"

"Derek has Alonzo."

"What?" I jumped to my feet. "That's impossible."

I'd left Derek knocked flat on his belly in The Body Shop with his gun tossed on top of his back. To seal the deal, I'd left the dope and money in the open safe with the deputies only minutes away. Derek *had* to be in jail.

"That's not right, Dad, you have to be mistaken."

"Margaret said that earlier today Derek came by the house on Laurel with the caseworker. They had court papers. Derek's parents now have legal custody of Alonzo. That's what Margaret said. There's nothing she could do about it. He should be with us, Bruno. Alonzo should live here with us. Not with those people."

I jumped up and paced the room. "No. No. No. This can't be. This is a huge miscarriage of justice. It's not right."

This was all my fault. The night I crushed Derek's fingers, I shouldn't have sent him into the police station alone. I should've gone in with him and made sure he told them what he'd done to Albert. A touchy situation though, with the way I had elicited the confession. In all likelihood, they would've kept me and let him walk.

Dad struggled to get up. His legs had to be as weak as mine from all the heated emotions. I gave him a hand.

He didn't let go; he just stared up at my eyes. "Derek is the boy's legal father."

I knew what Dad was trying to do. He wanted just a glimmer of justification, but no matter what Dad said, nothing would come out sounding right. I had told him about the incident three years earlier where I grabbed Derek Sams off Central Avenue in front of a pager store and drove him around. I didn't have to tell Dad what my intent had been at the time—he was a smart man and could figure it out. One of the biggest regrets of my life was that I had not carried through that plan and instead put Sams on a bus to Barstow. Now I saw that I'd made another big mistake letting Derek run loose. Dad stood before me worried I'd go back and finish the job I'd started. And he was right. Nothing in this world would stop me not this time.

"We'll get him back," I whispered.

But the law was against that ever happening.

"I called our attorney," Dad said, "and told him what happened. He said he was about to give us a call. He said the judge ruled against us. He said he could appeal but it would be a waste of money."

"Derek's in jail, Dad." I didn't know what else to say. At least with Derek in jail for a good long time, over the gun and the coke at The Body Shop, Alonzo wouldn't be exposed to him.

"No, Son. Before it got dark, not thirty minutes ago, he drove by the front of the house, twice. I opened the door the second time. He stopped in the street right out there in front of God and everyone, stuck his arm in the air, and gave me a vulgar gesture with his finger. He cackled loud like some kind of half-crazed fool. He only wanted Alonzo so he could get back at us. He's a vindictive little shit."

In all my life I had never heard Dad talk that way about anyone. And he had never used the word "shit." Tonight was a night of firsts.

I hurried to the phone and called the watch deputy at Lynwood Station. He told me when the deputies arrived on scene at The Body Shop, they only found the manager handcuffed in the repair bay. Derek wasn't there. I hadn't hit him as hard as I thought and the little weasel had been playing possum. He'd gotten away yet again. The kid had nine lives.

Dad sat at the kitchen table with a grim expression.

I sat down next to him. I took his hand. "I promise you this isn't going to stand."

"Son, please, don't do anything foolish."

"I don't have to. All I have to do is let the truth out to eat."

"What are you talking about?"

"Remember, a long time ago you told me that truth was a lion and that all you had to do was let it out to eat. That truth just needs a chance to defend itself."

"Yes, I know, but what *truth* are you talking about?"

My shame forced me to look away.

"What? Son, tell me."

"A while back, this was before Derek went to jail fighting that manslaughter case, I went looking for him. This was a second time I did it."

"Ah, Bruno."

"I know," I said.

Dad shook his head. "It's not your fault. Sin chooses us according to our weaknesses. You could never tolerate injustice. Tell me the rest of it. This was after Albert went missing and before Olivia—"

I squeezed his hand, interrupting him. "Yes, that's right. Remember we couldn't find Derek and I told you I thought he had something to do with what had happened to Albert?"

That had been when Olivia was still alive, emotionally crushed over her missing son. I had to do something.

He nodded.

"I caught up to Derek and he told me—"

"Oh, dear Lord, no."

"I'm sorry, Dad."

"Tell me. I have to know all of it."

I stared down at the floor. I could only say the horrific words to my shoes. "You know how Olivia was with the boys—she watched them like a hawk. She was a great mother. You know this part of it. She didn't do it often, but the day Albert went missing, she left the twins with Derek. It was only for a couple of minutes. She had to run to the store to get some diapers and baby food. Derek wouldn't go, so she had to. Derek told me Albert wouldn't stop crying. Derek couldn't take the constant crying and he—shook Albert too hard. Then . . . then he put Albert—"

Dad's hand came up out of the darkness and covered my mouth. He really didn't want to hear all of it after all. Good thing. To tell him the last part about the valise and the San Pedro Bridge—the long lonely drop to the ocean—might have been the end of me ever saying another word. No one knew about what Sams had done—not all of it—except me, a heavy burden to bear. Too heavy.

Dad sat quiet for a long while. "So that's it. Derek did do it and Olivia finally got it out of him. He either told her or she just figured it out. That's why she—"

I nodded and looked at his face through the dimness. "I dropped Derek off at the South Gate Police station. He was supposed to go in and confess to what he'd done to Albert."

"That was the right thing, Bruno. Let the law handle it."

"No, it wasn't, Dad. If I had taken care of it the right way, if I'd have gone in with him, told them it wasn't a missing person case, that it was a homicide, Olivia might still be with us. We might still have a family with her and Alonzo."

"You don't know that. You don't know *everything* that went on."

"What? What are you talking about?"

"I . . . I just mean, you don't know that's the whole truth. This story came from Derek, and I'm sure he didn't give you that information willingly."

That's not what he meant to say. I knew him well enough to know he'd changed his mind. "Wait, you were going to say something else. What is it?"

My cell phone trilled. Too early for Jumbo with a location for the deal.

I picked it up.

It was Ledezma from the Crazy Eight. "It's Nigel. Come quick."

CHAPTER FIFTY-NINE

"NIGEL, HE'S BAD hurt. You better hurry," Ledezma said over the cell phone.

"What happened? Hurt how?" But I knew.

"I'm not getting involved in this, Karl. You comin' or not? He looks like someone put him through a meat grinder, I'm not kiddin' here. It's bad. The worst I've seen, and I've owned this stinking bar for sixteen years."

"Did you call paramedics?"

"He said not to. He said he needed to talk to you first."

"I'm coming." I hung up.

"I have to go, Dad."

"I understand. We can talk later. You go."

I took off running out the door. Halfway across the front yard, I realized Junior Mint had followed along. No time to take him back and make him stay. For two blocks he ran alongside in a full sprint.

It was the gun deal. Johnny Sin used fear and confusion and tyranny to keep his opponent off guard. For the next few hours he didn't want me thinking about how I could rip him off and used Nigel as a distraction. A dangerous game, because now all I wanted to do was shoot the bastard.

We made it to the Opel, started up, and drove like hell. The Crazy Eight wasn't far, and I didn't let traffic get in the way or slow us down. Twice I banged over the curb and onto the sidewalk to get around cars lined up at an intersection. I drove with one hand, dialed 911, and got paramedics rolling. The same call would alert LAPD.

It couldn't have taken more than six or seven minutes from the time I hung up to when I pulled into the back parking lot of The Eight. I bailed out, leaving the car door standing open, the engine in smoking ruins and one blown tire. Junior Mint bounded alongside me. I burst through the back door into the near darkness of the bar. I shoved the crowd of regulars out of the way and went down on one knee. I couldn't see; my eyes hadn't adjusted.

"Ledezma, turn on the lights."

"Drag him outside, Karl. ABC will yank my license for sure over this one. You know I'm already on probation with those guys."

The drunks parted. Ledezma stood behind the bar.

"I said turn on the lights. Now."

He did. A couple of the folks in the crowd gasped. I wanted to weep. "Ah, Nigel." I sat down getting underneath him, his shoulders in my lap, his head cradled in the crook of my arm.

"Hey, Karl, good to see you, man." He reached out a bloody hand and clutched my shoulder, smearing the khaki-colored shirt. I didn't know how he could see anything; his eyes were welded shut with swollen purples and reds. His entire face was bloated, and the skin parted here and there with slices that seeped blood. The bones underneath were fractured, as were his arms and ribs and collar bones.

"You just lie still. Paramedics are on the way."

"It's okay. It's funny, I don't feel it anymore. You think you could get me a vodka tonic, hold the tonic?"

"Sure. You rest easy." Tears blurred my vision. "What happened?"

"It was Johnny." His tone came out singsong, as if the answer had been obvious to any fool who knew anything at all. "He used two black eight balls from a pool table, put 'em in a sock. Showed them to me first, told me what he was going to do, too. Said he was going to beat me to within an inch of my life, and boy he sure missed the mark, didn't he, Karl? Didn't he? I got at least a couple of feet left, don't you think?" He tried to laugh and coughed and choked. Blood sputtered into the air in a fine mist.

"Don't talk anymore, just rest. Ledezma, get me a wet towel with some ice. Hurry."

Outside, sirens echoed up and down the street. The police and paramedics.

"Karl? Karl, are you still there?"

"I'm right here, Nigel. Just take it easy."

"Karl."

"Yes."

"Johnny said something queer, real queer. He said . . . he said that you are really a cop. That's funny, isn't it, Karl? You of all people a cop." His breathing became more labored and he spoke with a heavier rasp. "Said your name was really Bruno Johnson. I told him he was crazy. He said he knew it the whole time. That bird is nuts, ain't he, Karl?"

"Yes, he's nuts all right."

"Bruno Johnson of all people, that guy's a brute, a real animal. You still going to do the deal with him if he's crazy?"

I didn't answer.

He said, "I know it's silly to ask this." Cough. "Especially under the circumstances."

"Go ahead and ask anything you want."

"I don't think I'm going to make the deal with you tonight . . . I . . . I'll still get my finder's fee, right?"

"You'll get it even if the deal goes sour, you have my word."

"You're a good man, Karl. I'm glad we met. Really, I am. Now, I'm sooo tired. I'm just going to take a little nap. Feels like I haven't slept in thirty years, you know what I'm sayin'? You going to stay right here, Karl?"

"Yeah, Nigel, I'm not going anywhere."

Paramedics didn't transport Nigel right away. They worked on him a long time. I stood by, looking on, dazed and confused. Johnny Sin got what he wanted. Confusion, disruption, hot emotions fogging clear thoughts.

Working patrol, I had stood tall over similar instances, good people down in the street or laid out on some grimy floor. But during all those times, I had been able to put aside my emotions in order to deal with the job: finding who committed such a hateful assault. This time I had a vested interest and it changed everything.

The paramedics finally got him on a gurney and strapped in. The filthy floor of The Eight was littered with torn and abandoned packages that had sheathed the medical supplies used to stave off death. The medics didn't have to tell me a status. Nigel was barely hanging on.

The two blue uniforms from LAPD weren't real interested in a beaten-down drunk, even one "beaten within two feet of his life." Not when it happened in the back parking lot of the Crazy Eight. A nightly event in their minds, the parking lot and bar a swirling vortex of the disenfranchised—no victims involved.

They asked me my name. I took out my wallet and gave them the TW driver's license that said Karl. I'd be Karl for a few more hours.

The two uniforms left following the gurney. I came out of my daze standing in the same spot with Junior Mint sitting by my foot leaning up and licking my hand. He'd sensed my need for consolation. How much time had passed? Forty minutes? An hour? I checked my watch. Fifty-three minutes. The other patrons had moved back to the bar to resume their drinking, the night's entertainment over.

The cell phone in my pocket trilled. I didn't have my own—this was the one Black Bart insisted that I carry. I took it out and flipped it open. "This is Karl."

"Bruno!"

"Dad?"

"Help, Bruno. Come quick."

CHAPTER SIXTY

I STEPPED OUTSIDE the front door of the Crazy Eight, panic-stricken. I needed a car. The Opel was around back and trashed. Traffic whizzed by. Night people were already out creeping the streets. I needed to get home. I fought the urge to step in the street, pull my gun, and commandeer an unsuspecting driver.

"Dad, what's going on? Where are you? Are you still at home?"

"Bruno! Oh, my dear Lord."

"Dad, what's the matter? Talk to me."

He continued to gulp and sputter, unable to put words together about what had happened.

"Dad, listen to me. Calm down and take some deep breaths."

"Okay. Okay." His loud breathing came over the phone.

"That's good. Now tell me where you are and I'll be there in two minutes, I promise. Are you at home?"

"What? No. I'm . . . I'm not at home."

"You're doing fine, Dad. Keep breathing. Deep breaths. Now tell me where you are."

"I don't know. I'm . . . I'm on Central, I think."

"Central? I'm on Central. Where on Central? What's the cross street? Describe it." I stepped out further to the edge—one foot on the curb, one in the street—and looked north and then south not seeing anything, wanting to see him close by, close enough to help.

"What's the cross street with Central?"

"The cross street?" He knew what I was talking about; he'd been a postman for forty years. He couldn't get his mind in gear.

"I . . . I don't know."

"Guess."

"The Seventies . . . I'm somewhere close to the Seventies. Yes, that's right."

"I'm coming, Dad. I'm coming."

I pivoted and took off running full out. Junior stayed with me, barking at people on the sidewalk to move them out of the way.

One block.

Two blocks.

From the middle of the third block, south of Seventy-Ninth and across the street, I spotted my blue Ford Ranger parked crooked. It was two more blocks north. I poured it on. Junior yelped. "I see my truck, Dad," I yelled breathlessly into the phone. "I'll be there in two minutes. Two minutes, Dad."

I cut across the street in front of headlights and misjudged the speed of the car coming south. Brakes squealed. I leapt in the air a second before impact, crashed onto the hood and bounced up onto the windshield, which caved in and knocked all the wind out of me. Bright lights of pain flashed behind my eyes. My rib cage crunched. At the same instant, I heard the second bump. Junior let out a howl.

I rolled off the car onto the street and down on my knees. A second car screeched to stop just short of running me over, its headlights bright in my eyes, the heat from the engine like a wild beast huffing in my face.

I looked back. Junior lay on his side in front of the first car, his legs still running going nowhere, a low whine coming from deep in his chest.

"Ah, man, I'm sorry, my friend."

No time. Had to get to Dad.

"I'll be back, boy, I'll be right back. Hold on."

I got up and stumble-ran. Half a block to go. My ribs ached something fierce. A couple of them were broken. I held my arm tucked tight. It hurt to breathe.

A group of blacks, seven or eight of them, all wearing gang-banger attire, stood close to a door cracked open to the business as they tried to peer in through the windows. The Ford Ranger sat in the street, right in front of that door with its tail end sticking out in northbound traffic. I recognized the fat gangbanger, a leader of a Crips clique, Mr. G or Big G or something like that. He owned and ran a pager/cell phone store. They turned and saw me coming on fast. One of the bangers next to the leader said, "Hey, hey, that's Bruno the Bad Boy Johnson."

I reached under my work shirt to pull out the .357.

Gone.

It had to be back in the street where the car hit me.

I yelled at them, "Get the hell outta here. Go on. Move."

They scattered, all of them running except for the fat one. He strolled. They wouldn't go far, and it wouldn't take them long to come back.

I grabbed the door to the pager store and swung it open.

CHAPTER SIXTY-ONE

DAD STOOD IN the center of the small store in front of the customer counter. His shoulders were slumped. He looked up when I came in. A deep sadness hung heavy in his eyes, his sallow cheeks wet with tears. "Bruno, what have I done? Dear Lord, what have I done?"

The air smelled of gunpowder. Dad held a gun loose in his hands, a gun I recognized, the .38 Colt taken from our house the day Olivia died. The one I recovered on the counter at TW during the deal with Leo from Sparkle Plenty. The one I had put back in the wall hide at the house.

On the floor at Dad's feet lay a dead black man. Underneath him a widening puddle of dark maroon blood grew outward on the scuffed white tile. I recognized him even from the back.

Derek Sams.

Dad had shot Derek.

Oddly, the back of Derek's pants were pulled down enough to reveal both buttocks.

I held out my hand and walked toward Dad. I whispered, "It's okay. It's going to be okay." I relieved him of the gun and put my arm around him. He latched onto me and buried his face in my chest. His whole body shook as he wept.

The door to the pager store opened. A man stuck his head in and saw the deadly tableau: the dead man on the floor, the gun in my hand. The dark maroon pool of blood. His eyes went wide. "Holy shit." His head popped back out the door, then popped right back in. He said, "I don't want any part of this mess, mister, but your dog's bad hurt. I'm taking him to the vet while you deal with all this."

"Thank you." He popped back out.

"Dad, what happened here?"

"Junior's hurt?" he asked, his words trailing off.

"Dad, what happened here? We don't have much time."

"It's not him."

"What?"

"I asked Derek to show me his butt. He laughed and jumped around. He laughed at me. It was like a cackle. A crazy man's cackle."

"Dad?"

He reached into his pocket and pulled out a jaggedly torn swatch of denim, one stained brown with dried blood. It looked like the rear pocket from a pair of pants. "It wasn't him, and I shot him."

"Dad, what are you talking about?" He was delirious and on the razor edge of going into shock.

"After you left, he drove by again to gloat—the son of a buck. This time I followed him. I don't know why."

But I knew. I shouldn't have told him what Derek had done to poor little Albert.

"I followed him here and"—he again held up the swatch of blood-dried denim— "it's not him." He pointed to Derek's ass. "I didn't want to believe he'd have anything to do with what happened to Olivia. I wanted to believe he had some good in him even if only a bit, and that deep down he really loved her."

He paused. I let him tell it.

"The day I found Olivia, I found this on the floor in the house. I didn't want to believe someone had purposely done that to Olivia, and at the same time, I didn't want to believe she'd do that to herself. I didn't know what to do. I did know I shouldn't show it to you. I knew what *you'd* do. I kept it to myself until you told me what Derek had done. Then I believed—no, I was sure he'd done it. He killed Olivia. She wouldn't do that horrible thing to herself."

He paused as he thought about it, stepping back from the edge of shock. "That day I found Olivia, Junior was there and bit whoever tried to hurt her. That's what I now believe. So when Derek came by again for the third time tonight . . . I grabbed this gun. I knew where you hid it in the wall and I followed him. It didn't make a lot of sense to blame Derek for Olivia. I know it didn't. Derek was in jail. Least I thought he was. But the bad guys get out all the time, right? For bail. To go to funerals and whatnot. I just knew he'd done it and had to find out for sure. Now look what I did."

I pulled Dad back into a hug. "Ah, Dad." I held him tight. My heart ached for him. His entire world had to shift in order for him to pick up a gun.

"Come on," I said. "We have to get out of here."

"No. Don't you see, it wasn't Derek. It must've somehow been something unrelated. A burglar or someone who came into the house. I found Junior out front that day and this piece of pants pocket in the house. I have to atone for my actions, what I did here. I was wrong, Son. Dead wrong and I'll have to pay for it."

"No, you don't. You have nothing to atone for, not after what he's done. You owe nothing to anyone. Had you not taken care of this problem the way you did, the law would have."

His whole body turned calm as he must've reconciled what needed to be done. He'd let the court decide his fate. And he'd go to prison. I wasn't going to let that happen even if I had to throw him over my shoulder and carry him out.

"Dad, truth caught up to Derek. That's all that happened here. You have to see that."

"I can't be judge and executioner. It's wrong." He swayed on his feet and his eyelids fluttered. The stress had been too much for him. I had to get him out of there with little steps. I knelt down and felt Derek's neck. Nothing. He was gone.

"He's still alive, Dad. We have to call paramedics." I took out my cell and pretended to dial. I spoke to no one and asked for help. I closed the flip phone. "Come on, we have to move the truck so the paramedics can get in here and you need to sit down."

Little steps.

He nodded. I took him by the arm and escorted him out. I got him in the truck and closed the door. I held up my finger. "I'll be right back."

I stepped into the pager store as I wiped Dad's fingerprints from the gun and made sure mine were on it. I got down on one knee while holding my aching ribs. I shot Derek in the back and tossed the gun down on top of him. I dipped my fingers in the pool of blood on the floor and smeared it on my shirt.

Outside, Dad had opened the door and was trying to get out. "Ah, Son, what have you gone and done?" He'd heard the shot.

"I let the lion out to feed, nothing more."

I eased him back in. "I finished what needed to be finished. Now we have to get out of here before the police show up."

He sat staring straight ahead. I ran around, got in, and pulled away as a black-and-white LAPD car did a U-turn and stopped in the spot we'd vacated. They had to have seen the truck and the plate.

Dad had turned catatonic.

"I'm going to drop you at home."

He didn't answer. We weren't far away, only minutes.

"He was alive," I said. "You're not the one who killed him, I did. You don't have to atone for it. I do—and I will. Dad, are you listening?"

He continued to look straight ahead. "What have we done?"

"You haven't done a thing. I did it. You understand? I did it. I pulled the trigger; you didn't."

I came to a red signal and stopped; the streetlight cast eerie shadows on his face.

"There's no reason for the both of us to go to prison. Dad, you hear what I'm saying?"

Small steps.

"Dad, Junior is hurt."

His head slowly turned to look at me.

"Junior's hurt? He's Olivia's dog."

"That's right. He was hit by a car. He needs you. I'm going to drop you at home. Can you call around and find out what vet the guy took him to and then go and be with him?"

"Yes, of course." He turned and watched out the windshield.

I wanted to ask him more about what happened the day he found Olivia. If he hid the swatch of bloodied denim, what else had happened that he had not told me? He wasn't ready to talk about it, and I didn't have much time. LAPD would be coming for me.

I pulled up and stopped in front of our house. "When they come, don't say a thing to the police. Promise me, Dad. I know a good attorney. We'll get through this."

He got out. "I know we will. We always do, don't we?" He said it in a monotone steeped in sarcasm. "Where are you going?"

I had to give him something to cling to. "Listen. All this time . . . the times you found me in that bar, I've been working undercover. I never gave up my badge. I'm sorry, I wasn't allowed to tell you."

A small glimmer of light returned to his eyes. He reached in and put his hand on my arm and squeezed.

"I have one more thing I have to do, Dad." What I left unsaid was, *Before I give up my badge for good.* "I'll be back soon, I promise. Take good care of Junior."

"I will."

CHAPTER SIXTY-TWO

I OPENED THE flip phone and dialed Wicks' cell while I drove obeying the speed laws, headed to Norwalk.

"Yeah," he said.

"Where are you?"

"Why?"

"You want me to guess?"

"You think you're so smart, go ahead."

"You're sitting down the street from Harry and Sons in Norwalk watching the front door."

Long pause. "So, what if I am? I'm not going to burn your precious gun deal if that's what you're worried about. I'm just keeping an eye on things."

"I'm not worried. You got eyes on Johnny Sin?"

"He pulled up driving a plumbing truck seventeen minutes ago. He's dressed like a plumber. Looks like he's got some blood on his shirt. He went inside. Why?"

"I'm burned. Johnny knows who I am. The gun deal's a no-go. I'm coming to you."

"Now you're talkin', buddy boy. What's your ETA?"

"Ten. Don't you do anything until I get there."

"What if he tries to go mobile?"

"Let's hope that he doesn't. It's still an hour and a half before he makes the call to me. But if he does try to leave, I know you'll figure something out." I closed the flip phone.

I drove slumped over, taking small breaths to avoid the sharp rib pain. I dialed James Barlow Jr. He picked up on the first ring.

"This is Johnson. Get rolling. Set up out of view, Firestone and the 605 Freeway. The location is going to be Harry and Sons Oil to Nuts. I'll give you the word when to roll in."

"Right. How much time do we have?"

"You should've been there ten minutes ago."

"Don't go without us. You hear me? Don't you go without us."

I closed the flip phone.

I still wasn't thinking straight, not about what lay ahead. Dad had shot a human being. The idea that an emotion so powerful overcame his moral resolve and allowed him to pull the trigger tilted my world out of balance. That whole scene, the way he described it, kept popping into my head and shoving out all else. Derek, jumping around in front of Dad, cackling like a fool. Dad thinking Derek had something to do with Olivia's death—Dad knowing Derek had a direct hand in Albert's death after what I'd just told him.

I went over everything I'd done at the scene in the cell phone store. I had it covered. But I still needed to make the narrative I'd created real. To do that I had to say it over and over in my head until it became natural: "I ran Derek Sams down and shot him. I cornered Derek Sams and gunned him. I shot Derek Sams in the back." It had to be real even to me. That's the way it would be from now on. There wasn't anyone else to say different. Not a soul.

And Derek did his part to make it real. He'd taken out a restraining order saying I was dangerous. He'd given a deposition that I'd been the one to crush his fingers. All of that worked in my favor.

I left fingerprints at the scene and I had Derek's blood on my shirt. What could go wrong?

When committing crimes on the fly, something always goes wrong. You can't think of everything.

Dad could go wrong. He could and would have a moral crisis and try to take the blame. But I had the evidence stacked in my favor, and if Dad tried to take the blame, I could easily say he was just trying to cover for his son. Nobody would believe him. I hated to do it to him but there wasn't any other option.

I ran Derek Sams down and shot him in the back. I ran Derek Sams down and—

I found Wicks' Ford Taurus parked in the shadows of a business closed for the day. I wouldn't have seen him had I not been looking for him and known he'd be in a position of advantage watching Harry and Sons. I parked around the corner and crept up on foot. I knocked lightly on his trunk so he wouldn't shoot me and came up on the passenger side. He had his interior dome light disabled. I crawled into the dark, stifling a pain-filled grunt and eased the door closed. "Any movement?"

Wicks leaned forward over the steering wheel looking through binoculars as he spoke. "Yeah, buddy boy, it's Christmas come early. We hit the jackpot."

"What are you talking about?"

He brought the binos down and faced me, but it was too dark to see his eyes. "Guess who just showed up?"

"I'm not in the mood for games. Tell me."

"Henry Bogardus."

"You're kidding me?" I took the binos from him and peered down the street at the front and side of Harry and Sons.

Old Henry Bogardus was on Wicks' A-list of fugitives. He'd been at the top of the list for three years that I knew of. Whenever Wicks wasn't working a directed target, he made another try at digging Bogardus out of his hole. Kind of like a hobby fugitive. Bogardus had killed three people—in a garage. Used an acetylene torch. Wicks had talked about him often and made up scenarios of what it would be like when he caught up to him.

"That's kinda hard to believe," I said.

"It was him, I'm positive. You can't see him right now. He went inside. He pulled up in that no-account Nissan Sentra parked right there in front of the primary loc. Stepped out in the light. I got a good look at him. It's Bogardus, all right. Like I said, it's Christmas come early. He was with another mope I couldn't identify. Both of them are armed, handguns. What do you want to do? I think we should go knock down their door."

I pulled back the binos and turned toward him. "Are you crazy? They have military-grade automatic weapons in there."

"What? Are you going soft on me? We hit 'em hard and we hit 'em fast. We do that, we'll catch 'em with their pants down. We can drive this car right through the front of that shop, it's all glass. We'd take both those glass doors down. I always wanted to do one that way. Hey, is that blood on your shirt?" He was talking wild now, as he gulped at the adrenaline he craved so much.

"Johnny Sin beat a friend of mine. He might not make it. I just came from there. That's how I found out Johnny knows I'm a deputy."

"And you're telling me you don't want to take this place head-on?"

Thinking about what Sin did to Nigel made me want to throw caution to the wind. But that's exactly what Sin wanted. We wouldn't catch him flat-footed; he'd be waiting for us.

In all my years working with Wicks, I had always been the voice of reason keeping him from burning down the world. That was the second reason why he kept me around, to keep at least one foot of his placed firmly in reality. Not this time. I no longer had to worry about the brass in the aftermath second-guessing poor tactics. In a few hours I wouldn't have a badge. And Johnny Sin, more than anyone else, deserved to have his world burned down.

"Tonight, I'm with you all the way."

"Now you're talkin', buddy boy."

"I need a gun."

"Glove box, there's a Glock with an extra mag. How do you want to do this?"

I pulled out the Glock and press-checked for a round in the chamber. "How about like Encinitas?"

CHAPTER SIXTY-THREE

"You think that's better than driving through the front window? I don't."

Wicks' cell phone rang. He picked it up. "Yeah." He listened.

I watched his eyes as he looked straight at me. They hardened as he said, "Is that right?"

The word had already gone out about what had happened at the pager/cell phone store on Central.

He clicked off still staring at me. "We're going to have to talk after all this is over."

"Yeah, I figured as much. I don't have a problem with it. I just want to make sure my dog's okay first. That's not asking for much."

He didn't answer.

I opened my cell and dialed the number to Harry and Sons Oil to Nuts. Someone picked up but didn't say a word, their breathing normal.

I made my voice urgent. "Cops are on the way. Get out! Get out!" I hung up.

Ten seconds later headlights came on around the back of the store and lit up the cinderblock wall to the rear. A large truck lumbered into view. I dialed James Barlow's number. He picked up on the first ring.

I said, "Okay, you're up. It's a large truck coming your way. Watch your ass, they're armed and dangerous."

"Got it."

Wicks said, "Hey, what are you doing? This is supposed to be our takedown."

The truck blew by, three people in the cab. Painted on the side in a professional elegant style were the words, scrolled in red in an arc over the top of a city's skyscrapers, "TransWorld Logistics." This was the load truck Johnny was going to drive to the gun deal. He had a sick sense of humor.

Wicks started the car and put his hand on the gear shift to throw it in gear. I stopped him. "Wait, our target isn't in the truck. He sent the truck out as a decoy, a distraction so he can weasel out. Keep your lights off and drive around back. You better hurry."

Wicks took off, the car accelerating fast. Behind us automatic gunfire ignited in a string of rapid pops from multiple guns that lit up the night. LAPD had engaged the truck. The gunfire continued after the first volley.

"Damn." Wicks slammed his fist on the steering wheel. "We picked the wrong end of this thing. All the action's back there." He whipped the car around to the back of the building.

Jumbo and Johnny Sin came out the back door on the loading dock. Johnny fired a handgun. His round spider-webbed the windshield. The round came at an angle and embedded in the back seat

"This is more like it," Wicks said. He skidded into the loading area and bailed out while Johnny let go with two more rounds, the noise loud in the enclosed area.

Jumbo threw his hands in the air and lay down. Johnny disappeared back inside. Wicks bounded up the concrete steps to the door, his hand on the knob when he turned, expecting me to be right there with him.

I held my ribs tight and ran out into the alley away from the loading dock door. I ran along the side of the building and came out into the front. Johnny had exited the front door seconds before and was running across the parking lot with a gun in his hand.

I stopped and yelled, "Hold it."

He stopped dead in his tracks still facing away. His back stiffened as he slowly turned. He held the gun in his hand down by his leg. I couldn't read his eyes behind his sunglasses—his intent.

"Don't do it. Drop it."

A slow grin crept across his face.

His gun rose in a flash.

I let go three quick rounds from a gun I'd never held before. The gun popped and kicked in my hand. Two rounds thudded into Johnny Sin's chest. He grunted, flew backward, and skidded along the asphalt. He was on his back and didn't move.

Wicks burst out the front door, gun up, eyes wild. He took in the scene. "God damn you, Bruno. You played me. Bogardus must've been in the truck, and I missed him, too. I got dick in there and you got to take the shot out here."

I slowly walked up on Johnny Sin, who didn't move at all. When he hit the asphalt, his gun had skittered away. I stood over him. Blood stains grew wider in the light-blue material of his security guard uniform. I couldn't see his eyes behind the sunglasses and maybe that was better. An uneventful end to a violent man's reign.

Three cars zoomed up and skidded to a stop. LAPD. James Barlow appeared at my side, breathing hard. "You okay?"

That's what Wicks should've asked instead of his mentally deficient rant about missing out on the shot.

"Yeah, I'm good. Anybody hurt at your end?"

"Amos caught some shrapnel in the face from a bullet fragment, but that's it. All three crooks are down hard. Is this the guy?" He pointed to Johnny Sin, who still hadn't moved and continued to bleed.

"Yeah, that's him."

James Barlow stepped in close, grabbed Johnny's limp arm, flipped him over, and knee-dropped the center off his back. Through clenched teeth he said, "Procedure states all suspects involved in an OIS are to be handcuffed." He handcuffed Johnny Sin. He turned him on his side and slapped the sunglasses away to get a look at his face. Johnny's eyes were slits exposing only the whites. A trickle of blood ran down the corner of his mouth.

Paramedics pulled up with rotating red lights, no siren. They got out and went to work on Johnny. I continued to look on, numb. Derek Sams' parents had legal custody of Alonzo. Dad had shot and killed Derek Sams. I wasn't a cop anymore and I was going away to prison.

Three paramedics worked on Johnny, their hands a blur.

Wicks put a hand on my shoulder and tried to spin me around. "Hey, pal, we need to talk." I pulled away and held my ground close to Johnny Sin.

James Barlow sensed the tone. "Leave him alone."

"Stay out of this, pal. Bruno, we're going to talk right now or I'm going to cuff you."

James Barlow shoved Wicks. "Back off. Cuff him? Are you out of your mind?"

One paramedic used a sharp pair of scissors and sliced up the length of Johnny's pants, cutting off his clothes in a search for other injuries. Johnny still lay on his side while the other two worked on his entrance and exit wounds. The paramedic exposed his right buttocks. The pale white skin on his ass cheek was marred with red ropy scars. The kind of scars I'd seen before and that could only come from one source. A dog bite.

Jessica Lowe had said William Butterworth had a scar on his butt. She described it as an old bullet wound.

Johnny Sin was William Butterworth, aka La Vonn Lofton. He was the one who'd killed the judge and his wife. He'd killed Twyla.

Then it all made sense. Butterworth had also come after me and started with Olivia. He had been the one to overdose my beautiful daughter. Junior Mint had been there that day and taken a bite out of Butterworth's ass. That swatch of bloodstained denim of Dad's came from Johnny's pants. That was why he told Nigel my real name. There was never going to be a gun deal. The whole time he'd been playing me, making my life a living hell. And if I had to guess, Butterworth had also been the one pulling the strings on Derek Sams, telling Derek the moves to make with the attorney.

Wicks came over for a closer look. "What is it?"

"It's William Butterworth, La Vonn Lofton."

"You're kidding me. Are you sure?"

"Yes."

"Son of a bitch, we closed both cases at once."

I turned to walk away. Wicks lost his smile. "Hey, buddy boy, where do you think you're going?"

"My dog's hurt. I need to go see to him." I also needed to tell Dad about Butterworth and about how Olivia had not taken her own life.

"Sorry, no can do. I have to take you in."

James Barlow stepped in between us. "You have to do what? Why?"

"No," I said. "It's okay. I do have to take care of what he's talking about. And I promise I'll do it as soon as I see to my dog."

"Can't let you do it, Bruno."

Barlow put his hands out, blocking Wicks. "Go ahead, Bruno. I'll stay here and talk with him."

"Hey, pal, you don't want to get in the middle of this. I'll kick your ass."

Did anyone else looking on, the paramedics or the other LAPD officers, notice how Wicks and Barlow looked like father and son? I couldn't allow them to go to blows.

"Wait. I'll go with him."

"You sure, Bruno?"

"Yeah, I'm sure. Come on, let's go."

I walked with him back to the car behind the auto parts store; Wicks didn't say a word. We got in. I grabbed Wicks' hand and cuffed it to the steering wheel, and in the same fluid motion, reached in and pulled his Colt .45 and his set of cuffs.

"Ah, man, you're making a big mistake here, Bruno."

"I'll turn myself in. You have my word. I just need to talk to my father first." I got out and moved around the front of the car to his side. He was scrambling to get his cuff key in the handcuffs. I punched him in the face as a distraction, grabbed his free hand, and cuffed it to the outside mirror.

"That tears it. You better run, Bruno. That's all I gotta say, you better run far and fast because I'm coming after you."

"I'm sorry it had to end this way."

I left him in the car and went in search of my dad to tell him what had happened—to tell him goodbye.

AUTHOR'S NOTE

Early on in my career as a young police officer, I believed novels and movies were overwrought with story lines involving hit men or contract killers. I thought people who took money to kill another existed, just not as frequently the world of drama would have us believe. Until a murder with a hit man struck our family.

My aunt Carol and cousin Danny were involved with the Mexican Mafia, selling tar heroin. I had no idea. They seemed so normal at family gatherings. My favorite uncle, Don, found out about their nefarious ways and told them to stop or he'd turn them over to the police. Aunt Carol—his wife—and cousin Danny hired a hit man from Orange County by the name of Cornelius to take him out.

Uncle Don was a supervisor for the Metropolitan Water District in Indio. Cousin Danny and Cornelius made a fake emergency call about one of the water plants. When Uncle Don got out of his car to open the gate, they shot him in the back of the head. There was little evidence of the crime for the prosecution. The police put a wire on my cousin's girlfriend and obtained a conversation about the crime. Of course, there is much more to the story.

Cousin Danny was seventeen at the time and was tried as an adult. He was convicted and sentenced to life without the possibility of parole. Only that's not the way it works in California. After forty years in prison, the governor released him. After forty years, cousin Danny is free, and my favorite uncle, Don, is still dead.

During my career, I became aware of two other contract killings. Only one of those was solved. The girlfriend of the killer was scared to death of her boyfriend. When he went to jail on another matter, she walked into a police station and told them about the unsolved murder.

The story line in *The Ruthless* depicts the murder of a judge and his wife. This really did occur in San Bernardino County. The method of the murder and the lack of evidence points strongly to a hit man.

* * *

In *The Ruthless*, Bruno Johnson goes undercover as Karl Higgins in a sting operation to bring down a huge illegal arms operation. Not even his family or his former cop colleaugues know that he is still a Los Angeles County sheriff deputy.

During my career, we used a variety of sting techniques to catch various types of criminals. In the more extensitve operations, federal and state grant money was available to lure the informants. I personally participated in two fencing stings similar to the one described in *The Ruthless*. Both were highly successful.

On another occasion, I wrote a search warrant for a house in the high desert that was selling rock cocaine—and a court order to use some rock cocaine from an adjudicated court case that had been sitting in our evidence locker. We executed the search warrant on the rock house—ironically, the "rock house" was constructed with a river rock exterior. We arrested several dealers and seized their rock coke. Then we set up shop selling "our" rock cocaine. We had a wild time with this endeavor. The prospective buyers would knock on the door; we'd answer and invite them in. The rock coke was spread out on a table in different-sized plastic baggies. They would select a bag; we'd hand them the rock; they'd hand us the money; then we'd arrest them. One crook was so high when I showed him the badge that he pushed it away—his focus still on the table filled with baggies of coke. He said, "Maybe I want that one instead; it's bigger." I showed him the badge again, said, "You're under arrest." He again pushed it away. "No, man, I want to trade this one for that bigger one."

In that sting, I realized that we had our prey cornered—something that doesn't happen in the wild kingdom. The crooks we let in were not searched beforehand and could've been armed. Several, once cornered, turned on us with weapons, and we had to confront them.

* * *

In one of my other favorite stings, we had CalTrans build a fake sign that looked like any other highway sign. This one was eight feet by four feet with a blue field and white letters that read, "Narcotic Checkpoint Ahead." Narcotic checkpoints are strictly illegal in the U.S. We didn't put up a checkpoint; we just put up the sign. Signs aren't illegal.

We posted the sign on I-40 in a known narcotic corridor. Farther along, where the nonexistent checkpoint might be, we parked a marked cop car with its overhead red and blue lights rotating. Then we sat on the off-ramp located between the sign and the cop car and watched all the craziness. We had one cop perched in a cedar tree at the bottom of the ramp with a video camera recording the cars running the stop sign as they made a left turn to go over the freeway and get back on the highway in the opposite direction. That's when we pulled them over—using the stop sign violation as probable cause.

We didn't have enough cops to stop everyone who turned around, but we arrested several heavyweight fugitives. We also made several large smuggling cases. One of my cases—a trunk full of naracotics—trailed in Barstow court for three years—some folks out of Oklahoma who'd come to California to buy their dope. They hired heavyweight attorneys who kept postponing the case. One time, yet again waiting on this case to go, I got into a use of force right in the courtroom, but that's another story.

All along that off-ramp, the cars that pulled off tossed their contraband, mostly open containers—alcohol, narcotics, narcotic paraphernalia, and weapons. The ramp was littered with these items. It looked like the aftermath of a huge rock concert. It was great fun, like shooting fish in a barrel.

ABOUT THE TELEPHONE ROBBERY

I lived next door to and became good friends with a kindly old gentleman who had worked forty years for the phone company. He told me stories of phone booths and of the millions and millions of coins he dealt with throughout his career and of the many cons used by reprehensible individuals to steal that money. He worked in some of the worst areas of Los Angeles collecting the coins where he was in constant fear of being chunked over the head and mugged for his bags of coin.

ABOUT BRUNO GETTING SUED BY DEREK SAMS

During my thirty-one years as a police officer, I was sued thirteen times. This was more than the average, but the kind of people I chased, once cornered, did not, as a rule, stop and throw up their hands in surrender.

ABOUT THE BRUNO JOHNSON SERIES

The Ruthless is the fourth and final Bruno early-years novel, finishing off the prequels to the real-time Bruno series, which begins with *The Disposables*. The four early-years novels begin with *The Innocents*—Bruno is a young cop when he finds out he is the single father of a baby girl, Olivia, who is placed in his care. That little girl grows up as Bruno battles a tough, brutal career throughout *The Reckless*, and *The Heartless*, and culminates in the *The Ruthless*.

Having read *The Ruthless*, you, the reader, can imagine what comes next.

That takes us to the first (in order of publication) Bruno novel, *The Disposables*. Current day Bruno is an ex-cop, and now, an ex-con. He no longer has Olivia, but he has a grandson, Alonso. He will do anything to protect this child—and other children.

The Replacements, *The Squandered*, and *The Vanquished* follow as Bruno is called back to Los Angeles County, time and again, to exact justice—and to save children.

The next Bruno Johnson novel after *The Ruthless*, *The Sinister*, will continue the current day Bruno series, where *The Vanquish* left off.